A BROTHER'S TALE

A Brother's Tale
STAN BARSTOW

London
MICHAEL JOSEPH

First published in Great Britain by Michael Joseph Ltd
44 Bedford Square, London WC1B 3EF

© 1980 by Stan Barstow

ISBN 0 7181 1893 6

Phototypeset in Great Britain by
Western Printing Services Ltd, Bristol
Printed and bound by
Billing & Sons, Guildford and Worcester

124612

I

He came in darkness, ringing the doorbell at five minutes to midnight, when I was preparing to go up to bed and Eileen was already there. I wasn't expecting him. I'd seen the papers and heard the talk about his absenting himself from a league game, being dropped for the next and turning up for training too drunk to stand. 'Cross-eyed and legless', an anonymous team-mate had described him to the press. 'It looks like our kid's in bother again,' I'd remarked to Eileen. But it wasn't his habit to run home, either to me or to our parents, so it was not without surprise that I opened the door to find him on the step.

'Room inside for a little 'un?'

'Well. Come in, come in.'

I went upstairs to speak to Eileen, who was still reading.

'Was that someone at the door?'

'It's Bonny.'

'Bonny?'

'Is the spare bed made up?'

'Yes, the sheets are clean. What is he doing?'

'Running for cover, I think. You go to sleep. I shan't be too long.'

I pondered the wisdom of offering him a scotch, then decided that it was up to him to accept or refuse. I all at once felt like one myself, and when he joined me he sipped it with no sign of unseemly appetite. In an odd way flattered that he'd decided to come to us, I didn't want him to feel that it was at the price of the kind of cross-examination and criticism he'd have been bound to face from our parents; so we talked around the subject until it couldn't be avoided.

'Somebody's got to win,' he said at one point then.

'I thought you liked that. You'd take anybody on, you used to say. "I'll be as good as anybody who walks on to the field".'

'I was.'

'But not any longer?'

'They've no mercy, once you start to slip.'

'Every coin's got two sides: love and hate; adulation and disdain.'

'What the fucking hell do you know about it?'

I shrugged and he twisted in his chair, as though he half regretted the brutality of his put-down. But only half.

'You're good with the words, our kid. Like, once you've tagged the ailment you've found the cure.'

I finished my whisky and got up. 'Anyway, I've got to work in the morning. Your bed's ready, so come on Twinkle-toes.'

He remembered who was talking to him, but not quickly enough to kill the sudden venom in his eyes. He was raw, his feelings flinching from every flick of the verbal whip. And he'd taken some whipping, from the bright boys of the press, from his team bosses, from the erstwhile loving fans on the terraces. There was a part of him that felt betrayed. Telling him for so long how brilliant he was, they left him no room for failure; and what he seemed intent on now was something I'd seen in more than one boy of apparently exceptional academic promise. Slipping from the rarefied heights and disappointing more than their average brethren could, they had, in face of criticism, set themselves on a downhill course seemingly perversely designed to prove how mistaken first expectations had been.

My mother had a simple phrase to describe it. 'He's cutting off his nose to spite his face.' My father contributed another: 'Give a dog a bad name ...'

I'd called to see them on my way home from school, without telling Bonny I was going to, feeling duty bound to let them know where he was, before someone else did and compounded the hurt they both felt at his not going to see them first.

I knew well enough why he hadn't. My mother's reaction, made perhaps still more unbearable by love, was no different in essence from that which assailed him from all sides. She knew only what she read in the papers, and only the simplistic verdicts of the popular tabloids at that, rammed home in a few short sentences – the lengthier, more subtle analysis of the posh Sundays being beyond her powers to tease out. His achievement had been the kind boys dream of and grown men envy, and, baffled, she frankly could not understand why he didn't behave himself.

'It's harder than a lot of folk realise, Dot,' my father said. He clamped his dentures round his pipe, his own disappointment no less for his awareness of what at least some of the pressures might be. No braggart, he'd all the same known quiet pride in being the father of

Bonny Taylor the hero, and the shame for the weak-willed rake whose achievement had turned rotten.

'Imagine,' I said, 'having to prove yourself time after time after time; on trial every Saturday afternoon. Thousands of fans watching your every move on the field and the press watching every move off it. It would drive me potty.'

'But you're not our Bonny,' my mother said. 'You never yearned for any of that. And you hadn't the gift for it, in any case.'

'No ...' I promised to bring him round home to see them.

'He'll come when he wants to,' my mother said, proud in her pain, 'and stop away the same.'

I left them, my mother brooding, no doubt looking back, trying to find the flaws of the man in the recollected shortcomings of the child.

'Twinkle-toes.' That had got to him. I remember afterwards that a sports reporter had dubbed him so in a piece which savaged him for playing to the crowd, showing off by displaying his individual dexterity at the cost of team effort and the necessary end of scoring goals. 'Pissing about instead of getting on with the game,' was a remark I'd heard in my local. In a team of hard tacklers he was the virtuoso of elegant footwork, suspected by some fans of being afraid to get hurt. Of course he didn't want to be injured unnecessarily. But physical coward? Not Bonny. I'd watched him through boyhood and adolescence as he fought anyone, bigger than himself or not, who dared to suggest unfortunate connotations in the nickname my mother had given him and which had stuck. Christened Bernard, he was a beautiful child over whom my mother crowed in maternal exultation. 'Ah! but he's t'marrer to bonny,' she would say, meaning he was synonymous with beauty, or contained the essential core of beauty in his physical person. We were, as it happened, not a bad-looking family. My mother, at turned fifty, was still a handsome woman. But of the two of us, it was Bonny over whom matrons had drooled, Bonny who had turned girls' heads from the time some admiring tot could toddle to his side and take his hand in a propriet-ary grasp. The blond curls had darkened now and lost their spring, but the blue eyes were still a blaze when turned straight on you, and his thin aquiline nose, cleanly sculptured thin-lipped mouth and neat but determined chin were a combination to draw women's attention even without their knowledge of his status as a folk hero. 'It's not fair,' a woman colleague had once said, 'that a man should be so good-looking and have an exceptional talent as well,' Or that he should have both and not know, as my mother put it, 'how to behave himself.' And be happy. For I had no doubt that however much his behaviour might upset others, it hurt him more; and happy he was not.

I caught a glimpse of his face behind the rain-splattered window as I walked the last few yards to the house. He'd kept indoors all day.

'I expected you sooner than this,' he said as I went in. 'Don't you drive to school?'

'Eileen takes the car,' I told him. 'She's farther to go than I have.'

'You could have used my car. It's standing idle.'

'Imagine the raised eyebrows and questions if I rolled up in a dusky-pink Jag.'

'Enjoying your rich kid brother's handouts, eh?'

'I didn't mean it that way. I thought you didn't want your where-abouts broadcast.'

'The neighbours can hardly miss seeing the motor in the drive. They'll all know by now; everybody round here.'

'Well ... What have you been doing all day?'

'Nothing much.'

There was a scattered pile of old Sunday colour magazines, and a couple of books he'd taken from the shelves and dipped into. In the kitchen I found a coffee cup and the plate from which he'd eaten the sandwiches Eileen had made for him before leaving the house.

'The phone rang a couple of times, and somebody came to the door. I didn't answer.'

The telephone rang again as I was cleaning vegetables for the evening meal.

'Mr Taylor?' the man's voice asked.

'Speaking.'

'Mr Gordon Taylor?'

'That's right.'

'I understand your brother, Mr Bonny Taylor, is visiting you just now, Mr Taylor.'

'Just a minute. Who is this speaking?'

'Oh, I'm sorry, Mr Taylor. Didn't I say? This is the *Gazette*.'

'Oh, the *Gazette*.'

Bonny was in the doorway now, watching me. He lifted one hand, palm out, and slowly moved it through the air.

'Where did you get your information?' I asked the reporter.

'It came to us through a member of the public.'

'I'm sorry, but you appear to have been misinformed.'

'That's too bad. We wondered if Mr Taylor had any comment to make about the reports in the national press on disciplinary action by his club.'

'I'm afraid I can't help you.'

'We'd be glad to send someone round and give him a chance to put his side of the case.'

'I'm afraid that's not possible.'

He had the wit not to push it. 'Sorry to have bothered you, Mr Taylor.'

'They'll be back,' Bonny said as I left the phone and returned to the kitchen. 'If he's daft enough to let it slip to a mate on one of the nationals, they'll come and camp on the doorstep. And you're a rotten liar, our kid,' he added as an afterthought.

'You said yourself, the car's in the drive for all to see.'

He shrugged, watching me as I dropped sprouts into a pan of water.

'Do you do all the cooking?'

'I do very little actual cooking. But as I'm usually home before Eileen I do the preparation. It's a fairish division of labour.' I paused. 'My *macho*, such as it is, operates in other areas.'

He eased his shoulder off the doorpost and half turned.

'I only asked a question.'

'If you'll give me your keys I'll put the motor under cover.'

He dipped his hand into the pocket of his slacks and held out the purse. It was of a soft, rich pliable leather: expensive, like all his accessories. 'It's a bit late for that.'

'We can always let them think you've been and gone.'

'Can you drive a Jag?'

'I learned this morning. I had to shift it while you were still asleep, to let the Mini out.'

I'd sat for some minutes in the stationary car after I'd started the engine, enjoying the threatening growl of power as I gently depressed the accelerator, the smell and comfort of the leather upholstery, the battery of dials and switches on the dashboard. I tried again now to decide if I felt envious. No more, I thought, than one felt on seeing a man with a really beautiful woman. Every man ought some time in his life to make it with a stunner; every man should sometime have the chance of driving a powerful and well-equipped motor car. It was the longing to possess that beggared a man. I wondered if my awareness of that was a sign of maturity.

I was shutting the garage doors in the dusk when the headlights of the Mini swung into the drive.

'Is he staying, then?' Eileen asked.

'It looks like it.'

'How long is he staying?'

'I haven't asked him. He's welcome, isn't he?'

'Of course he is.'

She'd been to the supermarket. She shopped for the weekend's food after school on Thursday, that being a quieter time than Friday evening or Saturday morning.

'This one feels heavy.'

'Support it underneath. There's a couple of bottles of wine in it.'

'Two?'

'They had an offer on a new line. And we've got a guest.'

'I don't know how much Bonny's drinking nowadays.'

'You should read the papers more often.'

It was said drily and, I thought, without malice. I wondered as I followed her into the house what Eileen really felt about Bonny, because I didn't know. By the time we'd met and married, he was already famous and no more than an occasional visitor home. It was, in any case, her way to be quiet and unimpressionable. I found her stillness reassuring. In discussion, be it about education, the arts, politics or any topic of the day, she preferred listening to talking. My typical mind picture was of her sitting forward, elbows on knees, taking sips from a mug of coffee or tea clutched between both hands, a small, almost secret smile touching her eyes and lips as someone made a point she felt no need to contradict or to amplify. But anyone who was lured by her quietness into thinking her unintelligent, or suspected from her undemonstrativeness a lack of passion, was wrong on both counts.

It felt cold enough for snow now. I shivered as I stepped into the warm hall and shut the door.

There was a bottle of Spanish Rioja in the drinks cupboard. I put the new bottles away and opened that while Eileen lit the gas under the vegetables and grilled pork chops. Bonny glanced at the bottle as I held it over his glass at table. He nodded. 'Thanks.' I noted, though, that he left it untouched until he had nearly finished his main course, when he took no more than half an inch of wine into his mouth, rolled it for a moment before swallowing, and replaced the glass, holding the stem with his neat square-tipped fingers, before picking up his knife and fork again to strip every last shred of meat from his chop. I found it hard to reconcile this abstemious behaviour with his reputation. Unless he was trying very, very hard to demolish that, in our eyes at least.

Eileen had pushed the vegetable dishes towards him without speaking. He waved his hand in refusal.

'Thanks. I enjoyed that, Eileen.'

'I called round home this afternoon,' I said, 'and told mother and dad you were here.'

'Oh, did you?' Bonny fingered the stem of his glass again, but didn't lift it.

'I thought I'd better do it before somebody else did.'

'I suppose you're right. What did they say?'

'They'd like to see you.'

'Uh-uh. They could do with something to take their minds off me. Isn't it time you and Eileen gave them a grandkid to coo over?'

'I don't think you can count on that,' Eileen said.

'Oh?' Bonny looked from her to me.

'There's something wrong with Eileen's plumbing,' I told him. 'She went into hospital last autumn for an examination and a minor op. They told her then it was unlikely she'd ever conceive.'

'I'm sorry, Eileen,' Bonny said. 'I'd no idea.'

'Oh, I've told her it's grounds for divorce,' I said lightly.

Bonny's gaze flicked once again from face to face, as if he were wondering how much the fact could have damaged our relationship, how much, while Eileen might feel deprived, I might feel both deprived and cheated. I noticed that a faint colour had tinged Eileen's cheeks.

'So it looks,' she said, reaching for our plates, 'as if that particular task must be left to you.'

'That'll be the day,' Bonny said.

I wondered which of the dolly girls he'd been photographed with had come anywhere near qualifying for the role of mother of our parents' first grandchild. He must have had what the average man would regard as some very pleasant screwing, nonetheless: a model, a member of a pop group, a girl who'd appeared in a couple of minor (and, I gathered, very bad) sexploitation films. All in, or from the fringes of, showbiz; but none with any real talent – nothing to match his. Was this his choice, or what his way of life had limited him to?

The doorbell rang as Eileen had got up to serve the rice pudding. Being nearest, she went to answer it and was back almost immediately. 'It's two men, asking for Bonny.'

Bonny muttered something I didn't catch.

'I'll talk to them.' I went into the hall. Eileen had left the door open, but not asked them in. It was snowing now, thin and grey. They were both bareheaded and drops of melted snow glistened in their hair. One was a photographer. He stood a little behind his companion, a camera and light-meter in leather cases hanging from straps round his neck.

'We're from the *Gazette*,' the first man said. 'We wondered if we could speak to Mr Taylor.'

'Are you the man who rang up earlier?'

'That would be the editor.'

'I told him there was nothing doing.'

The reporter had sideboards and a *Viva Zapata* moustache. The photographer, an older man, looked as if he didn't care one way or the other. There were plenty of pictures of Bonny; the story was the important thing and that wasn't his pigeon. He shifted his weight in the cold, alternately tapping one heel against the other. I felt churlish for not asking them in; but how long they stood there depended on them.

'This is your brother's home town, Mr Taylor. The editor thought he might welcome a chance of explaining himself to the people who know him.'

'*Explaining* himself?'

'Putting his side of the matter.'

'I see. Well, I'm afraid he's not here now.'

'Oh?'

The photographer glanced up the drive to the garage and the Mini standing outside the closed door. Neither of them believed me. 'It's a pity,' the reporter said. 'A statement from your brother would have been useful in setting the balance straight.'

'It's half past six, Harry,' the photographer said.

The reporter made no reply, but looked at me for a moment longer.

'I'm sorry. I can't help you.'

'We'll leave it, then,' the reporter said. 'Sorry to have disturbed you.'

The *Gazette* was a weekly. 'They print on Thursday night,' I told Bonny. 'You've robbed them of their scoop.'

'That's their poor lookout,' Bonny said. 'Yours would have been hawks from all the nationals running your doorstep off tomorrow, if you'd let those two in. They might turn up yet,' he added in a moment.

'Didn't you fancy a chance of putting your side of it?'

'What side? I've been a bad lad. How many ways does it need saying?'

'There seems to be no shortage of other people ready to say it.'

'Oh, sure!'

'That bird in the *Sunday Globe,* for instance.'

'"The Bonny Taylor I know," you mean,' Bonny said. '"Bonny is a deeply divided man." She's as thick as two short planks herself. The only division she knows about is what's between—' Eileen was bringing my pudding. She looked at the back of Bonny's head as he broke off. 'You know what I mean.'

The first spoonful of pudding scorched my mouth. I gasped, wordless, reaching for the remains of my wine.

'Don't bolt it, Gordon,' Eileen said.

'I'm going to be late.'

'Have you got to go out?' Bonny asked.

'Afraid so. Evening class. There'll be twenty-two people waiting for me.'

'What are you teaching?'

'It's a creative-writing class I was talked into taking.'

'Do you do any yourself? Creative writing, I mean.'

'Oh, the occasional poem.'

'Does that make you an expert?'

'Has every football coach you know been the best player of his day?'

I took the things from the table into the kitchen and managed a moment alone with Eileen.

'I'm sorry about this. It's damned inconvenient. Will you be all right?'

'Of course I shall. Television will save us if conversation flags.'

'I can't let them down at the last minute.'

'You go on. I don't expect you'll be late, will you?

'No, no. I'll be back as soon as I can.'

I fondled her behind. The roughish wool mixture of her skirt

13

slipped silkily over the taut stuff of her pants. In the routine of married life desire gets used to awaiting its appointed hour. But I wanted her now, and given a different evening, with no one else here and no need to go out, we might have enjoyed reverting to the snatched opportunities of our courting days with a half-dressed clinch on the rug.

'Go on,' Eileen murmured. 'You'll be late.'

'I have an urgent desire to possess your milk-white flesh.'

'It'll still be here when you get back.'

'And that's the great joy and comfort of my life.'

She turned and smiled, giving me that sidelong, hooded-eyed look of pleasure that I knew so well, before she pushed me aside to get to the sink.

Bonny appeared in the doorway. 'I'll help Eileen with the pots.'

'There aren't many,' Eileen said. 'And we don't dry. We leave them to drain.'

'Put your feet up,' I told him. 'Open another bottle, if you want to. I wouldn't go out myself on a night like this if I didn't have to. And by the way,' I said to Eileen, 'in case anybody else rings up or comes looking for Bonny, the story now is that he *was* here for a while, but he left.'

2

The class met in a Victorian house, in a residential suburb of the town, that the authority had bought for use as a teachers' centre and adult education institute. It was the English Adviser, an Irishman named Noonan, who had persuaded me to mount the course in response to requests for it from the public. I'd spent part of the winter trying to find a professional or semi-professional writer willing to take it over next autumn and give it a much needed tilt towards the practical. For I was aware that I erred too much on the side of literary appreciation, when what nearly all of them wanted was to be shown how to make their own work better – at whatever level it aspired to – and given solid advice about how to market it. Some of them, in fact, had sold quite a bit, and who was I, with a mere three or four poems published in pamphlets from obscure presses, to lay down the law? Noonan had shrugged away my scruples.

'They've all got one thing in common,' he said, 'they're lonely. They want to talk about what they're doing. We give them the chance. I expect three-quarters of them are wankers, anyway.'

I had to laugh, because in his direct, disenchanted way Noonan had put his finger on a characteristic of this – and, I supposed – most other writing classes. There was some 'wanking' going on, both in the metaphorical sense of work which substituted cosy fables for the complex and often messy realities of life, and more directly, I suspected, in the case of one bespectacled, plain-faced plumpish girl who took no particular care with her appearance but who wrote verse for me to appraise containing the most startlingly overt erotic images. I had one in my case to hand back to her tonight. In it a woman with few physical inhibitions said things she was otherwise too shy to let her lover hear, only when he was made deaf by the pressure of her thighs on his ears. Though I'd laughed and passed the piece to Eileen, who had giggled in her turn, it was in its way a quite telling comment on the sexual climate of the 'Seventies: of desire without tenderness, of the death of courtly love in the face of a readily assuagable lust. But Eunice I'd always previously seen in trousers. Tonight, despite the inclement weather, she wore smoke-grey nylon stretched over unexpectedly shapely legs; legs crossed one over the other, inescapable to my line of vision, on the front row, their owner expectantly waiting with pad and ballpoint to capture any recordable nugget of truth I might produce during the proceedings. I found myself willing to revise my conviction that the images in her work were no more than the product of a fevered imagination. Perhaps she'd had her moments, after all. And I wondered if Eileen would find cause to giggle were she to know about the stir of flesh that came on me at one moment when those legs uncrossed, recrossed and settled themselves, drawing down my gaze for all to see in mid-sentence. Had I actually caught a pale glimmer of inner thigh above a stocking-top?

'So it seems to me,' I was saying, 'that any class like this is bound to be full of contradictions, because, unlike most other subjects we might study, we're faced with the many things that the term "creative writing" embraces, and the many different levels it aspires to and achieves in practice. Ask the average well-informed football fan to name the six best current players, and his list will roughly tally with that of the sports writer – the expert – as well as that, for instance, of the intellectual who follows the game. They all subscribe to the same criteria of what is the best, and the best is what they all enjoy the most. But ask the average man what he has been reading and he's more likely to say Harold Robbins than Saul Bellow or Marcel Proust or any book of poetry. No, the consensus doesn't exist. Much work with a wide circulation has only a brief life. Much work which will be read fifty years' hence for entertainment, for aesthetic pleasure, for the picture it gives of life in our day, has in that day a limited circulation and brings its creator only a meagre financial reward. Much the same applies to music and the visual arts, of course. Van Gogh never sold a painting during his lifetime; he existed on handouts from his brother Theo, a man we now remember only because of his connection with the artist, but who was the success of the family at the time. "Why can't you settle down and earn a respectable living, Vincent, like your brother Theo?"' A few chuckles here.

'Put briefly, what I'm saying is that teaching someone to write well is by no means synonymous with teaching him or her to make money by writing. It's also true that some of us will not see this as a problem at all. We shall be satisfied to find a level we can operate on and a market we can cater for. And it's because creative writing is on one level a commodity and on another an art that makes this course so tricky to teach, unlike mathematics or physics or carpentry or needlework.

'I suppose I could have said all this when we first met, but I thought it might confuse the issue, and I wanted to get to know you and find out something about you through your written work. I've been thinking about it more and more, however, and since it's become something of a burden on my mind I thought I'd offer it tonight as a kind of interim summing-up and a possible topic for discussion.'

I paused, looking round them. The harsh weather had reduced their number to fifteen. Perhaps I should have waited, I thought, and made my statement when I had something like a full class.

Jack Atherton, a bearded lad in an anorak on the second row, put up his hand. I nodded at him.

'If you're having doubts about the success of the course, wondering if it's been worthwhile, I can tell you that as far as I'm concerned it's been a big help.' There were a few murmured hear-hears. 'I mean I'm a lot surer of what I'm doing and what I ought to be doing than I was when we started.'

Mrs Brotherton leaned forward: a trim, tweed-coated woman in her fifties. A couple of spots of colour had appeared in her cheeks, and her voice, as she half turned her head to look at the others, had that earnest, slightly wavering note of one who is not sure she ought to speak at all, but who has something she's determined to say.

'I don't know what other people's experience is as regards personal contact with Mr Taylor, but though I certainly wouldn't describe my work as great art, he's been able to point out technical improvements which have helped me to submit it to editors with more confidence; and in fact since this course started I've sold three stories and I've got editors asking for more.' She nodded, sat back, gave me a shy little smile, then looked at her hands.

'All I want,' Eunice Cadby said, with her slight drawl, 'is to be encouraged to see how I can express my experience, my feelings and my observation more fluently and honestly. Though I'd obviously be thrilled to be published, that can wait till I'm ready for it. But I do feel I'm nearer to it than I was four or five months ago.'

No one else spoke up, but they were beginning to talk among themselves. I raised my voice.

'Well, thank you all very much for the vote of confidence. Perhaps one of you might like to kick off a general discussion on the topic.'

'Standards,' Mr Lazenby said. 'That's what it should be about. The world has no standards any more. The pen is a mighty weapon. It should be used with responsibility.' He was a retired bank manager, in his early sixties, with sleek grey hair and a face made ruddy by tiny broken veins. His style of dress – thornproof tweeds, Viyella shirts, polished brogues – always reminded me of my father, except that *he* bought his suits from a multiple tailors, his pastel-coloured shirts from the supermarket, and marred the nevertheless dapper result by adding fancy cardigans between jacket and shirt.

'The only responsibility of the pen,' Jack Atherton said, 'is to put down the truth. Whether my truth is your truth is another matter.'

'I always remember what an editor once told me years ago,' said a thin, mousy, sweet-voiced woman whose name constantly escaped me, but who I knew had, under various pseudonyms, published more than all the rest of us together. 'She said that when I wrote for her magazine I was being accepted as guest in my readers' homes, and that I should always comport myself accordingly.'

Jack Atherton, his back to the woman, raised his eyebrows, sighed and muttered something under his breath.

'You might just as well not have bothered,' he said to me afterwards, 'for all it meant to most of 'em.'

'I know. But it was worth it for the ones who did understand. And I suppose that also answers the question I was asking myself – is the class worthwhile?' The door closed behind the last of the stragglers. I fastened my briefcase.

'Have you time for a drink?' Jack asked.

'I haven't really. I've got somebody waiting for me at home, and I promised not to be late. But I could murder a pint, and I'd like a word with you about your playscript.'

'Fine. Let's go across the road.'

Eunice Cadby came out of the ladies' cloakroom as we walked along the corridor. There must be something revealing about the demeanour of two men bound for a pub, because she said, though she couldn't have heard our conversation, 'Mind if I come with you?'

'Our pleasure.'

Jack walked a few paces ahead. As I held open the door and let Eunice pass through, the cold draught from outside brought the heavy musk of her scent to my nostrils.

'I rather thought you'd be going on somewhere tonight, Eunice,' I said.

'Oh, why?'

'You're wearing perfume and stockings. I can't remember you in anything but trousers before.'

'Oh, I got fed up of the jeans and mucky sweater bit,' she said airily. 'You can let yourself go before you know it, these days.'

'"There are no standards any more," as Mr Lazenby would say.'

'Quite.' She chuckled. 'Anyway, I took stock of myself and decided it was time I changed my image. My legs are my best feature in any case, so why should I keep them hidden?'

'Why indeed?'

Some people were leaving a corner table as we went into the pub lounge. 'Bag that,' I told them, 'and I'll get the drinks. What'll you have, Eunice?' Jack, I knew, would have a pint of bitter. Eunice asked for a half of lager. I went to the bar, slightly relieved that her new image didn't call for vodka martinis. Lazenby was standing at the counter, drinking bottled Guinness.

'Mr Lazenby ... can I get you a drink while I'm in the chair?'

'I have one, thanks.' He looked over his shoulder to see who I was with. 'I'll join you for a few minutes, though, if I may.'

'Sure.' I watched him cross the room as I waited for my order. I knew that neither Jack nor Eunice would welcome his company, but it was unavoidable. I hoped he wouldn't stay long, though, as I wanted to talk to Jack about his play.

'Did you manage to look at my poem?' Eunice asked, when we'd taken the top off our drinks, said 'Cheers' and 'All the best' and settled in our chairs.

'Er, yes, I did.' I gave a quick glance at Lazenby. Even less than Jack's play was Eunice's poem something I felt like discussing in front of him. 'I was going to give it back to you. I've made a few pencilled comments in the margin.' I opened my briefcase, took the sheets from the folder and passed them to her. 'Perhaps we can talk about it when you've had a chance to study my notes.'

'The main thing is whether you thought it worked. In general, I mean.'

'Oh, yes. I was quite impressed. The notes are in places where your metre falters a little, and where I think you might be overstating your metaphor and imagery.'

'Do you mean the cunnilingus bit?' Eunice asked.

Jack leaned back in his chair. Over the rim of his glass he glanced at Lazenby, then at me, his eyes dancing with mischief.

'No, no—' I began.

'Do we really have to have all that, for goodness' sake?' Lazenby said. 'Is that all that writing can rise to nowadays: perversion and debauchery?'

'Just what do you mean, Mr Lazenby?' Eunice challenged him.

I put my hand on her arm and turned to Lazenby. I found myself mildly surprised that he'd recognised the term.

'As a matter of fact, Mr Lazenby, Eunice uses it to create a very telling image. Here are a man and a woman involved in perhaps the most intimate of sexual acts, yet unable to communicate verbally. To my mind it comments perceptively on the sexual climate of the 'Seventies: a climate in which a man and a woman can engage in what used to be the ultimate intimacy, sexual congress, on the basis of an acquaintance which finds them like shy fumbling strangers when they come quite simply to talk to each other.'

'We don't all live that way, you know,' Lazenby said, his mouth prim.

'Perhaps that's what Eunice's poem is saying: that people shouldn't live that way.'

'I don't know why anybody should want to know about it.'

'Well, at least,' I said, 'it's an honest attempt to come to grips with a situation that exists. And it may well be more important as an expression of our times than the assumptions you make in a lot of your work.'

'And what assumptions might they be?' Lazenby asked.

I'd started, so I might as well go on, though I'd have preferred to attack Lazenby's work without an audience, particularly this audience, which I knew would be on my side.

'I mean the assumptions you make instead of looking squarely and directly at a subject, and describing it in vivid concrete detail and leaving your reader to draw his own moral and emotional conclusions from it. What you do is load your work with abstract concepts designed to arouse an automatic and predictable response in your reader.'

'To what concepts are you referring?'

'I mean concepts like honour, truth, justice, courage, loyalty, love, God – even right and wrong.'

'We all know what they mean.'

'No, we don't, Mr Lazenby. You know what they mean to you, but you can't automatically assume they mean the same to anyone else. They're not certainties that we all share any longer.'

'More's the pity. I told you that what the world lacked was standards.'

'Just because people don't share your standards,' Eunice said hotly, 'you think they haven't got any values.'

'You've only got to look at the world today to see the answer to that,' Lazenby said.

This finally stung Jack to speech. 'It's not a world we made, chum,' he said. 'It's the one you've left us with.'

Lazenby gave a short mirthless laugh. 'I'm afraid I'm not accepting the responsibility for that.'

'You built an empire,' Jack said, 'but you won't accept responsibility for the consequences of it.'

'I didn't give the Empire away.'

'No, I expect you'd have fought for it to the last drop of somebody else's blood.'

'I seem to remember spilling some of my own blood to make the world safer for the likes of you,' Lazenby said stiffly.

'There's no need to get personal about all this, you know,' Eunice told him.

'Isn't there? I must be old-fashioned, then, because I still take insults personally.' He emptied his glass and began to button his raglan overcoat.

'I'm sorry, Mr Lazenby,' I said. 'I didn't intend it to take this turn, but you did rather start it yourself with your criticism of Eunice's poem, offered, what's more, without your having read it.'

'I don't need to read it,' Lazenby said. 'I don't want to and I don't intend to.'

'You won't be asked to,' Eunice said, flushing, 'don't you worry.'

Lazenby stood up. 'I'll leave you, then, to carry on your – ah – literary discussion.' He nodded curtly at me. 'Good night.'

'Silly old sod,' Jack muttered as Lazenby walked, straight-backed, head up, to the door.

'Oh, Lazenby's all right in his way,' I said. 'A good solid citizen, all of a piece. But you'd have to take him apart and put him back together again to make a writer of him. And who am I to try to do that, even if he'd let me?' I glanced at my watch. 'God! Look at the time.'

Jack got up. 'I'll get another round.'

'Just a quick half for me, Jack. I shall get shot as it is.'

'Isn't Bonny Taylor, the football player, your brother?' Eunice asked, when Jack had gone to the bar.

'Yes, he is.'

'I suddenly remembered tonight, when you were making that analogy between football players and writers.'

'Bonny's a great player. Everybody knows he is, and he gets rewarded accordingly. It's different for writers. That's the point I was making.'

'The rewards don't seem to do him much good, do they?'

'No.'

'I'm sorry if I'm being personal.'

'Bonny's failings are common knowledge.'

'He'd make a fascinating subject.'

'There's been a lot of print expended on him already.'

'That's all superficial. I meant in depth, as a biography or the basis of a novel.'

'Hmm . . . It would probably need a talent as fine as his to capture him.'

Jack came back.

'Listen, Jack. I've got to dash in a minute. But about your play-script.'

'Yes?'

I took the bundle of haphazardly typed sheets out of my case.

'I think it's got a lot going for it, but first of all it seems to me – and I'm a bit out of my depth here – it seems to me that you haven't made up your mind whether it's a stage play, a radio play or one for the telly. It's got elements of all three forms and it doesn't work completely in any of them. I'd get hold of some books about the different techniques, if I were you, and read up. But the dialogue and character confrontations are vivid, though you could lose a lot of the four-letter words without diluting its grainy realism.' I smiled at him.

'It's how people talk, you know. I don't know if you've ever worked on a factory floor or a building site, but I can assure you it's how people talk.'

'Okay, but one of the problems in portraying poverty of vocabulary is to do it without numbing your audience's sensibilities or boring them out of their minds. What I think is that you'd benefit from hearing the script read.'

'How would I manage that?'

'I mean get a number of people together, cast it and read it. You might find enough suitable members of the class. I'll listen in, if you like, but I think you should do it on a separate evening from class. You don't want an audience of Lazenby, Mrs Brotherton and some others we all know tut-tutting and cramping everybody's style. Perhaps Eunice would be willing to join in and help you choose the others.'

Eunice reached for the script. 'May I?'

'Sure.' She scanned the first couple of pages.

'If you'd let me take it home to read, I could perhaps come up with some names for next week.'

'Okay.'

I swallowed the rest of my beer. 'And now, kids, I must be on my way.'

'Are you going through the town centre?' Eunice asked.

'I am.'

'I'd appreciate a lift. I can catch a bus from there.'

'Right you are.'

Jack still had a three-quarters full pint of beer.

'I'm not going to rush this,' he said. 'I'll see you later.'

It was only a four- or five-minute drive into town. Eunice's perfume was noticeable again in the confines of the Mini. I found myself catching the intermittent glitter of light from streetlamps on the grey sheen of her stockinged knees. Perhaps, I thought, the poems were not the product of a frustrated sexual drive. Perhaps she has a lover. Perhaps those are the actual thighs . . . I found myself speculating what she was like between them: the odour, the taste. A couple of weeks ago, if I'd brought myself to wonder, I should not have dwelt on the thought. Now I asked myself if she might not match the tangy succulence of Eileen.

'I'd like to meet your brother,' Eunice said, after a silence.

'Oh?'

'I think a woman might achieve an insight that a man wouldn't.'

'I've not noticed much success so far.'

'Oh, I don't mean those shallow, decorative bitches he's been linked with.'

'Are you sure your interest is entirely artistic?'

'What d'you mean?'

'Bonny's a celebrity, and an attractive man.'

'I shouldn't think I'm his type.'

'Do you know anything about the game?'

'Quite a lot. I've always been a keen fan.'

I pulled up at a red light. A fine drizzle was falling now and the air was milder. But the town looked black, drawn into itself. It was beginning to feel like a long winter and I found myself yearning for the spring.

'He doesn't get home very often,' I said.

'I heard he was here now.'

'Oh? Where did you hear that?'

'A friend of mine works for the *Gazette*.'

'Yes,' I admitted in a minute, 'he's here. But he's not going out and I don't know how long he'll be staying.'

She let it drop. We were in the town centre now. I asked her where she wanted putting down.

'Near the bus station, please.'

'Let's see, don't you live out on the Moor?'

'Yes. It's only a short bus ride.'

'Do you live on your own or with family?'

'On my own. I have a council flat.'

I couldn't recall what she did for a living. I didn't bother to ask.

'Here we are, then.'

'Thanks very much for the lift. And special thanks for defending my poem.'

'I shouldn't have been able to if I hadn't liked it.'

'It was sweet of you and I'm both grateful and encouraged.' She turned her head and looked at me. She seemed to move her face a fraction closer. For a surprised second I thought she was going to kiss my cheek. Then, briskly, she gathered her coat about her and got out of the car. 'Good night.'

''Night, Eunice.'

There was a bus for the Moor standing at one of the platforms. I watched her as she trotted towards it, with that outward throw of the legs from the knees down that some women have when they run. I felt the creep of skin on private flesh again. It wasn't until I'd seen her out of sight behind the bus and moved the car off that I noticed she'd taken Jack's script but left her poem.

Bonny was alone downstairs, watching a feature film on television.

'Eileen gone to bed?'

'Yeah. When you didn't hurry back she said she'd have a bath and an early night. Where've you been till this time, anyway? In a pub?'

'I got tied up with a couple of pupils.'

I slumped beside him on the sofa, thinking there was something vaguely familiar about the film, though I couldn't remember the plot, nor even how this scene developed. Robert Mitchum was confronting an ingratiatingly smiling Kirk Douglas in a huge comfortable room with a log fire.

'Douglas is a gangster,' Bonny said. 'Mitchum's tried to get out of the racket, but he's marked down to be the fall guy.'

'*Build my Gallows High.*'

'That's it.'

'Did you have a drink?'

'No, I didn't bother.'

'Like a nightcap?'

'If you're having one.'

I got the bottle of Bells out of the cupboard and poured two doubles.

'One of them said she'd like to meet you.'

'Who did?'

'Eunice Cadby. One of my pupils.'

'Did she?' his tone said. 'Not bloody likely.'

'Somebody on the *Gazette* told her you were in town. She said she thought somebody ought to write you up in depth. She said she thought a woman might do it with more insight than a man.'

'Very amusing.'

'She referred to your women as "superficial, decorative bitches". Or was it "shallow, decorative bitches"?'

He looked at me, curiosity stirring. 'Did she?' he said again. 'Is she any good as a writer?'

I reached for my case and took out the poem she'd left in the car. 'Judge for yourself. That's her latest opus.'

He took it and scanned it quickly, letting out a softly explosive and amused 'Jesus!' as he came to the end. He shifted his position on the sofa and, smiling slightly, settled down to read it more carefully.

'Well, well!' His smile broadened into a grin. 'So that's the kind of stuff they write in evening classes.'

'Not all of them, I hasten to assure you. We've got our share of Empire-mourners and cuddly-rabbit makers.'

25

'It's not bad, though, you know,' Bonny said, glancing at the poem again. 'Not bad at all.'

'I rather thought so myself.'

'What's she like, then, this Eunice?'

'If you'd asked me before, I'd have said she was a plain and rather slovenly lass with too much imagination for her own peace of mind. But tonight she turned up wearing silk stockings, make-up and half a bottle of perfume. Good legs. It was quite a transformation.'

'She's been turning you on, our kid.' Bonny's grin came again. 'Go on, admit it. The legs and the poetry together turned you on.'

'Well, okay. I mean, you can't exactly control these things, can you?'

'You ought to get paid danger money.'

'Yeah, well. I've got all the turning-on I need in this house, so that makes a difference. And speaking of that, I'd better go and see if I'm still in Eileen's good books. Are you stopping up a bit?'

'I'll see this picture through, if you don't mind.'

'Help yourself. And by the way, don't think you're not welcome for as long as you like, but it'll help to know what your plans are.'

'I haven't any plans. I ought to go and see mum and dad.'

'It's Friday tomorrow. They'll be in the shop most of the day.'

My father, made redundant at fifty-five in his job in the stores of a local engineering works, had put part of his savings to his redundancy money and bought a lock-up fish and chip shop a couple of streets from where he and my mother lived. He'd turned out to be a good fish-frier and the business was prospering.

'I suppose I can go before they open again at night.'

We talked briefly about how he was going to get there and whether he minded being seen, then decided to discuss it again in the morning. I said good night and went upstairs.

Eileen was an inert shape under the duvet, her face hidden from the light which burned at my side of the bed. I undressed and got in as quietly as I could, and took up my book. I'd done no more than find my place and pick up the thread from the previous page, when Eileen turned and tucked up behind me, her arm moving over my hip, hand searching my groin. I switched out the light and twisted to face her. Her habitual receptive languor had left her tonight. She was setting the pace. When her mouth found mine it was a ferocity of desire that seemed to have no memory but thwarted longing, no promise of a future beyond now. But it was my knowledge of precisely what she liked that hardened her nipples between the roll of finger and thumb, tightening her breath to catch in the throat and vaulting her want beyond an attempted caress between her thighs to the moment when she turned on to her back and drew me over to where her urgent hand could guide me into her. The speed at which she'd come for me rushed me to the edge of climax. Drawing her legs together between mine, I sought a depth and drag of penetration that would pleasure her to the bounds of her need while sparing me. I cast for diversion in thoughts: Bonny turning on me, eyes full of venom; the fifteen faces of tonight's class, intelligence, gentle forgiving incomprehension; Jack's glee and anger in the pub; Eunice's poem; Eunice herself ... Unbidden, bold, obliterating all else, a picture came of drawn-up silken legs and parted white thighs. For a second I tensed flesh, contracted muscles. Then, knowing my failure, I drove deep and came.

3

I was usually up first, taking Eileen a cup of tea before I made a quick trip through the bathroom while she went and started breakfast; but when the alarm clock rang the next morning I reached to stop it and found myself alone in bed. I went straight down. Eileen was scrambling eggs in the kitchen.

'I didn't know what Bonny might want,' she said, 'so I thought I'd do something more substantial than usual.'

'Usual' was a bowl of muesli or cornflakes followed by toast and honey or marmalade.

'I'll take him a cup of tea and ask him. If he wants to lie in he can do. He knows how to boil an egg, or fry bacon.'

Before pouring the tea I reached for and cupped one of her unencumbered breasts through her dressing-gown. The beauty of Eileen's breasts had almost stopped my breath with excitement the first time I saw them. I was already three-parts in love with her by then, in a tender unfocused way that had grown out of my pleasure in a calm womanliness which, if initially suspected as lack of imagination, had soon revealed its true nature as something approaching serenity. But that night in her room, when she pulled the sweater up over her head, unhooked her bra and turned, frankly but without demonstration, to face me as I lay in her bed with the sheets to my hips, brought the searing ache of passion into our relationship. From that night I knew that I could not be with her without longing to touch, could not touch without yearning to fondle, could not fondle without aching to possess. And in what way did I possess her? In what way was she mine? The uninhibited but relaxed and undemonstrative manner of her lovemaking gave me joy succeeded by foreboding. We had already been dating for several weeks, but I could not bring myself to feel that tonight marked any clinching commitment. Rather, from the easy, unfussy way she gave herself, that I'd only needed to make a move earlier; that this might be merely a physical extension of her serenity of manner, something she had naturally offered as such to men she had liked in the past and would offer similarly to other men than myself in the future. And so in the fear of losing her, of forcing the day when she would say with gentle regret, 'I'm sorry; it's been fun, but now it's getting too serious,' I lived under the strain of seeming not to want to possess her, not to want to monopolise her free time; the strain of allowing no give-away utterance to escape me when we lay together in the narrow divan bed in her room. Until, one night, she confronted me. We'd been to a film. Back in her room she made coffee and brought me it with brandy from a duty-free bottle she'd acquired on a weekend trip to Holland. When I moved to sit beside her on the divan and took her hand, she released herself, threw a cushion on to the floor and sat down there in front of the gas-fire. I waited, not daring to speak.

'Gordon ...'

'Yes?' I felt my heart contract, then step up its beat.

'Can I ask you something?'

'Yes.'

'Will you promise to answer truthfully?'

'If I know what the truth is I will.'

I was acutely aware of the thick weave of the Italian blanket under my hand, of the blue- and orange-covered paperbacks in the book-shelves she had made by resting lengths of planed timber on white-painted house bricks; the welded sculpture of woman and child by the heavy stone ashtray on the low table; the picture postcards from friends in foreign parts that stood across the top of the cheap tiled fireplace. All of it I took in again, along with the way her dark hair with the deep chestnut lights curled over the roll neck of her jumper, the slightly bowed line of her long back as she sat, half-turned away from me, supporting herself on one hand. All of it my mind regis-tered, as though I would never see it again.

'Are you seeing me these days because you feel you ought to be kind to me?'

'What makes you ask that?'

'You did say you'd answer truthfully.'

'But I don't know how to put it till I know why you ask.'

'I feel you've been different, somehow, lately. You always used to make another date before you left me; now you say you'll ring up, and it's longer between.'

'You've not been long in this town,' I said. 'I don't want to monopolise you. I want you to make other . . . other friends. Give you a chance to turn me down, see me when you can.'

'But you're not at ease like you used to be. You don't laugh as much. You're even . . . well, you're different in bed.'

'If I seem different it's because I *am* different. Because *things* are different. With me, at any rate. The trouble is, I . . . the trouble is, I don't know if they're different with you.'

'They're no different with me,' she said after a moment. She was looking away from me, at the fire.

'Aren't they?'

'No . . . they're just like they always were. Only more so.'

I let my held breath go on a long sigh as she turned her head and gave me a shy upward smile. I put my glass on the table and went down beside her.

'You've just taken a tremendous burden off my mind, young woman.'

'And you off mine.' I kissed her. 'The trouble with the times we live in,' she said, her voice lifting, light and buoyant now, 'is that all the stages of a proper courtship have been jumbled up. We don't know what the rules are any more.'

'I suppose it means there are fewer uncertainties left to gamble on.'

'I suppose so.'

Of course neither of us knew then that while the pill she took might lighten and regularize her periods, as a contraceptive it was redundant. I kissed her again. She swallowed her coffee and then reached for and took a sip from my glass.

'Would you like to go to bed now?' she asked.

'Yes.'

'And can we have it with the words this time, please?'

'Yes, love. Yes, we can.'

Yes, if Eunice Cadby's legs were her best feature, then Eileen's breasts were Eileen's. And what the hell had Eunice to do with anything? I recalled the trigger image of last night's lovemaking and told myself to ignore a small but definite twinge of guilt. It had, after all, come as a consequence of my trying to please Eileen.

She removed my fingers from her stiffening nipple. 'If you carry on doing that you'll get no breakfast.'

'You mean the girl could be ready for more? I thought last night it was going out of fashion. I shall have to have a look at what you'd been reading.'

She turned, smiling that hooded-eyed smile, and reached out to tap the side of my nose with her forefinger, a gesture of hers which sometimes expressed pleasure, sometimes an amused criticism.

'Anyway, thank you for your consideration.'

'That was just the economy flight, love. If you can calm down a bit next time, we'll travel first class.'

'Take Bonny his tea and see if he wants some breakfast.'

He was stretched out under the sheets, face down, legs apart, arms crushing the pillow into a ball beneath his head. I debated with myself whether to wake him or let him have his sleep out. I couldn't remember what traits of personality expert sleep-watchers said a position like that revealed. To me, it was simply characteristic of Bonny, remembered from the time when, as boys, we had shared a room. I tried something. Standing there, making no sound, I looked steadily at his face. Perhaps, to work, it needed a charge of feeling as intense as that which had burned across the space between our beds in that occasion all those years ago ...

There had been a girl, called Frances McCormack. I met her through a friend from university. University wasn't far away and I was coming home every other weekend. Frances was tall and slim, with blue eyes and red-gold hair. She came from a well-heeled family, but the town was not big enough for money to cut her off. Besides, her father, who was a builder, had only prospered with the building boom of recent years. They were Catholics, we merely notional C of E; but I'd fallen for her so fast and hard I refused to see that as any problem. Frances was eighteen and taking her time deciding what kind of work she wanted to do after leaving a convent school. I was going on twenty-one, Bonny a year or so older than Frances. She let me take her out. The second time I introduced her to Bonny. There wasn't a third time. She made a date but broke it and after a couple of refusals I gave up. I lost sight of her. My mother took to kidding Bonny about a girlfriend he was reported as having, but he always slow-timed his way out of discussing her and it wasn't for several months that I got to know who she was. Or, more accurately, who she'd been.

I was coming out of a pub a couple of miles from town with a friend, one Saturday night, when she called to me from where she was standing by a low two-seater Triumph. She wore a sheepskin coat over a white sweater, and close-fitting boots of soft black leather which covered her knees. I'd never seen boots like those before. She

31

looked beautiful, radiant with health and cocooned in material comforts. I knew as I walked towards her that, although resentful, I was still vulnerable.

'Hullo, Frances. I didn't see you inside.'

'Gordon, are you going straight home?'

'More or less, yes.'

'Will you let me give you a lift? I want to talk to you.'

'Well, I . . .' My friend had got into his car and started the engine.

'It's very important.'

It was after closing time. People were calling good-night and cars were moving off all round us. There was a touch of desperation in her manner as she looked at me, plumes of breath between her parted lips visible on the still, cold air.

I said, 'Hang on a tick,' and walked to Richard's car and tapped on his window. He wound it down.

'Look, would you mind very much if I went home by alternative transport?'

'Who's your chauffeuse?'

'Somebody I haven't seen for a while.'

'Ask her if she's got a twin sister.'

'Sorry, old lad.'

I said I'd let him know when I was coming home again, and he drove off. We'd been going to call for some fish and chips on the way and eat them in the car. I wondered what Frances could have to say to me that was more important at this stage in the game than fish and chips. I didn't want to start all that again. I'd assigned her to the ranks of the desirable but unattainable.

She was in the driving-seat. I got in beside her.

'Well,' I said, 'where have you been hiding yourself?'

'Oh,' she said, 'so you *don't* know.'

'Know what?'

'About Bonny and me.'

I was about to try to cover the feeling of absolute foolishness that hit me then by asking, 'What about Bonny and you?' when she started the engine and put it into gear. So I said nothing.

'I've been seeing him,' she said, when we were moving along the road and she'd changed through the gears to top. The business of driving seemed to make it easier for her to talk and gave her actions with which to punctuate what she was saying. I wished I'd something to occupy *my* hands. 'Or I was seeing him. That's why I refused your dates,' she said in a rush. 'I'm sorry, Gordon, but we had only been out a couple of times, hadn't we? I mean, I wanted Bonny to tell you and get things straight, but he said he didn't want trouble in the house, and there was plenty of time. Besides, he—'

'What do you mean you *were* seeing him? Aren't you still?'

'No. He's thrown me over.'

'Why?'

'I don't know. I mean I don't know for sure. He knew I was a Catholic when we started going out together and I didn't think it mattered. It didn't to me, at any rate. Then one night I did a silly thing. I told him that Dad was very keen and that he'd always talked against mixed marriages. Bonny surely knew I wasn't like that. I mean, I was brought up that way and I believe in God and all that, but all the rest of it is just going through the motions.'

'You're both a bit young to be talking about marriage, aren't you?'

'Well, of course, that's what *I* thought. And I thought that given time there'd be nothing to worry about.' I looked round at her. She was biting her lower lip in agitation, but her driving was still proficient, carried out with due care. 'I may as well tell you,' she went on. 'I'm sorry, but . . .'

'Tell me what?'

'I'm absolutely bloody mad about him. I've cried myself to sleep every night since he began to avoid me.'

'Haven't you seen him?'

'No. I've written to him, but he won't answer. I don't want to wait for him and stop him in the street. I just want a chance to talk to him quietly, make him see that we can work something out; make him understand that I don't want him to do anything he doesn't want to do.'

'And you'd like me to try to arrange that for you?'

'Yes.'

'What if he still won't play?'

'I don't want to . . . Oh, God! I want it to be his way; what he wants to do. But I've got to talk to him. I don't want to—'

What she said then was overlaid by what I said to her, interjected in caution, but without panic. And what it was she said was obliterated from my memory for some while by what happened during the next few seconds. We had reached a new bypass which ran along a ridge and connected with the old main road into the town. Here she'd put her foot down, picking up speed: too much speed, I thought, for that

33

slow, deceptive right-hand curve, with the fifteen-foot drop beyond it.

I said, 'Take it easy, Frances, or you'll run out of road.'

Then the nearside front wheel hit the kerbstone. We lurched. She said 'Jesus and Mary' as she pulled on the steering-wheel. I thought later that I remembered it wresting itself from her hands, her hands themselves lifting to cover her face as she screamed and we were launched over the edge of the bank towards the fence below . . .

I woke in hospital to the sound of my mother's voice.

'Gordon . . .' She leaned into my field of vision, running her hand over the bedclothes to find and press mine through them. 'You're all right, son. There's nothing to worry about.'

Yellow curtains with a pattern of flowers enclosed my bed-space. It was daylight. Bewildered, my head throbbing, I tried to struggle up. I almost yelled then. I was sore from head to foot. My left leg ached abominably. I felt the tug of something heavy holding it down. As my mother said, 'Steady, son. Just rest easy,' I slowly explored with my right foot. Plaster.

'Is my leg broken?'

'Yes, but that's all. You were lucky.'

My memory was full of blank spaces, like the morning after a really heavy booze-up.

'We had a crash, didn't we?'

'Yes. But don't think about it now.'

I'd been in the pub with Richard but not gone home with him.

'What happened to Frances? Is she all right?'

My mother's eyes shifted. If she'd prepared the outright lie, she couldn't now deliver it. And anything short of that told me the truth.

'Oh! God.'

'They say she was such a lovely lass, an' all.'

My mother's eyes brimmed with tears, and in a moment I began to weep with her.

I was kept in hospital through another night while they watched me, probably for the effects of shock, and then they sent me home to be put to bed in the room I shared with Bonny. I'd not had a previous chance to speak to him alone.

'It was a lousy thing to happen.'

'We were talking about you.'

'Oh?'

'She wanted me to try to persuade you to meet her. Get things sorted out.'

'They were sorted out.'

'She was all worked-up. At her wits' end because she couldn't get to you.'

'Did you tell the police that?'

'No. I didn't think it was any of their business.' I looked at him. 'She said she was absolutely bloody mad about you.' He shrugged uneasily and screwed his face up. 'Are you upset?'

'I'm *sorry*, Gordon. She was a nice kid. But she was a mick. I've got nothing against them, but I didn't want to get involved in all that rigmarole. She was too serious and we were both too young. I've got things to do. When she started talking about mixed marriages and what her father thought, I decided it had gone far enough. There were a couple of scouts at Saturday's match. I think I'm going to get a trial with a third-division club. I couldn't be bothered, Gordon. I'm sorry. I didn't want her to be unhappy, but I couldn't be bothered with it all.'

I asked myself how I should have seen it if I hadn't once wanted her myself; if it hadn't been my own brother who had spoilt my chances.

My mother came up that evening to tell me there were two policemen downstairs.

'Two?'

'They're plain-clothes.'

'But I gave a statement at the hospital.' That had been a uniformed constable, on his own.

'If you don't want to see them now I'll tell them you're not well enough.'

'No. They'll only come back. Better see what they want.'

She looked at me, her handsome face serious. 'What d'you think they want?'

'I don't know.' She regarded me for a moment longer. 'Don't worry, Mother, I haven't broken any laws.'

'Well, then,' she said, 'I'll make you comfortable and fetch them up.'

I pulled myself up in the bed and she plumped my pillows and wedged them behind my shoulders. I'd seen enough police series on television to know that when they visited in pairs it was either for safety, or the second one was a witness. But since I'd done nothing I waited for them as placidly as my aching bones would permit. My mother hovered after showing them in, but they said they would like to speak to me alone. She went out. They were a detective-sergeant and a detective-constable. The sergeant, who did all the talking while his colleague took notes, had fair wavy hair and prominent eyes of a washed-out blue. He apologised for bothering me, enquired about my health, then asked me how well I'd known Frances.

'Not very well.'

'Well enough for her to offer you a lift home.'

'People do it all the time.'

'Had she been drinking, Mr Taylor?'

'I don't know. I wasn't with her earlier. She gave me no impression of having had too much. Don't you know?'

'She wasn't over the legal limit,' he admitted, and paused. 'Did she give you any impression that she was upset about anything?'

'No. We just chatted about this and that. Commonplaces.'

'Was there anything erratic about her driving, that you noticed?'

'No. Not until we got on to the bypass. Then I wouldn't call it erratic: she just misjudged the road and went rather too fast. I don't like that road. It's all right coming up on the inside curve, but going down I think it's dangerously misleading. I'm surprised there haven't been more accidents.'

'Do you drive yourself?'

'I have a licence, but no car at present.'

'And Miss McCormack was driving that night?'

'Yes, of course she was.'

'So, will you tell me what happened.'

'On the bypass?'

'Just before the accident, yes.'

'I felt she was driving too fast for the road and I asked her to be careful. Then the front wheel hit the kerb, she couldn't correct and we went over the bank. I knew nothing after that till I woke up in hospital.'

'Did you know that Miss McCormack was two months pregnant?'

It came quietly, intended to jolt, and jolt it did. For in the instant his voice died I remembered the last thing Frances had said as I spoke my warning over it. 'I don't want to blackmail him,' she had said, and I didn't think she'd intended to give away her secret, had probably determined not to tell Bonny except as a last resort, and perhaps not even then.

'Hell, no ...' I must have gone pale, and he didn't miss it.

'I seem to have given you a shock, Mr Taylor.'

'Yes.'

'Any particular reason?'

'I fancied her at one time myself. Had a bit of a crush on her. I took her out a couple of times, but it came to nothing.'

'How long ago was that?'

'Oh, several months.'

'Can you be more accurate?'

'The back end of last summer. September time. Look,' I said, 'I wish you'd tell me what this is all about. She didn't crash the car on purpose. Not with me in it with her. It was an accident.'

'We're just trying to clear the ground for the coroner.'

'It needn't come out, need it, that she was pregnant?'

'Does it matter to you, Mr Taylor?'

'It doesn't matter to anybody else, either, except her family. She's dead. Can't she rest?'

'She can unless it's relevant.'

'I don't see how it can be.' The gaze from those washed-out popping eyes rested on my face. 'If you're thinking,' I said as it dawned, 'that it was my baby, you can think again. I hadn't even seen her for months till the other night.'

He reached for his hat.

'Well, then, it all seems straightforward,' he said, preparing to get up. 'Whoever it was might be a sad man, or he might be indifferent. But it's got nothing to do with the police.' The constable closed his notebook and stood up with him. They manoeuvred round each other to reach the door. 'Thank you for your co-operation. I hope you'll be up and about again soon.'

The bed shook slightly to the heavy tread of their feet on the stairs. My parents had recently bought a new stair-carpet and I could smell it through the open door. Ever afterwards the smell of new carpets brought back that interview, my lying in bed, the accident, Frances ... I heard my mother's voice in the hall, then the thud of the closing house-door. She came straight up.

'Well?'

'They were just getting the facts right for the coroner.'

My leg ached in slow throbs. My head ached too, and I felt slightly sick.

'Would you like a bit of supper?'

'No, thanks. If you'll get me a hot drink to wash my pills down I'll call it a day. Is Bonny in?'

'No. He said he might be late.'

'Ask him to be quiet, will you, when he comes up.'

And so I woke next morning to contemplate Bonny's face across the gap between our beds: looking and looking until he came quietly and quickly awake and looked back.

'What . . .?' he said, as though conscious that my stare had willed him out of the refuge and ignorance of sleep.

'She was pregnant, you bastard.'

'What?' he said again. He struggled up on to one elbow. 'What are you talking about?'

'Frances was two months pregnant.'

'How do you know?'

'The post mortem found it. There were two cops here last night, trying to find out if it had any bearing on the way she died.'

'It hadn't, had it? How could it have?'

'No way, except she was even more upset than I realised. No way, except with a thing like that preying on your mind and a feller you can't get to, it might just affect your judgement behind the wheel of a car.'

'Lay off, will you. I didn't know.'

'No. She was a mick, and you didn't want to get mixed up in all that rigmarole. But you had to slip her a length just the same.'

'Listen, Gordon, she might have been a Catholic, but she was no nun. She had hot pants, kid. I wasn't the first, so why should I have been the last? She knew more fellers besides me.'

'She was also stuck on you. Right in. She obviously knew whose kid it was. And the funniest thing is I'm nearly convinced that if you'd met and talked and she'd seen it was no go, she wouldn't have embarrassed you by telling you. She was worth more than you knew, more than you could recognise.'

He threw back the sheets and swung round to sit on the edge of the bed, glaring at me.

'Oh, piss off, will you! I don't have to take your sermons, just because you once fancied her yourself. I'm sorry, d'you understand? I'm even more sorry now I know she was pregnant; but unless you know how I could have stopped her car running off the road, just piss off and leave me alone.'

My mother opened the door without knocking, and came in.

'What are you two squaring up about?'

'Nothing, nothing,' Bonny said. 'Just a little brotherly tiff.'

'Well, your breakfast's ready. You'd better come down and get it, or you'll be late . . .'

Eileen spoke quietly from the landing, outside the open door. 'Gordon, your breakfast's on the table. Hurry up, or you'll be late.'

I called back softly to her. Bonny's eyes opened. They focused on me. 'What . . .?' he said.

'I've brought you a cup of tea.'

'Thanks.' He turned over and lifted himself on to one elbow as I set the cup and saucer down beside him.

'Do you want some breakfast now, or will you make your own?'

'Don't bother about me. I'll manage.'

'Are you going to see mum and dad today? Shall I run you round when I get back from school?'

'Okay.'

Mr McCormack came to see me after the inquest. He was a stocky, balding man in his late forties, with hard-skinned hands. I could see little of Frances in him, except in the fading colour of his hair. I wondered if his having several other children offered him the slightest consolation. He fenced for a while until he found out I knew she'd been pregnant. I asked him if it had been made public.

'No. The coroner had a word with me and the wife. He said he didn't see any point because it had no bearing. It'll get about, though, I expect. Things like that always do.'

'It won't from me, Mr McCormack.'

His gaze flicked on to my face, away, then back again.

'I have to ask you . . . you weren't responsible for that, were you?'

I met his gaze, which was holding steady now.

'No. As I told the police, I hadn't seen Frances for months until that night.'

'You're ready to swear on the Bible to that?'

'No, Mr McCormack, I'm not. You'll just have to take my word for it.'

He sighed and looked away. 'And I don't suppose you know who it might have been?'

'She was an attractive girl. Popular. She had lots of friends. A lot of them I didn't know.'

'God knows,' he said then. '*He* knows, and He'll punish him.'

For what? I asked myself when he'd gone. For succumbing to the pleasure of an attractive and willing girl, while refusing the trap of an unwanted marriage in a faith he didn't believe in? For the manner of his rejection, perhaps; though who knew the truth of that, and that it had not been the only possible way? Bonny and I never talked of it again; but as McCormack had predicted, there was a short season of rumour. It was put to me in a pub one weekend. I turned it aside with 'Oh? I wouldn't know about that.' But when my mother brought it up I had to do a little better.

'I hear that McCormack lass was pregnant when she was killed.'

'I've heard that as well.' I waited for a moment before putting down the magazine I was reading and looking up at her. I shook my head. 'Not guilty, Mother.'

If she mentioned it to Bonny, I never knew. I'd never heard his and Frances's names coupled. He'd kept their relationship as secret as an illicit affair, and I couldn't believe the only reason was to hide it from me.

The telephone rang while I was eating my scrambled egg and toast. I answered it still chewing. It was Eunice.

'Sorry to disturb you at this time of the day, but I thought I'd try to catch you before you went out. Have I interrupted your breakfast?'

'Just finished.'

'I left my poem somewhere last night. Did you find it in your car?'

'Yes, I have it.'

'Oh, good. I haven't got a copy.'

'Always keep a copy, Eunice. First rule of the writing game.'

'But it's only in rough first draft, and I'd like to do some work on it this weekend.'

'Would you like me to post it to you?'

'Oh, I'm afraid that even locally and first class it might not turn up till Monday. Would you mind awfully if I came for it?'

'There'll be nobody in all day.' Except my brother, I might have added, who won't answer the door.

'I'm busy myself all day. Would half-past seven this evening be all right?'

'Okay.'

'You're sure it's not an intrusion?'

'No, that's all right.' You've worked for it, young miss, I thought

40

as I put the phone down, even though you can't be sure that I won't meet you at the door with the poem and not let you across the threshold, let alone give you a sight of Bonny.

Eileen came down, combed and dressed, as I was making fresh tea. 'You're going to be late this morning, Gordon.'

'I've got a free first period. By the way, you won't be late back with the car, will you? I've offered to run Bonny round home before mum and dad leave for the shop.'

'I'll be coming straight back. Did I hear the phone ring?'

'Yes. It was Eunice Cadby, one of my writing pupils. You know, the one who wrote that sexy poem.'

'Oh?'

'I gave her a lift into town last night and she accidentally on purpose left it in the car. She's coming round to pick it up tonight.'

'Hmm.' Eileen checked the contents of her handbag. 'I'd rather like a look at her.'

'Oh, it's not me she's interested in, love. It's Bonny.'

'Does he know that?'

'I told him last night. He doesn't know she's calling yet, of course.' I grinned at her. 'It might be amusing.'

Eileen stood in the kitchen doorway, pulling on her topcoat. '*Has* he said anything about how long he's staying?'

'Not yet. Why?'

'It's just that ... well, with the weekend coming up it could be tying. If we wanted to go anywhere, I mean.'

'He doesn't need a sitter to look after him.'

'No but ... Oh, I must fly. We'll talk about it later.'

She gave me a swift peck, grabbed handbag and briefcase and flew. I looked at my watch. Even with that free period I'd be none too early. I poured myself a cup of tea from the fresh pot and took it with me to the bathroom, picking up the morning paper from the hall table as I passed. Bonny had been suspended by his club.

4

'Is there anything you can do about it?' my father asked.

'I can appeal and go up in front of the Board. Promise to be a good lad in future. Or I can ask to be put on the transfer list.'

'Putting it bluntly,' my father said, 'is there anybody ready to pay the money for you? They won't *give* you away, will they? They'll want their money back and a profit on top. Would you say your market value had gone up from two years ago, or gone down?'

My father was pulling no punches, in his dry, unemotional way. It was how he had always slated us: little direct criticism, just a statement of the facts as he saw them and what disadvantages our behaviour was creating for us.

'There are still plenty of managers who think they can handle me.' Bonny hooked his fingers behind his head and stretched in his chair. I couldn't tell now whether his nonchalance was genuine or assumed.

'Maybe I'll chuck it altogether and buy a business.'

We were sitting by the gas-fire in the living-room of the house our parents had lived in since before we were born. The kitchen, opening off this room, ran the width of the house. There were two bedrooms and a bathroom (which they'd had made from a third bedroom) upstairs. Behind the house, separated from it by a right of way giving access to the other houses in the row, was a long, pleasant garden with a lawn and vegetable plots which my father tended; at the front a square of garden between the stone-faced wall of the house and a main road along which ever-increasing traffic belted. A cosy, comfortably appointed house, with fewer corners knocked off things than when Bonny and I were at home. I had always enjoyed it in childhood and adolescence, only coming to find it constricting as Bonny and I grew up and began to bump each other. My mother now was moving between kitchen and living-room, carrying in scones and jam and a home-baked apple pie, despite my protest that Eileen would have a hot meal ready for us. In fact, knowing my mother, Eileen was more likely to wait and see what appetite we had left before preparing anything.

'Anyway,' my mother said, bringing in the teapot and setting out cups, 'your dad and me always have our teas about this time, so you can please yourselves whether you join us or not.'

I'd offered on the way here to drop Bonny at the house and clear out for an hour, but he had said he would prefer me to stay. Now I wondered if my presence might be inhibiting my mother's speaking her mind. For though I knew that her undemonstrative pleasure in seeing Bonny was marred by her bewildered disappointment with his shortcomings, she had so far uttered not one word of criticism beyond reproaching him for the infrequency of his visits. Had Bonny remained lost in the obscurity of some humdrum trade, my mother would have thought no less of him. What grieved her was his having given her cause for an exceptional pride which was now soured into shame; and that shame was less important as an embarrassment than as a barometer of his failure. She asked him who was looking after him these days.

'I look after myself. I eat out when I can't be bothered.'

What I thought she wanted to know was whether anybody was living with him; though so far as I knew none of his attachments had embraced that kind of domestic arrangement. His women were not the sort to wear aprons.

'They keep on to me to go and live in these digs.'

'Digs?'

'There's a woman who runs a place. They put the young lads in there when they first join the club. She sees they get properly fed and don't stop out late.'

'But you've no need of that kind of thing,' she said sardonically.

'I'm not having it, anyway.'

'Bonny,' my mother said, 'what *do* you *want,* son? That's all your father and me are bothered about. It gives us no pleasure to keep picking up the paper and reading how you've upset somebody again. If you can't be happy and play football, then it's time you packed it up and did something else.'

'He's got six or seven good years left,' my father said. 'All that experience . . .'

'If you ask me he's had too much experience of the wrong kind. That young dolly in the Sunday paper the other week; giving all and sundry your private life to chew over.'

'She never wrote that. A reporter asked her questions and wrote it for her.'

'She'd plenty to say, whether or not.'

43

'You shouldn't believe all you read.'

'You mean it was lies? Isn't there a law against that?'

'They can twist things without actually telling lies.'

'They've got to have things to twist.'

We came away when it was time for my father to go and get the pans started at the shop, my mother making Bonny promise to call again before he left. She saw the life he was leading as destroying him, and she could only stand helplessly by and watch it happen. 'You talk to him, Gordon,' she said in a low voice at the door, as Bonny went ahead to the car. I promised to try, but it was only to pacify her. I only partly understood the world he lived in; the constraints and disciplines, the rewards and disappointments of my world were different, and I had enough arrogance to believe that he wouldn't have survived a week in it. But men did survive and fulfil themselves in his world without all that destructive trampling, and if this was all that talent, fame and money could bring him it would have been better had it been his leg that was broken in the wreck of Frances McCormack's car, putting paid to his chances of a first-class career at the same time that her life was snuffed out with that of their unborn child. I was getting impatient with him.

We'd driven for some time in silence when Bonny suddenly said, 'I could drink a pint.'

'Could you? Don't you mind going into a pub?'

'Gordon, the whole bloody world isn't waiting for a look at Bonny Taylor.'

I glimpsed a Tetley's sign along a side road as we passed and ran on to a filling-station forecourt to turn. 'I've never been in here before,' I told him, 'so I don't know what kind of place it is. I'll bet you a quid you're spotted inside ten minutes.'

'Okay, you're on.'

There was no one in the lounge except a shirt-sleeved man replacing stock on the shelves behind the bar. He was thickset, paunchy, with iron-grey hair brushed straight across his scalp from a low side-parting. I asked for two pints. He gave us a quick summing-up as he was drawing them, his gaze drifting back a couple of times to Bonny, who was looking at the beer foaming into the glasses and seemed unaware of this appraisal. I reckoned I'd already won my pound.

'You're very quiet,' I said to the barman.

'Give 'em another hour and they'll roll in.'

I was getting out a handful of coins when Bonny tossed a note on the counter, picked up a glass and walked across to a table. I followed with his change.

'You've lost the bet.'

He threw a quick glance at the bar. 'Have I?'

'Pretty certain.'

He shrugged. 'Well . . . give him something to tell his regulars.'

Our visit home had turned him morose again. He drank from his glass as if it were something he kept noticing; but he'd finished before I was halfway down. He took a fold of notes from his pocket.

'D'you mind fetching?'

'No, but it's my shout.'

'Don't be daft. You've been keeping me for the last two days.' He pushed the pound note across the table. 'Have a scotch with it.'

'No thanks.'

'Bring me one, anyway.'

'Just the one scotch?' the barman asked.

'Just the one. Make it a double.'

I got change out of my pocket and added some coins to Bonny's note. The barman glanced across at Bonny as he turned from the optic. For some reason I couldn't fathom I felt then the smallest touch of unease. I wished we weren't there. It stayed with me as I went back to the table.

'You know,' I said, 'the trouble with Mother is that she's quite simply baffled.'

'Everybody's baffled,' Bonny said. '*I'm* baffled. Why doesn't it work, eh? Why doesn't it work?'

'She'd be happier if you were a plumber or some such, living round the corner and bringing the wife and kids to Sunday afternoon tea.'

'Oh, she would *now*, now it's gone wrong. But it's too late to take up an apprenticeship now, Gordon. And I'm not coming back to settle in this midden, either.'

'There are worse places.'

'Not if you've once got clear.'

'Where do you fancy, then?'

'Somewhere where I've got no history. Where they know nothing except what they've read in the papers.'

'You're content to let the legend speak for you?'

'Why not? Then I can charm the arses off them by showing them what a good-natured, easy-going bloke I really am.'

'And what would you do for a living?'

'I could buy a pub. A free house. The old-timers, they used to go cap in hand to the brewers and run them for *their* profit, or scrape together for a newspaper and tobacco kiosk. But I could *own* a pub, Gordon. That must be some kind of progress, mustn't it?'

'What about carrying on with your career, then coaching or managing.'

'I haven't got what they call the qualities of leadership, have I? I can't even bend down to pull my own socks up. Some can manage it, stick the course, but every time I step on to that field now I wonder what the hell I think I'm doing. You've heard that roar. You should hear it from the middle. Do they love you or do they hate you? They love you when you're on top. They don't know what it can be like till you show them, and then they hate you when you slip below that standard you've set for yourself. Then they want to destroy you. You're proving what they think they've always known: that nobody can be that good. And they love that, too. It gets the blood running. They'd destroy you then just like they destroy pubs and trains and buses, and one another. You can hear that note in the roar; you can tell when it changes to that. And then you either slip further and play worse, or you put on a show for the bastards. Only you're just pissing about, because you can't do what you really should be doing with all that contempt and fear in you. And you know then, in your heart of hearts, that you haven't got what it takes. You're a dazzler, but you haven't got the guts and the sticking power to turn that dazzle into really great football. I've blinded 'em, Gordon. I've blinded them with science, but now it's all coming out. There are some who've suspected it: some pro's, one or two writers. After the last few matches even the yobboes on the terraces know.'

The barman had been moving about the room, drawing crimson curtains across the windows. I didn't think Bonny had even noticed him. Now he stopped at our table and put his fingers into our two dead glasses, drawing them together in one hand.

'Is your mate who I think he is?' he said to me.

It had taken him a long time to get round to it, and I didn't care for his tone.

'He's my brother, and who do you think he is?'

'His picture's in the paper – behind the bar. I thought I knew his face when you came in. Think they'll manage without you to-morrow?' he said to Bonny.

'It looks as if they intend to.'

'Aye. They'll manage. No man's indispensable, though some like to think they are.'

'Look,' I said, 'we came in for a quiet drink.'

'All that money for all that bother,' the barman said, warming up fast. 'What was that last transfer fee – four hundred thousand?'

'You're a touch on the low side,' Bonny said. 'But what's fifty thou between friends?'

'A bloody expensive headache, I call that. Some of them old-timers must be turning in their graves.'

'They lived in the wrong age,' Bonny said.

'A good job some of 'em didn't live long enough to see the game dragged down like it has been.'

'Look,' Bonny said, 'how are you on sex and travel?'

'You what?'

'Why don't you fuck off and when we've finished these drinks we'll do the same.'

'You'll drink off now, and fast,' the man said. 'I won't be talked to like that in my own pub; not by anybody, let alone the biggest little shithouse in football.'

I'd seen Bonny eyeing that overhanging gut and thought he might be judging the distance; but now he moved so fast I could do nothing to stop him beyond saying 'Bonny' and lifting my hand. He stood up and struck in the same movement, doubling the landlord over and fetching the wind out of him in a long spoken gasp. 'Oo-oogh!'

Bonny knocked back his whisky and said, 'Come on.'

We were at the door when I heard another sound. I looked back to see a woman coming in through a door in the far corner. I had time to notice that she was wearing a black frock with plenty of ripe white flesh in its low neck before she saw the landlord on the floor and shouted, 'Ey, you two, what d'you think you're—?' and then we were out.

'He'll have summat to talk about now,' Bonny said as we drove back to the junction. 'And just watch how it'll get embroidered. In a couple of days I'll have gone berserk and wrecked the place.' I said nothing. My pulse was still racing and I had to concentrate on my driving. 'Remind me, by the way, I owe you a quid.'

Hearing the familiar note of the Mini's engine. Eileen met us in the hall.

'Where have you been till this time?'

I looked at my watch. It was twenty-past seven. I'd intended to ring her from the pub.

'We stopped off for a pint.'

'You should have let me know. That girl's here and we haven't eaten.'

'Eunice? She's early. Where is she?'

'In the sitting-room. I had to ask her to wait because I didn't know where her manuscript was.'

'It's in my case, upstairs. And don't bother about food. We'll eat later. Mother filled us full of scones and apple pie.'

'Sorry, Eileen,' Bonny said. 'It was my fault.'

'Listen, Bonny,' I said to him, 'this is that girl from my writing class I was telling you about last night. Would you mind saying hullo to her? You can make your excuses any time you like, then.'

I shouldn't have been surprised after the incident in the pub if he'd said no, he'd had enough. But he shrugged. 'Why not?'

We lived in one of a pair of rather ugly but solidly built 1920s semis which plugged a gap for some reason left between Victorian and Edwardian villas along one of a series of interconnected backwaters off a main road. It was roomy, which we both liked; but in the knowledge that there would be no children – at least, of our own – to help fill it, we had furnished sparingly in the unspoken assumption that we might yet move into something more compact. The sitting-room, I sometimes joked, looked like a Habitat sale. Eunice was sitting forward on the squashy cushions of the sofa, one elbow resting on the white-enamelled arm, her ankles crossed, as Bonny and I went in.

'Eunice, sorry we were out when you arrived.'

'I was rather early. I think there's something wrong with my watch.'

'Bonny, this is Eunice Cadby. My brother Bonny.'

Bonny nodded. 'Eunice ...'

'Hullo.'

Bonny flopped into the nearest chair. 'You're doing some writing, then, Eunice?'

'A little.'

'You're not full-time?'

'Heavens, no. I'm not even published yet.'

'So what do you do for a living?'

'I work for the local authority, in the public information office.'

'Is that interesting?'

'Frustrating, sometimes. When people want answers you can't give.'

'You'll see a bit of human nature, though, and know a lot about how the town's run. I should think that's good for a writer.'

'Oh, yes.'

I left them, to fetch some drinks. I got out one of the bottles of wine that Eileen had bought and went into the kitchen to open it.

'How are they doing?' Eileen asked.

'Bonny's talking to her as though she were the most interesting person in the world.' I found the corkscrew. 'You must be famished. I'm sorry we got held up, but when Bonny said he'd like a pint I thought it might be good for him after keeping his head down.'

'And was it?'

'Well ... I'll tell you about that later. Have a glass of wine.'

'Are you taking them some?'

'I thought I would.'

'How long will that girl stay?'

'I've no idea.'

'Will she want to eat with us?'

'I don't know. Would you mind?'

'It's up to you. I'm doing a chicken casserole. It'll stretch for four, if I do some rice.'

'Let's play it by ear. If Bonny suddenly gets bored and turns off, I'll get rid of her.'

I went back into the sitting-room, carrying a glass of wine apiece for Eunice and me and a scotch for Bonny.

'It seems to me,' Bonny was saying, 'that there are similarities. The world's full of people who'd love to be a star of the Saturday afternoon match, but apart from the lack of talent, they wouldn't want to put in all the hard training that makes it possible. And there must be lots of people who'd like to hold out a book and say, 'I did this,' but they don't want the labour of sitting down for months and actually writing it. In any case,' he went on, 'these things always look more glamorous from the outside. The difference between your situation and mine, you see, is that you're in no hurry. You've got all

49

the time in the world to come good, but me, I'm already going downhill.'

'I don't believe that.'

'Oh, but it's true. Apart from everything else, I'm simply not the player I was even two years ago. It's not something I generally admit, but it's a fact, and there are people who've noticed.'

'I saw your last away game against United,' Eunice said.

'Oh, did you?'

She made a comment whose perception made Bonny narrow his eyes, watching her as he reappraised her, then followed with a number of questions which were intelligent and probing.

Bonny's candour surprised me. I brooded on the implications of what he'd said. Men such as Bonny flashed like meteors across the pages of football history. Not for them the steady maturing of an art, the writer, the painter, the composer producing the masterpieces of old age; not even the golden twilight of the interpreters, the Stokowskis, Boults and Rubensteins bringing to their final performances the accumulated wisdom of generous lifetimes. No, they blazed, illuminating the heavens for a few brief years, then burned out. The rest was no more than memory and perhaps a few feet of film. 'I could do that once.' 'I saw Bonny Taylor play.' 'Who was Bonny Taylor? One of those old-timers, eh?' Who cares? There are others now. When men in other fields were approaching their prime, they were gone to their managers' boxes, their pubs and hotels, their sports shops, watching new talents flare, unable to prove that they could do it once, could do it better. What must it be like to have been glorious once?

Eileen came into the room, closing the door behind her. She bent and spoke into my ear. 'There's somebody to see you.'

My heart gave a nasty little anticipatory lurch. 'Who is it?'

'Two policemen.'

Bonny caught the last word. He was looking at Eileen. Eunice's voice tailed off as she realised he wasn't listening to her.

'Eunice,' I said, 'I wonder if you'd mind going into the other room with Eileen for a few minutes.'

She didn't know what was happening, but she reacted without loss of composure. 'I really ought to be going, anyway.'

'No, no. This shouldn't take long. And you haven't got your manuscript in any case. Ask them to wait, Eileen. I'll fetch them in.'

Eileen took Eunice out, shutting the door again.

'Well ...' I said to Bonny.

'It hasn't taken them long.'

'No. Do you want to flannel?'

'There's not much point in that, is there?'

'I shouldn't have thought so.'

He shrugged. 'Well, wheel 'em in.'

I went into the hall, which seemed full of navy-blue uniforms.

'Good evening,' I said to the sergeant.

'Mr Taylor?' he asked. 'Mr Gordon Taylor?'

'That's right.'

'Is that your car in the drive, sir?' He recited the registration number.

'Yes, that's mine.'

'Sorry to trouble you, sir, but we've had a complaint.'

'Will you come through here.'

I showed them into the sitting-room – 'This is my brother' – and sat them side by side on the sofa.

'Have you been out in your car this evening, Mr Taylor?' the sergeant asked.

'I have, yes.'

'Was your brother with you?'

'Yes.'

The sergeant glanced at Bonny, who nodded. 'Yes.'

'Would you mind telling me where you went?'

'Would you mind telling us what the complaint is you mentioned?' I asked him.

'Have you no idea what it might be, sir?'

'We'll know better when you tell us,' Bonny said.

'We've had a report that two men assaulted the landlord of the Criterion Hotel on Northfield Road earlier this evening. They were seen driving off in a motor car, orange Mini, registration number ...'

He read off the number again from his book and looked at me. 'That's your car, isn't it, Mr Taylor?'

'What did I tell you, Gordon?' Bonny said.

I already had the feeling that there was something odd about this exchange, as though it had somehow kicked off on the wrong foot. The sergeant's attention was now on Bonny.

'What did you tell him, sir?'

'I told him the facts would get blown up. My brother had nothing to do with it. He just happened to be there.'

'You mean you assaulted the landlord single-handed?'

'I don't know about "assaulted". It seems a big word for just one punch. I hit him, just once, in the gut. If he says anything else he's lying through his teeth. My brother would have stopped me if he could have reached me in time.'

'Perhaps you'd like to tell us what the circumstances were surrounding the alleged assault.'

I noticed that he'd stopped calling Bonny 'sir' and again that quality of oddness struck me.

'The landlord recognised Bonny and began talking about football.'

'By the way,' the sergeant said to Bonny, 'could I have your full name?'

'Bernard Lewis Taylor,' Bonny said. Impatience touched the corners of his mouth as the sergeant wrote in his book, then nodded. 'Carry on.'

'He got stroppy,' Bonny said, 'made cracks about my last transfer fee and people bringing the game down.'

'I told him,' I chipped in, 'that we'd just called in for a quiet drink.'

'There was nobody else in the room during this time?' the sergeant asked.

'No.'

'What time did you leave the premises?'

'About ten-past seven.'

'And you'd been there how long?'

'Since about a quarter-to.'

'Why do you think he wanted to be offensive? You didn't know him, by the way?'

'Never saw him before, never been in his pub,' Bonny said. 'And I suppose I'm barred from now on.'

I didn't expect any reaction from the sergeant, but I looked for a flicker of amusement on the young constable's face. He glanced at Bonny, but he wasn't laughing.

'Anyway,' Bonny said, 'I'm a target for clever buggers like him; chaps who think they know the game, and believe everything they read in the papers. When he wouldn't back off I told him what my brother had told him, only in slightly stronger terms.'

'Can you remember exactly what you said?'

'No, I can't,' Bonny said, with the first sign of self-preservation. 'But I can tell you what *he* said. He said he wouldn't be talked to like that in his own pub by the biggest little shithouse in football. That was when I dropped him one on.'

'And you struck him just the once?'

'Yes. In the belly.'

'And he didn't retaliate?'

'No, he went on to the floor, winded, and we left.'

'And there were no witnesses to verify what happened?'

'There was a woman who came in through another door as we were leaving,' I said. 'And I'll verify what happened. Unless,' I added, 'I'm accused of something myself.'

'What does *he* say?' Bonny said. 'That's what I'd like to know. He was a real charmer, that one.'

'He's not making any statements just at present,' the sergeant said. We both looked at him. 'The landlady, his wife, saw two men leave and gave us the description of the car. The landlord managed to tell her he'd been assaulted just before he had a heart attack. He's in hospital.'

Bonny sighed. 'You didn't know who you were looking for when you came here, then?'

'We had the description and number of the car and the computer gave us the name and address of its keeper.'

'So there's no charge at present?' I asked.

'Not at present. We're just making preliminary enquiries. It'll be up to the landlord to bring a charge.'

'Oh, don't worry,' Bonny said, 'he'll do that. He'll love it.'

'That's assuming he recovers,' the sergeant said. 'If he doesn't, it might rest with us. I take it this isn't your permanent address?'

'No, I'm just visiting.'

'If you leave we'll be obliged if you'd inform us where you can be reached.'

They went. When I returned after showing them out, I found Bonny brooding in his chair.

'There's another fan of mine,' he said, inclining his head towards the door. 'Not a reassuring word out of him.'

'He was only doing his job.'

'He should have asked for my autograph, Gordon,' he said, quite seriously. 'It's a bad sign. And we told 'em everything, when we'd no need to.'

'It would have looked worse if we'd held it back.'

'But what can they do?' he asked. 'What difference does it make if he had a heart attack? What difference will it make if he snuffs it?'

53

'I don't know. But I think you ought to talk to a solicitor. Do you know a good one?'

'Oh, yes.'

'It's the weekend.'

'I can get him at home.'

Eileen came in. 'What was all that about?'

'Just some enquiries about the car.' I didn't want to go into the real reason with Eunice in the house.

She looked from one to the other of us, knew she was being fobbed off and tactfully changed the subject.

'I'm cooking. What about that girl? Do you want her to stay?'

I noticed how she always called Eunice 'that girl', like a mother referring to a dubious female her son has brought home.

'What do you think, Bonny?' I asked him.

'What?' he said. He hadn't been listening.

'Would you like Eileen to ask Eunice to stay for supper, or would you rather she went?'

'I thought she'd just called to collect something.'

'She did, but it was an excuse to meet you.'

'It's up to you.' His mind wasn't on the subject. He bit at the corner of a fingernail.

'I'll get rid of her.' I moved towards the door.

'No,' Bonny said. I stopped. 'Look, she probably had something before she came out anyway. I'll take her off your hands.'

'How d'you mean?'

'If you'll shunt your motor out of the drive I'll give her a lift in mine.'

'You're not going out again?'

'Why not? You and Eileen would probably like to be on your own for a while in any case.'

'What about your supper?' Eileen asked.

'Honestly, Eileen, I couldn't eat a thing. Really.'

I went upstairs to the bedroom I used as a study and got Eunice's manuscript.

'Bonny says he'll be glad to give you a lift home, Eunice,' I told her. She was sitting in the living-room. Her glass was empty and she looked spare now: someone to whom the household had suddenly ceased to adjust. But if we were getting rid of her, it was surely with an unexpected prize. 'Were you going home, or somewhere else?'

'Well, I . . .'

'Is that all right, Eunice?' Bonny said. He had appeared in the doorway.

'Thanks, but you needn't trouble.'

'Oh, I've been getting under the feet here a bit, the last couple of days. I'll be ready in a minute.' He disappeared up the stairs.

There was the tiniest burn of heightened colour in Eunice's cheeks. She examined her hands, then glanced round the room without looking at me.

'Did you manage a look at Jack's play?' I asked her.

'Yes. I glanced through it when I got home last night. I think I know an amateur group who might read it for him.'

'I shouldn't like him to be led into an embarrassing situation.'

'I don't follow.'

'Professionals have a sort of disinterested interest, if you see what I mean.'

'He can't hope for a professional reading, can he?'

'Not at this stage, no. But there are amateurs and amateurs.'

She pondered this for a moment. 'You mean some amateurs might get sniffy about some parts of it?'

I laughed. 'Yes. I don't want a reading to throw him. That's not the idea.'

I saw that, with her own habit of candour in her writing, this was something she'd not thought of.

'He's surely prepared to stand by what he's written, isn't he?'

'With the authority of a production behind him, or with people he repects, yes. But the play's not finished yet and what he needs are technical insights, not censorious judgements from people who don't understand what he's up to, but feel they've been given a right to pronounce. Jack's a sensitive man.'

'He can be touchy at times.'

And you can be stupid, my girl, I thought.

'I don't mean that. I mean he's vulnerable, artistically. He hasn't established the validity of his own artistic feelings and his voice yet. He has no recognition to fall back on.'

'I know a man who produces for them. I'll have a word with him first.'

Bonny came in, pulling on his car coat, the fresh smell of toilet soap hanging about him.

'Ready, then, Eunice.'

She asked if she might visit the bathroom, and left us alone.

'Will you want to put your car away again?'

'No, it can stand out. Everybody knows I'm here now.'

'Are you going to ring that solicitor?'

'I'll perhaps try him in the morning. Anyway, there's not a lot he can do till there's a charge.'

'He can maybe tell you how much you have to worry about – or how little.'

'Hmm, there is that.' He seemed to have pushed it aside now. Listen, Gordon, have you got a spare latchkey, just in case I'm late?'

'It's less than ten minutes to Eunice's place.'

'The night's young, man, and I've been cooped up.'

I slid my key off its ring and gave it to him.

'If anybody else needles you, will you promise to smile and walk away?'

'I can't guarantee the smile.'

Eileen came into the hall from the kitchen to say good-bye to Eunice.

'So, what was all that about?' she asked me, when I'd garaged the Mini and got back into the house.

'He's either mounting the horse again before he loses his nerve, or he doesn't give a damn.'

'I'm no wiser.'

'He hit the landlord of the pub we called in at. That's what the police came about.' She listened in silence as I told her what had happened and what the police had said.

'He draws trouble to himself,' she said, when I'd finished.

'It certainly seems to like him.'

'I don't want him to draw it to you. To us.'

'I'm his brother, love. He wanted to drop out for a few days, so he came here.'

'And already we've had the police at the door.'

'I'm in the clear, Eileen. They can't touch me.'

'Mud sticks.'

'Hey, when did you get so toffee-nosed? You'll be telling me next you're bothered about the neighbours.' She knocked the sieve with the rice in it on the edge of the sink with unnecessary force, and didn't answer. 'What did you and Bonny talk about last night?'

'You mostly. Us.'

'Oh?'

56

'He was trying to find out if I knew I couldn't get pregnant before I married you.'

'Come off it, Eileen.'

'Oh yes, he was. He didn't accuse me straight out, but that's what he was driving at. Well, *I* know I've short-changed you, but I don't need him to make out it was deliberate.'

She left the rice, turning away and putting her hands to her face. I went and put my arms round her from the back. It was a moment before she allowed herself to be drawn round to face me.

'Now you know *I* don't think I've been short-changed.'

'Don't you?'

'You know I'd have married you anyway.'

'Would you?'

'Haven't I told you so before?'

'It's like you to make the best of things.'

'Oh, is it? I didn't know that. I'm long-suffering, am I?'

'I didn't mean that.'

'Is that why you were so randy last night?'

'Why shouldn't I be?'

'No reason, except that it's not your usual style.'

She freed herself. 'What do you prefer – a complaisant *hausfrau*, who rolls over and opens her legs only when you tickle her under the chin?'

'Eileen . . .'

'That Eunice . . . I don't suppose there's anything wrong with her insides. And she's got good hips. I reckon she'd drop babies as easy as having a shit.'

That kind of vulgarity wasn't Eileen's style either. I was shocked, but tried not to let her see it.

'Well, that'll be nice for whoever marries her; providing he's the fatherly type.'

'Aren't you the fatherly type?'

'I've never given it much concentrated thought.'

'I don't believe you.'

'I can't force you to.' I took a swallow of wine. It tasted bitter now, setting my teeth on edge. Perhaps, I thought, it would improve alongside the food. Except that I still wasn't hungry.

'It's one thing thinking there's no hurry, that it'll happen in its own good time,' Eileen said. 'It's another altogether knowing it can't happen at all.'

'When we're ready, love, we can look into adoption.'

'Haven't you heard, there's a waiting-list? Haven't you read those childless cretins who write to the papers, complaining that the pill has dried up the supply of little bastards?'

'There must be somebody a pair of enlightened young liberals like us can give a home to.'

'I don't want any black kids. I want a couple of white ones, of my own.'

I had known the depth of Eileen's disappointment, witnessed her tears, when the consultant gynaecologist at the hospital had given the verdict; but this impotent railing at misfortune was new. The irony was that we both had colleagues who, though capable of it, declined to bring children into the kind of world they saw about them. They saw a violent world, a world with little law, and that little corrupt. They saw the ineffectiveness of their institutions, at the mercy of so many outside forces, but were terrified of the monolithic alternatives and retreated into pessimism. Would they, I wondered, have felt differently in a different age? For, I guessed, in every age there must have been such: men who saw a future with little hope and refused to deliver hostages to fortune. I had lied to Eileen: I did think about it, and I found it disturbing to contemplate the deliberate curtailing of a line, to reflect on an attitude which said, 'Well, we find ourselves here, through no fault of our own, so we'll make the best of it; but when we're gone, that's the end.' Eileen, the born mother, discerned arrogance in that pessimism. Who were they to decide that the human race was not worth perpetuating; that because they could not see how man might prevail, they would take no part in ensuring his survival? Eileen, the born mother, projecting her longing into me, foresaw a day when she might have to step aside.

I recalled the tolerant smile with which she had listened after supper one night while Tony Mair expounded his theory of men's essentially polygamous nature. Tony, a lecturer at the local polytechnic, still single in his thirties but known as a fancier of the ladies, explained his unmarried state as due to the impossibility of his undertaking to be faithful to any woman for any length of time. 'Look at it this way,' he'd said. 'A woman is physically incapable of bearing more than a comparatively small number of children. Oh, I know you hear about some who've managed twenty, but they're rare and there is a limit. But a man, well, theoretically he could score every time he screwed. He could, without physical hardship, father kids on ten, a dozen, twenty women. He doesn't, unless he's a sheikh with a harem, because it's not practical; but the knowledge that he could is built into his genes. The urge is atavistic. The wonder is not that he's a sexual roamer, it's that he curbs the instinct as much as he does.'

This was before Eileen's inability to conceive had become common knowledge, or Tony would not have spoken as he did. Eileen did not show that she was upset till he'd gone, and then only in a subdued way. But I guessed the way her mind must be working. If men were naturally sexual roamers, how much less chance had a woman of holding one to whom she could not grant his most basic human right – that of perpetuating his kind?

I chewed my way without appetite through half the food she put before me, then gave up. Eating slowly, she managed to finish, then took my plate away without comment.

'I haven't got a pudding,' she said. 'Would you like coffee and some cheese?'

'Coffee,' I said. 'No cheese.'

I felt I ought to reassure her, but my mind would shape no new formula, and the old one – 'I don't mind' – implied a magnanimity out of key tonight. I *did* mind. And in letting me see again just how bitterly she minded, Eileen acknowledged the possibility in me of an understandable grievance. A thought of a kind I'd never felt the need to entertain before sidled into view: it was a grievance that one day might be put to use. I didn't like myself for it. It marked a stage in our marriage, a moving away from candour to storing ammunition for some future struggle.

5

Saturday dawned hard and bright. It was still very cold out of the sun. I put on a thick sweater and went out to take the first cut of the year off the lawns. Bonny's car blocked the drive and I had to carry the Flymo high, clearing the Jag's roof, to get it to the front of the house. I'd not heard him come in last night, though Eileen and I had sat up late, watching television in the kind of torpor the medium has introduced to the nation's households: when you are physically relaxed, your critical faculties are anaesthetised and you can't summon the necessary effort to get you to bed. I had ended feeling sluggishly irritable at the waste of time; but I'd been too restless to listen to music, and to have immersed myself in a book would have seemed like deliberately shutting myself off from Eileen at a time when anything shared – even a mild boredom – was preferable.

This morning she was fidgety. Looking from the breakfast table at the sunlight outside, she had said we ought to have gone away for the weekend. I asked her where to.

'To Somerset. I haven't seen mum and dad since Christmas.'

'They weren't expecting us.'

'You know we're welcome any time.'

'It's a bit late now. And I shouldn't have fancied driving all that way in the kind of weather we've had this week.'

'Look at it now, though.'

'It's not to be trusted.'

'Well, why don't we just have a run out somewhere; take a packed meal, or buy a pub lunch?'

'What about Bonny?'

'What about him?'

'It looks a bit inhospitable to buzz off like that.'

'And it's a bit much if he expects us to drop everything just to keep him company till he decides to go.'

'He won't.'

'Well, then. In any case, he might have plans of his own. Do you know what time he came in last night?'

'No, it was after I went to sleep.'

'What time was that?'

'About one, one-fifteen. I was reading till then.'

'It's a long time to drive a couple of miles and back.'

'Do you think he was with Eunice all that time?'

'I don't know. But wherever he was, he left us to our own devices and we can leave him to his today.'

'Where would you like to go?'

'We needn't go very far. We could go to Haworth and come back over the moors, make a round trip. We haven't been to Haworth for a while.'

'Hmm.'

Eileen, brought up in the lush valleys of Somerset, had quite fallen in love with the West Riding, especially the north-west area where the country ran up from the textile towns into bleak moorland tops, and I had enjoyed showing her the parts she had not already found for herself, seeing it afresh through her foreign eyes and listening to her exclamations of pleasure. 'Oh, they don't know how beautiful and grand it is, and they won't believe you when you tell them.'

'Well, don't tell everybody or they might all want to come, and then there'll be no room for us.'

I took my coffee to the window and looked into the back garden.

'I think it's dry enough for me to cut the lawns.'

'Does that mean you don't want to go?'

'It'll only take ten minutes. You wash up and get ready. But don't pack food; we'll get something in a pub.'

Our neighbour was washing his Marina in his drive. He must have seen the Flymo held aloft like a banner with a strange device, because he came to the dividing wall as I struggled clear and put the mower down.

'A bit early for that, isn't it? There could be some frost.'

'I thought I'd risk it.'

'That couple of days' mild weather we had a fortnight ago. It lulled us into a false sense of security.'

'I wish it would come again.'

'I expect it will, if we're patient.'

It would come when it was ready, I thought, whether we were patient or not.

Norton was an accountant at an engineering works; a burly man in his late forties, with gold-rimmed glasses and a loose wet mouth. He and his wife lived alone, after the death of a teenaged son from leukaemia, in that gloomy-looking villa which I guessed he had bought cheaply before the boom in house prices, and which must be far too big for them now. We saw little of his wife. She was a strange thin, dark woman who was permanently tipsy on grocer's sherry bought from the cask, who had run up bills at all the local shops and several in the town centre until Norton had stopped her credit, and whom Norton was said to beat up at intervals.

He cocked his head at Bonny's car.

'Been changing your motor?'

'Jaguars are just a little out of my league.'

'Yes. Nice work if you can get it.' He nodded. 'Er, by the way, do ask your visitor not to rev his engine and slam his car door at twenty minutes to two in the morning. Don't like to complain, but don't like to be wakened out of my first sleep, either.' He smiled.

I apologised, said I'd mention it, and went back into the house to plug in the mower cable and pass it out through the window. There was a distinct pleasure in uncovering the bright green turf under that lumpy last growth, and there was no easier or more immediate way of transforming the look of the garden. Neither Eileen nor I had much interest in horticulture, though we were diligent in doing the minimum needed to keep things tidy. Grass cuttings clung to my shoes and the bottoms of my trousers. I was standing for a moment, enjoying the scent of it and, on that sheltered side, feeling the warmth of the sun on my shoulders, when Bonny came out, holding a mug of tea.

'Eileen says you're going out for the day.'

'We'd like to. Will you be all right?'

'Oh, sure. I'll watch the match on television this afternoon. Will you be late back?'

'I shouldn't think so. Why?'

'I thought, seeing as you've given me board and lodging this last couple of days, I'd take you out to dinner. My treat.'

'That's handsome of you. Any special place in mind?'

'I'm a bit out of touch with local catering. You and Eileen think of somewhere. Eunice said she'd make up the four.'

'Where did you get to last night?'

'We went to the pictures, then took some fish and chips to her place.'

'Hmm. Does she live up to her poetry, then?'

'You've got a mucky mind, our kid. You might think they're

all for screwing, but some of 'em like to be loved for their minds.'

'Touché.'

'In fact, they all like to be loved for their minds – first.'

'That must be hard-going at times. By the way, you woke our neighbour in the small hours.'

'I didn't waken you and Eileen, did I?'

'No. We must have been fast on.'

'Is Eileen all right this morning?'

'What d'you mean?'

'I thought she was a bit – oh, I dunno – different.'

'She needs a change of scenery. We're off as soon as I've finished this mowing.'

He offered to do the rest for me, but I told him I quite enjoyed it and he went inside while I carried the Flymo back over his car, to the patch of grass behind the house. We left him, a little while later, eating cornflakes in the kitchen while he kept an eye on sausages frying in the pan.

'His night out with that girl seems to have done him good,' Eileen said, when we were on our way.

'He certainly needed something.'

'Is she as sexy as her poetry?'

I laughed. 'Now that I couldn't tell you. I asked Bonny as much and he told me I'd got a mucky mind.'

'Do you find her sexually attractive?'

'I find you sexually attractive.'

'Come on,' she persisted, 'tell me the truth. I'm not suggesting you'd do anything about it.'

'Well, since she worked the transformation in her appearance, I suppose I do.'

'Do you like her, as a person?'

'Now that's a different matter. I don't think so. Not very much.'

'Why not?'

'Because I think she's probably self-centred, if not selfish. I think she's probably quite a cold person at heart.'

'Then she's probably met her match, in Bonny.'

'D'you think Bonny's cold?'

'I've always thought he doesn't care tuppence about anybody but himself.'

'I'd be interested to know what evidence you have for that.'

'It's just a feeling.'

I'd remembered Frances as I spoke. Eileen didn't know about Bonny and her. But if you rejected a girl who later found she was pregnant and then killed herself in a car smash, did that make the rejection more reprehensible? If you struck a man you didn't know, did his suffering a heart attack add culpability to the blow?

'People accused Bonny of putting on side as soon as he started to take off; as soon as those who knew spotted his talent. Of course his talent made him different; it set him apart and made him impatient with those who simply didn't know as much as he did, but talked about it just the same.'

'You mean none of us can understand him.'

'I think there are complexities and pressures in his life that we can't understand.'

She said no more on that probably because she did not wish to challenge what she regarded as loyalty.

She pointed. 'Look, they're knocking that down now.'

We were driving towards the roofless outer wall of a nearly demolished mill. The sky could be seen through the window apertures and blocks of fallen stone lay piled in the foundations. It had been a proud building in its way, built to stand for centuries, its destruction after a mere eighty or ninety years another blow at the battered identity of these textile towns to which the coming of synthetic fibres and cheap imports had shrunk manufacturing space and reduced the numbers of hands needed to do the work. 'We shall have the ten-hour bill, yes we will, yes we will,' men had chanted in these valleys. But their inheritance had become the transistor-radio production line and the anonymous prefabricated warehouses where monstrous container lorries brought and took away the convenience foods of supermarket shopping.

Well ... in lonely Haworth in the year the ten-hour bill was passed, the year that *Jane Eyre* was published, with an open sewer running down Main Street and polluted water as the daily drink, life expectancy had been twenty-nine. Anne Brontë's term on earth matched that expectancy as though measured for it. She had seen her sister Emily die the year before, at thirty. Charlotte, who had watched them both enter the world, watched them leave it, and achieved thirty-nine.

At the bottom of Main Street I braked and stopped. Since we'd been here last, the traffic had been made one-way and a new bypass skirted the village on the low side. It also gave access to a large car park, offering more space for vehicles of both those who made long and deliberate pilgrimages and others, like ourselves, who had decided on a whim to 'have a run out' to the home of those famous young women who themselves thought nothing of walking four miles to Keighley station. One evening, Charlotte and Anne walked that road through a snowstorm and took the nightmail for London, where they confronted their astounded publisher with the news that Currer, Ellis and Acton Bell were indeed three different people and, moreover, unmarried sisters from a remote Yorkshire parsonage.

But I didn't want to go into the cramped rooms of the Parsonage today and look again at the touchingly tiny shoes, the unyielding sofa on which Emily had died, the minute script of the Gondal stories; nor gaze out at the weather-stained gravestones, rank on rank. What communicated itself to me today was not the achievements of the lives lived in that house, but the sombre brevity of their span. I thought that Eileen shared my mood, if I'd not, in fact, caught it from her. So we sauntered part of the way down Main Street, until the cutting wind slicing through the ginnels and courts drove us to seek shelter. We went into a bookshop where, attracted by handsome new paperback editions, I bought copies of the two major novels; then we crossed the square to the Black Bull.

'Would you like to go into the dining-room?'

'No. I'll be happy with a beer and a bar snack.'

I ordered the food and we managed to find seats. Eileen went to the lavatory and I opened my copy of *Jane Eyre* and read passages at random till she came back. I marked a place with the till-slip as she sat down beside me.

We had finished some rather tasty chicken soup with croutons and were about to start on the sandwiches, when I was hailed by John Pycock's high reedy voice, which was always a surprise when you saw the bulk it issued from. 'Gordon!' He beamed across the heads of the people sitting between us and what there was of open space by the bar counter. His wife, a shapeless body in a baggy skirt and a windcheater, nodded and smiled from beside him. 'May we join you?' Pycock asked.

I looked round, somewhat at a loss to see how they could. But there was an empty stool and a place on the bench seat, two tables away, and Pycock set about persuading seven people to re-deploy themselves, their possessions and their food and drink – 'So kind. How nice of you. I do hope I'm not putting you about.' – until he and his wife were seated across the table from us. A red faced, short-back-and-sides man, with a bright yellow shirt under his blue car coat, asked dourly, 'Are you all right now?' and Pycock beamed amiably across at him. 'So very kind of you.'

He was near retiring, taught chemistry in senior school and was deputy headmaster, the top job having gone to a younger man from another part of the country, though Pycock, as the only surviving member of staff from the time before it went comprehensive and was a grammar school, could not be beaten in seniority. He had a massive bald head, with a tonsure of crinkly grey hair, big fleshy features and powerful arms and legs. I knew the strength of those legs: I'd once been with him on a fell-walking expedition and had exhausted myself trying to match his furious pace. That had been while I was in the sixth form, for Pycock had also been one of my teachers and as I'd not been back long at my old school I still sometimes found it strange to be not a pupil but a colleague. To the staff he was known as Juno, because of his old-fashioned way of signing his name: 'Jno. Pycock.' The girls, I believed, referred to him likewise. Among the boys – well, his surname offered many pos-sibilities, but none had stuck except the name passed to us as we entered the school, which we passed on in our turn, and by which he was still known. They called him 'Bunprick.'

'Well, John,' Monica Pycock said dryly, 'now you've got us settled, don't you think we should have something to drink?'

Pycock chuckled and slapped his knee. He was notorious for his meanness in small financial transactions and it occurred to me that he had probably been waiting for me to offer a round.

'And what would you like?'

'A lime and lemon, mixed, in a tall glass, topped-up with soda water and ice.'

'It shall be yours. What about the fair Eileen?'

'A half of bitter, please.'

He looked at me. 'Same for me, John.'

'So – what are you two doing up here today?' Monica Pycock asked, her fingers tucking away straying lengths of grey hair. The mother of four children, she was a dingy woman in appearance, who I could not imagine had ever possessed sexual charm; but she did own a pair of clear and shrewdly appraising blue eyes. I suspected she

66

could produce character sketches of all Pycock's colleagues with whom she'd had more than one encounter.

'Everybody you know will turn up in Haworth, Monica, if you wait long enough.'

'Yes. The Brontës draw people to this place like some extra natural phenomenon such as a waterfall,' she said. 'So convenient that the Parsonage isn't in a back street in Cleckheaton.'

'Have you been in today?'

'Oh, yes; but we really came on another errand. I wanted to buy some tweed for a cloak, for next winter.' She indicated the parcel at her feet.

'You could find a use for one today,' Eileen said.

'Yes, isn't it bitter? But I was looking ahead. It's devilishly expensive, but I expect it will cost more by the time I get it made up and in service. It's a present from John. I let him talk me into it.' She smiled as her husband came back with the drinks.

'I've ordered some food,' he said.

'Oh, good.'

I pointed to our sandwiches. 'Would you like to stave off the pangs while you're waiting?'

'No, no. We'll be having soup first, thank you. And, please, you carry on.'

He took a good swig of beer. I guessed from the deliberate way he put the pint glass down, settled on his stool and lifted his chin that he was about to relate something in length.

'We came along the road today,' he said, 'behind a rather shabby F-registered Vauxhall saloon with a youngish couple in it. To the back window was stuck a small replica of the Union Jack. I pointed it out to Monica and we agreed – alas – that it could only indicate the presence of the National Front. We parked near them and found ourselves following them into the Parsonage. They looked round in there with a kind of dim and uninformed curiosity and then, in an upstairs room, we came upon a well-dressed black man who was expressing his opinion of the real cause of Charlotte's death to the white woman he was with. He went on to say – you know what clear sonorous voices those chaps have – he said that while we now looked at all those early and untimely deaths with a pitying curiosity for a medically and hygienically unenlightened age long gone, there were areas in his part of the third world in which they were still an everyday reality. The difference was that he and other educated men knew how to deal with the problems of today and the only thing they lacked was the wherewithal. The man we'd followed was in the room at the time. He didn't once look directly at the black man, but he was looking at him all the time with everything except his eyes.'

'*Was* he a National Front man, d'you think?'

'Oh, yes. He left leaflets about in the Parsonage.'

'*Did* he?'

'Yes. I picked them all up as we went round after them. I have them in my pocket now. I shall look carefully at them when we get home, but I've no intention of bringing them out in here and drawing people's attention to the fact that pollution has returned to Haworth, though in another form. It occurred to me as someone who spent six years of his life helping to rid the world of one racist tyranny that I ought to get one of those little replica Union Jacks and stick it to my car window, with a little added legend: "This flag is not the property of the National Front." '

'And you'd probably have your car vandalised within a week,' Monica Pycock said.

'No doubt,' Pycock conceded. 'No doubt, no doubt.'

'You didn't vandalize *his* car, did you?' I asked.

'No,' Pycock said, 'but that's rather different. I've no doubt we have some colleagues – perhaps a sixth-former or two as well – who, given an opportune time and place, would be capable of emptying his tyres or treating his bodywork to a pot of paint, but I personally feel that playing them at their own game is playing into their hands.'

There was a constant movement of people coming and going, but something made me look up at the door as Pycock finished speaking.

'I assume that's your black friend,' I said.

Pycock turned his head. 'Yes.'

He was wearing a well-cut fawn overcoat and a grey suit. Though not handsome by Western European standards, and not especially tall, he was quite a striking figure as he stood just inside the door and looked round the room with perfect composure. I couldn't see much of the woman he was with, except a grey suede topcoat trimmed with fur, until he moved towards the bar and turned back to speak to her. Then I said, 'Good lord!'

'What's the matter?' Pycock asked. 'Do you know him?'

'No. I thought for a second I knew the woman.'

This of course drew Eileen's attention to her so that when, standing alone while her companion was at the bar, she turned idly to glance about, the woman found all four of us appraising her. She averted her gaze, tilting her head back slightly, and turned away again. She might, I thought, have had to learn to cope with a good deal of that kind of summing-up.

'Do you know her?' Monica Pycock asked, her shrewd eyes on me now.

'No. I was mistaken.'

But I thought I knew who she must be. For in the instant that her profile had been revealed she had looked for all the world like Frances McCormack could have looked had she lived through those lost years. In full face, a different placing of the eyes, slight but decisive, at once banished the illusion of being in the presence of a girl long dead; but the resemblance was still remarkable.

Monica began talking about having been south for the christening of their eighth grandchild. She produced photographs.

'You're getting to be quite the patriarch, John.'

He smiled with quiet satisfaction.

'Oh, our tribe's nothing compared with some,' Monica said. 'The woman who cleans for me was telling me last week that her mother has just acquired the grand total of fifty children, grandchildren and great-grandchildren; and what's more she can read off all their names.'

'How old is she, ever?'

'Only just eighty. It can be done, if everybody starts early enough.'

'And manages to keep it up,' Pycock said, with a sly grin at me. His brand of sexual innuendo was always mild but nonetheless surprising because rare and unexpected.

'She looks lovely,' Eileen said, passing back the pictures.

I had always to remember when the subject of progeny came up in conversation that, though known about, Eileen's condition was not the first thought in other people's minds.

The black man and his companion were now standing together with their drinks. I excused myself and wove a path past them to the corridor leading to the lavatory. When I came back they were sitting at a small table by the stairs. I stopped and stood over them, addressing the woman.

'Excuse me. You won't know me, but could I ask you if your name is McCormack?'

'It was, yes.'

'My name's Gordon Taylor. I believe you had a sister called Frances.'

'Yes.' My name had registered. 'Weren't you with Frances the night she . . .?'

'Yes. I was struck by the unmistakable resemblance when you first came in. That's why I might have seemed to be staring.'

But I should never have fallen for this girl, I was thinking. Odd what a difference that tiny variation in facial composition could make.

'I'm Mary McCormack,' she said. 'There was hardly twelve months between Frances and me. I was just that bit older. People often took us for twins. This is my husband, by the way. Robert –' She gave me an African name which I couldn't take in at one hearing and I held out my hand, which he took into his firm grip.

'How d'you do.'

'How well did you know Frances?' Mary McCormack asked.

'We'd dated a couple of times. Then we ran into each other and she offered me a lift . . .' I shrugged.

'You were injured rather badly yourself, weren't you?'

'A broken leg, a few bruises. Nothing that wouldn't mend.'

She looked directly at me. 'You know, of course, that Frances . . .' She stopped. She knew that I knew. It was how I'd known that interested her.

I nodded, looking back at her. 'Yes. The police told me. And then your father came to see me. It was news to me and I couldn't help him.'

'I'm afraid he hasn't got over that . . . that aspect of it. I wish he could.'

'It's surely best forgotten, after all this time.'

'That's what I think. I think it's the mystery, you know. The thought that he doesn't know what kind of a man – or boy – was responsible.'

'Can I get you a drink?' Robert asked. He'd probably heard all this before. I wondered how Mr McCormack, with his views on mixed marriages, had taken to *him*.

'I've got one over there, thanks. I'm with my wife and some friends.'

'We mustn't keep you, then,' Mary said. 'But by the way, now I come to think of it, aren't you the brother of Bonny Taylor?'

70

'Yes, I am.'

'You know Bonny Taylor, the football player, don't you, Robert?' she asked her husband.

'Yes, I do. I've seen him play several times. A fine talent, but' – he hesitated – 'a somewhat mercurial temperament.'

'Do you still live in Yorkshire?' I asked Mary.

'We're in Leeds at present. My husband's a doctor. I'm a nurse. That's how we met. But we're probably going to Nigeria. Robert wants to work among his own people.'

'That's natural, I suppose.'

I left them and went back to the table. Monica and Eileen had gone to the ladies. By the time they came back, John's and Monica's food had arrived. Since we'd eaten ours and wanted nothing more to drink, we parted from them there and walked straight back to the car.

'You did know that woman, then?' Eileen asked.

'She's Frances McCormack's sister, Mary.'

'The girl who was killed?'

'Yes.'

'Is she like her?'

'So much so, I thought at first I was seeing a ghost.'

We reached the car and got in. The wind was still cold, but the sun was hot through the glass.

'Would you like to go back the long way, over the top?'

'Yes.'

I started the engine.

'Fifty descendants,' Eileen said. 'That woman Monica was talking about. Fifty descendants in her own lifetime.'

'Thank goodness not everybody's as fertile, or we'd soon be standing on one another's heads.'

Eileen said nothing.

'I found something in *Jane Eyre*, while you were in the loo.' I reached the book from the back seat and opened it at the page I'd marked. ' "It is weak and silly to say you *cannot bear* what it is your fate to be required to bear." Stern counsel, but true in the end.'

'That's Helen Burns,' Eileen said. 'She carried the consoling knowledge of another life to come.'

'And we who can't must make the best of this one, and count our blessings.' I looked round. There was no one near enough to matter. I leaned towards Eileen and kissed her cold cheek, at the same time sliding my hand under her coat to fondle her breast. 'What, no bra?'

'I didn't feel like wearing one today.'

'There's no earthly reason why you need.'

'Suppose I had to have one removed?' she said.

'What? What on earth are you talking about?'

'Women quite often do, you know. Monica Pycock had one taken away last year. Suppose I had to have a breast removed? What would you do?'

'I should learn to love the other one twice as much.'

6

Eunice was waiting in the house with Bonny when we got home. She was wearing a loose smock dress and either the same smoke-grey stockings or an identical pair, with high-heeled gloss-black shoes. They were drinking tea and watching the early news and sports reports on television.

'How'd you get on?' I asked, meaning Bonny's side.

'Lost,' Bonny said. 'Three, one.'

'See any of it?'

'No.' Bonny nodded at the fast-talking head on the screen. 'This guy just gave us a run-down: "It's obvious that the absence of the suspended Bonny Taylor is making a marked difference to the performance of this faltering side," he said. All of a sudden, I'm a miracle-worker.'

Eileen had disappeared upstairs soon after coming in. I found her in our bedroom, getting out clothes for the evening. Finding Eunice here, at Bonny's invitation, had annoyed her.

'This is *our* house, Gordon,' she said. 'We invite who *we* want to invite.'

'He probably thought it would be easier than picking her up later.'

'I just don't like to come into my house and find strangers sitting around.'

'Anybody would think he'd thrown a party while we were out. After all, the girl is making a four for dinner. Don't you want to go?'

'I do want to go. I'm getting ready to go. I just don't care for the way Bonny makes free with this place, as though it were an hotel.'

'But what has he done? In God's name, what are you so touchy about?'

She would say no more. I laid out suit and shirt and tie, then followed her to the bathroom. I was irritated to find that she had locked the door, then remembered that, after all, we were not alone in the house. The door of the smallest of our three bedrooms stood open next to the bathroom. This was my study: mine because Eileen preferred to do written work downstairs, on her knee, and it was I who dabbled in the field of creative writing, which called for quiet and solitude. 'Dabbled,' I'd admitted to myself, was a word quite strong enough to match the level of my commitment. While it seemed to me that more and more people felt literate and sensitive enough to try to describe on paper what it was like to be human, I knew only too well the difference between indulging the occasional impulse and the dedication that set aside regular hours for the struggle between language and the blank page.

On my desk was a pile of essays I must read and mark before Monday morning. I glanced idly at the top one then put them to one side. Water ran into the depleted hot-tank in the cupboard in the corner. Someone came up the stairs. It was Eunice. She met the closed door of the bathroom, then turned and saw me.

'Occupied,' I said.

'I'm not desperate.' She came a few steps into the room.

'You'd perhaps better hang on, though, and get in before me.'

And now, I thought, I'd given her an invitation to stay where her presence could irritate Eileen further. 'Or I'll give you a shout,' I said.

'I'll wait,' Eunice said, 'as long as I'm not interrupting anything.'

'No, no.'

She approached the end of the desk, then glanced round the room at the bookshelves, the filing cabinet, the posters, prints and photographs on the walls. 'Cosy little den you've made.'

'Yes, isn't it? It ought to be conducive of sustained creative effort.'

'Isn't it?'

But I was her teacher. It was one thing admitting my shortcomings to myself, another confiding them to her.

'Time,' I said, offering the lamest excuse of all, 'time is of the essence.'

'I'm afraid that's what we all say.' She picked up a magazine. The cover carried a picture of a lush-mouthed beauty lying back on satin pillows, one full-nippled breast exposed, her hands laid between her spread legs. There was a similar picture inside with the hands relieved of their coy guard. 'Not much creative in here,' Eunice commented.

'If your poem had been a story you might have found a market for it there.'

'Do you really think so?' She flipped the pages.

'Well, no. A few years ago, perhaps. But the death of euphemism has killed literary content as well.'

She stopped at a page of text and read a little. 'I see what you mean. Now you can say the words the only satisfaction is to go on saying them, *ad nauseam*.'

'Close encounters of the most primitive kind. How are you getting on with Bonny?'

'He takes a lot of getting to know. I don't think he's used to intelligent women.'

'Ah! There could be some truth in that.'

I felt ill at ease. Not because of the magazine, which she'd put down, but because I'd run out of small talk. I had run out of small talk because I didn't want her here in this room, didn't want her imprint on its atmosphere. It was private. The next time we met in the class she would imagine me here, know what surrounded me during my deepest and most serious thought, perhaps wonder why I didn't in any significant measure do what I was paid to urge them to do.

'I like that.' Her gaze had fallen on a small watercolour hanging on the wall opposite my desk. It was of a millyard with a hoist and two men handling bales of wool.

'Local painter,' I told her.

She went up to it and peered intently at it, adjusting her glasses. 'Hmm ... yes.'

The bathroom door opened. Eileen came out, saying, 'Gordon?'

'Here.'

'Oh.' She came in. 'It's all yours now.' Her mood seemed to have changed, as though her bath had also washed away her bad humour. She saw the magazine. 'How d'you like the imperfections of the real thing?' She opened the thin silk wrap she had bought at a Help the Needy shop, before we were married, and stood with hands on hips, giving an exaggerated shrug of one shoulder, as she showed me briefs, suspendered stockings, the jut of a towel-rosy breast. Then she saw Eunice.

'Oh.' She pulled the wrap about her.

'I was waiting to use the loo,' Eunice said.

'You'd better get in, then, before Gordon beats you to it.'

Eunice smiled slightly and walked past her, out of the room.

'Christ!' Eileen said, as the bathroom door closed.

My colour had risen to match hers. 'Sorry about that.'

'Oh, *hell!*' Eileen said.

''Leen, you're on a knife-edge,' I said. 'There's no need for it, love.'

But she whirled and was gone, her rapid movement leaving the scent of talcum powder behind her on the disturbed air. I breathed in the invisible particles. In a moment I began to sneeze repeatedly. It had once happened while we were making love, but that time we had both laughed.

When we went out to the car, Eunice did something I thought pushy. It would have been usual for us two men to sit together up front; but when Bonny reached over and opened the passenger door Eunice got in beside him, leaving me to sit in the back with Eileen. Not that Eileen, I guessed, did not prefer this arrangement. I caught her glance. She raised an eyebrow, then turned her head away.

She didn't speak as Bonny threaded his way to the first main road, crossed that and drove down a steep hillside through a semi-derelict area of four-roomed houses, pruned sparse by demolition, and on to a second. The headlights picked out the flimsy, brightly coloured trousers, tight at the ankles, of a Pakistani woman as she walked, head down, with short hurrying steps along the broken pavement. I was enjoying the smooth ride of the Jaguar, the quiet purr of its engine and the smell of Eileen's perfume. I should have enjoyed them more if I could have fathomed Eileen's mood. It wasn't, I thought, simply dislike of Eunice: that merely intensified it. I didn't know how to cope with it because it was new to our relationship, a side of her no more than hinted at before. I supposed I'd been extraordinarily lucky in having such a calm and compatible wife. The change in her did not seem due to any shortcoming of mine; nevertheless, I felt the stirring of some nameless guilt. As she sat beside me, still silent, I wanted to reassure myself by taking her hand, and felt the novel fear of a rebuff. A small knot of tension began to tighten in my stomach. I hoped it wouldn't spoil my appetite for dinner.

We began to climb the other side of the valley. When Bonny gave way to oncoming traffic at a fork overshadowed by the looming bulk of two great warehouses, I said, 'It's your road to the left. That's the quickest way.'

'I know,' Bonny said. He swung right. In a couple of minutes we had reached the ridge. I had hardly realised just where we were when Bonny stopped the car, engine still running, outside the Criterion Hotel.

'Eunice,' he said, 'would you like to do me a little favour?'

'If I can.'

'Would you mind popping across to see what the licensee's name is, painted over the door of that pub.'

'Are you serious?'

'Perfectly.'

For a second I thought she was going to tell him to go and look for himself, but after a glance at him she got out and walked across the car park.

'What are you up to?' I asked him.

'We don't know his name, do we?'

'No, but—'

'Eileen knows all about it, does she?'

'Yes. What about Eunice?'

'No. I'll mebbe tell her later.'

Eunice was in the lighted porch. Two men came out and spoke to her as one held the door open to let her in. She took hold of the door for a moment, then released it as they walked away. She came back and got in to the car.

'Did you see those two men? I suddenly felt a fool. I wouldn't have known what to say if they'd asked me what I was doing.'

'Oh, I'm sure you'd have thought of something.' Bonny eased the car away from the kerb. 'What's the name?'

'Thomas Arthur Grint, it says.'

'Thanks.'

'Do you mind telling me what it was in aid of?'

'Oh, I was just settling a little argument,' Bonny said easily.

'Who was right?'

Bonny did not answer directly, but half turned his head to speak over his shoulder. 'Thomas Arthur Grint, Gordon,' he said. 'Did you get that?'

'Yes,' I said, playing along with him. 'Tom Grint. I couldn't have told you his middle name.'

'His middle name is "Charming",' Bonny said. 'Thomas Arthur Charming Grint.'

'It's not a pub I've ever been into,' Eunice said, when it seemed that no one was going to enlighten her.

'Oh, you don't know what you've missed,' Bonny said. 'The landlord's real charming. A man of wide knowledge. You ask Gordon. Isn't he charming, Gordon?'

'Charming,' I said.

'He knows a lot about all kinds of things,' Bonny said. 'He knows all about football. I'll bet he knows a lot about mucky books as well. Especially mucky poetry. Mucky poetry's bound to be one of

Charming Grint's specialities. He'll have very firm opinions about mucky poetry.'

Eunice gave a short puzzled laugh. 'Do they often play games like this?' she asked, twisting round to address Eileen.

'They're brothers,' Eileen said. 'You'd better ask them.' She was looking at the back of Bonny's head. She raised an eyebrow again and let an odd little smile touch her lips, without glancing at me.

'Did you hear about the schoolteacher who asked the little lad to give her a sentence using the word "charming" twice? He said, "Our kid came home last night and told me dad she was up the spout with a baby. 'Charming,' me dad said, 'fucking charming'."'

We were moving quickly now, but with no sense of haste, towards Leeds.

'I hope this place you're taking us to is charming,' Bonny said. 'Eunice likes things to be charming, don't you, Eunice?'

'I've no doubt it will be,' Eunice said.

'You've no doubt it will be what, Eunice?'

'Charming,' Eunice said, drawing out the word.

'Ah, now you've broken the rules. You're not supposed to say "charming". That's my word and Gordon's. I shall have to think of a forfeit.'

When I'd suggested a Chinese restaurant which was a favourite of mine and Eileen's, Eileen had come in with: 'You must let Bonny choose. Our taste might not be his and Eunice's.' We visited the Silver Dragon perhaps a dozen times a year, more than we went to any other restaurant. We had found it by accident a few days after we had declared ourselves to each other, and thought of it as our special place. Having once taken a couple there who hadn't cared for it, and so tarnished our pleasure, we had been wary ever since of recommending it. I hoped, as we waited for a table, that it would not be like that tonight.

The headwaiter motioned to us, smiling broadly. He was the only member of the staff whom we had ever seen smile. The others, men and women alike, were as inscrutable as legend made their race out to be.

'Now he *is* charming,' Bonny said, as we followed the man. 'Nobody could deny that.'

We were left the menu.

'The best thing to do, after soup,' I said, 'is to order a main dish apiece, perhaps one extra, then all share.'

'Okay,' Bonny said.

'What do you like, Eunice?' I asked. 'Chicken, duck, beef, prawns?'

We selected and I jotted the numbers on a paper napkin.

'Chopsticks for everybody?'

'Why not?' Bonny said. 'Chopsticks are charming. Knives and forks aren't charming, but chopsticks are. And we'll have a bottle of champagne. What say you, Eunice?'

'Whatever you say,' Eunice said.

'How easy it is to please her,' Bonny said.

'Champagne's so expensive,' Eileen said. 'I'm quite happy drinking lager with Chinese food.'

'There's nothing charming about lager, Eileen,' Bonny said. 'What's lager, Gordon?'

'Lager is boring.'

'That's what it is. Now, champagne is charming and we're out for a charming evening.'

'I'm certainly not going to refuse it,' Eileen said.

'That's right,' Bonny said. 'A refusal never charms. It often offends, but it never charms.' He took some change out of his pocket, looked at it on his palm and said to me, 'Is there a telephone?'

I had to think for a moment. 'On the wall, in that passage over there.'

'Excuse me,' Bonny said, getting up.

Eunice watched him as he made his way across the room.

'Is he often like that?'

'Like what?' I said.

'Childishly facetious.'

'He's just trying to be charming.'

'Oh,' Eunice said, 'you're as bad.'

'It's in the blood.'

'You're not really all that alike, though, are you, for brothers?'

'In personality or appearance?'

'Both.'

A waiter came. I gave him the order. 'And a bottle of number thirty-nine, please.'

'Champagne?'

'Champagne. It will be nicely chilled, won't it?'

'Yes, sir.' He went away.

'Have you any brothers or sisters, Eileen?' Eunice asked.

'A brother.'

'Is he like you?'

'We look alike, yes.'

'You're an only child, aren't you, Eunice?' I asked.

'How did you know?'

'I guessed.'

Bonny came back. One or two heads turned as he walked across the floor. A man leaned across and said something to the woman he was with. She looked round as Bonny reached the table.

'Engaged,' he said as he sat down. 'Have we ordered?'

'It's on its way.'

'Would you mind showing me where the loo is, Eileen?' Eunice said.

'Sure.' Eileen took her bag and got up with her.

It was the first time I had been alone with Bonny since morning.

'I saw Frances McCormack's sister Mary today.'

'Oh? Where?'

'In the Black Bull at Haworth. She gave me a shock for a minute. I thought it was Frances herself.'

'Is she that much like her?'

'Remarkably so.'

'You didn't know her before?'

'No. I spoke to her. She was with her husband. He's a doctor. African. Black as an undertaker's hat.' I looked at Bonny and waited.

'Maybe he's a Catholic.'

I had to laugh. 'You know, I hadn't thought of that.'

Bonny drummed on the tablecloth with his fingertips. I wondered whether to tell him what Mary had said about her father.

'Anyway,' I said in a moment, 'it just goes to show.'

'Show what?'

I shrugged. 'That you can do anything you really want to. Providing you're willing to carry the can for it.'

'There was only one thing I really wanted, Gordon,' Bonny told me. 'And I got it.'

'What do you want now?'

'Ah, now there's a question. There *is* a question.'

The waiter came with plates, bowls, spoons and chopsticks. The soup arrived as the women came back. Eileen began to serve it into the bowls. A young couple of about twenty came by, on their way out, approaching from Bonny's rear. I saw the boy glance at Bonny as they passed. Then the lad must have plucked up his courage, because he turned back. I looked up at his earnest, fresh-complexioned face.

'Excuse me, Mr Taylor ... You are Mr Taylor?'

'That's Mr Taylor,' Bonny said, waving at me. 'I'm his brother.'

The boy coloured a little. 'I don't want to intrude.'

'But you feel you have to tell me I'm a shit,' Bonny said.

The boy's colour deepened. 'Oh, no. I wanted to tell you that some of us don't believe all we read in the papers, and my fiancée and I, we think you're great.'

'Thank you,' Bonny said.

The lad managed a smile. 'Enjoy your meal.' He nodded and went.

'Now I thought that was charming,' Bonny said. 'Didn't you think it was charming, Eunice?'

'Yes, I did.'

'What did you think it was?'

'Delightful and enchanting.'

'Delightful and enchanting as well as ...?'

'As well as,' Eunice said.

'You've been thinking them up,' Bonny said. 'What do they call words that mean the same as other words, Gordon?'

'Synonyms,' Eunice answered for me.

'Very clever,' Bonny said.

'Except there are no such things as precise synonyms,' I said. 'Even the closest have slightly different meanings.'

'I'd never call Thomas Arthur Grint "enchanting",' Bonny said. 'And you're cheating, Eunice. You're cheating while everybody else is trying to be charming.'

'I thought you said I wasn't to say "charming".'

'There!' Bonny said. 'You've done it again. That's another forfeit.'

Eunice nodded as Eileen held the full soup-ladle over her empty bowl, for seconds. Then: 'Charming, charming, charming, charming,' she said. 'Charming, charming, charming.'

'Eunice doesn't like our game, Gordon,' Bonny said. 'She's trying to spoil it.'

'I think your game is boring,' Eunice said.

'Oh, do you now?' Bonny finished his soup without looking at her and shook his head as Eileen proferred the ladle.

'What are we going to do with her, Gordon?'

'I think it's boring, too,' Eileen said.

'In that case,' Bonny said, 'I'm surrounded and I give in.'

The main dishes came. The headwaiter brought the champagne himself. 'You ready for this?'

'We ready,' Bonny said. He held out his hand and felt the bottle. 'Okay.'

The cork came out with a deep plunk. Heads turned. A woman smiled. Bonny raised his glass. 'Here's to poetry, wherever we may find it.'

'Mmmm ...' Eunice said. 'There's nothing quite like it.'

'Poetry or champagne?' Bonny asked.

'Champagne,' Eunice said. 'One thing at a time.'

'Don't say that, Eunice,' Bonny said. 'Champagne goes with everything. One of the best screws I ever had was while we were drinking champagne.'

'Was it really?' Eunice said. Eileen was filling the bowls with fried rice. Eunice's dexterous chopsticks topped hers with chicken and cashew nuts.

'I hate that word,' Eileen said.

'What word?' Bonny asked.

'Screw.'

'We're really short of words for it,' Bonny said. 'What do you call them again, Eunice?'

'What?' Eunice said, mouth full, bowl to chin.

'Hey!' Bonny said, turning his head and looking at her. 'You've done that before!'

'Synonyms,' I said.

'Synonyms. That's the word. Now think of a synonym for screwing that isn't crude.'

'Making love,' Eileen said.

'Jane Austen and George Eliot talked about their characters making love,' I said, 'but they weren't talking about what Bonny's talking about.'

'I don't think so,' Bonny said.

'Well, what happened to her, Bonny?' I asked.

'To who?'

'The girl you had the best screw with. Or one of the best screws.'

'I don't know what happened to her. But it couldn't have been enough. She threw the bottle at me. I told you that champagne goes with everything. I fielded the bottle. Then she tipped the ice-bucket over me. That cooled things considerably.'

'Ice-bucket?'

'We were in a very high-class hotel,' Bonny said. He pointed with his chopsticks at the dishes. 'You ordered. What do you recommend?'

'This is good,' Eunice mumbled.

'You could have fooled me,' Bonny said.

'Try the duck,' I suggested. I passed the dish. 'Do you remember drinking champagne sitting outside that corner café opposite Rheims Cathedral, Eileen?'

'Yes. We were plagued by wasps.'

'There's something to spoil every romantic story,' Bonny said.

'We managed,' Eileen said.

'They used to sell champagne on draught in Yates's Wine Lodge in Blackpool,' Bonny said. 'So my father says.'

From our attic in a Blackpool boarding-house, Bonny and I, on holiday with our parents, had watched one afternoon a couple make love in a bay-windowed room diagonally opposite and one floor down. The woman had positioned herself on the edge of the bed, her skirt up. The man was in shirtsleeves, his trousers round his ankles, as he entered her. A little while later we had run down into the street as the couple left the house. Both man and woman were plain, squat, without elegance, and indistinguishable from thousands of other couples on holiday in the town. 'Hell's bells!' said Bonny, who had shown marked symptoms of sexual excitement upstairs. 'Better him than me.' With that, he seemed to dismiss the incident. But later I found myself brooding about the implications of what we'd seen. Were that man and woman making the best of a life in which they had little choice; or did each, in fact, possess an attraction for the other impossible to find so intensely elsewhere?

Eileen and I, amorous on champagne, had made love in the afternoon in an hotel in Rheims (not a high-class establishment, but a simple bed-and-breakfast place) and fallen asleep, finding when we went in search of dinner, at nine, an astonishing lack of choice as that provincial town put up its shutters for the night. Apart from the magnificence of the cathedral, I had said, as we tramped from one closed restaurant to another, we might as well have been in Barnsley. Better off in Barnsley, Eileen had pointed out, for there we should surely have found a Chinese restaurant open till midnight. But we had found a place whose proprietor was waiting to close, and with whom I had quarrelled, I in my limited French, the man in his limited

English, about the authenticity of the still mineral water Eileen asked for, which came in an already open bottle that I suspected of having been filled at the kitchen tap. Not ready for bed again, but with nowhere else to go, we had slept badly that night. The next morning I'd driven twice round the ring road before finding our route south. We were on honeymoon.

The headwaiter came up, having shown four people to a nearby table. Seeing Eunice's empty glass, he refilled it and topped-up the other three. It was an attention which always irritated me, in as much as it subsidised greed: the more quickly you drank the more you got, until the bottle ran dry and left everyone else on short rations.

Bonny gave the waiter a nod, eyed Eunice, intent on her food, for a moment, then asked with bland innocence, 'What was the best screw you ever had, Eunice?'

'I beg your pardon,' Eunice said.

'Was it the one in the poem?'

'Which poem?'

'The one you came to collect from Gordon, last night.'

'You've read that, have you?'

'Gordon showed it to me. I'm sorry, was it meant to be private?'

'It's not published yet.'

'Well, you shouldn't be shy about it. I thought it was good. I'm no expert, mind, like Gordon, but even I could see it had something going for it. And you will try to get it published, won't you?'

'Eventually, perhaps. But what makes you think it's auto-biographical?

'Well, you're a dead ringer for the girl. I mean, you're quiet and you don't push yourself forward. You obviously think a lot, but you don't say much.'

'Are you putting me on?'

'No, seriously. How do you get an idea for a poem like that? I can see how people get the idea of writing about daffodils and trees, but how do you come by an idea like that?'

'Poets must have *some* power of imagination,' Eunice said.

'Oh, *imagination,*' Bonny said. 'I thought experience came first.'

'Poets don't necessarily write everything from direct experience.'

'Well, no, not murder and torture and beating people up. But sex is something we can all enjoy, isn't it? I mean, I can't ask Gordon and Eileen what was the best screw they ever had, because they'd have to say with each other, wouldn't they? But you and I, we're free agents.

The world's our oyster. And I do think this women's lib is a marvellous thing.'

'In what way?'

'Because it lets them be honest about such things. They can admit they enjoy sex as men do – if they do. They don't have to be victims any more. They don't need to use it as a weapon or a meal ticket. I mean, they don't if they're as obviously modern and tuned-in as you are, for instance. 'Course, there are still a lot of 'em about who want it both ways. They want the bun and the ha'penny as well. So, anyway, answer the question if you want to and if you don't, don't. And if you're still a virgin, say so and I'll apologise for asking.'

'You are a sod, you know, aren't you?' Eunice said.

'Am I? Why? I thought we were having a friendly conversation about a pastime we all have in common, while drinking champagne and eating delicious food. I thought we were having a charming evening.'

'Oh, sod you and your charm,' Eunice said. She flung her napkin on the table, bent for the handbag at her feet, then walked away across the room.

Eileen's face was scarlet as she looked into her bowl and scored lines on the tablecloth with her chopsticks.

'She's right, you know,' she said finally, looking at Bonny.

'I don't know what you mean, Eileen.'

'Yes you do. What I can't understand is why you want to pick her up only to put her down.' She screwed up her own napkin and got up. 'I'd better go to her.'

'Go on, then,' Bonny said to me, when Eileen had followed Eunice.

'Go on what?'

'Let's have your two-pennorth.'

'You've been building up to this,' I said. 'I don't know why.'

'Have you never heard of a professional foul?' Bonny said. 'When you can't take the ball, you go for the player.'

'Did you make a pass at her last night?'

'Of course I did. After I'd eaten my fish and chips and wiped the grease from my lips, I made a pass.'

'And there was nothing doing, I take it?'

'You take it correctly. There was nothing doing.'

'Do you expect them all to drop their knickers the minute they see you coming?'

'What a gift of tongues you have, Gordon.'

'Well, I mean, why should she?'

'Why? Because she knew she would when she was ready. She had it in her power to give me – well, let's call it comfort. But no, she's like all the rest; she dangles it in front of you then pulls it away, till she's ready. When she's got what *she* wants.'

'There are plenty of others, aren't there? You're not going short, are you?'

'They like to be seen about with you,' Bonny said, 'in all the so-called smart places. Suggest a quiet evening by the fire and they throw a moody. The ones who do come at you head-on, and no messing, always end up calling you a bastard when their consciences start to trouble them.'

'It's generations of conditioning, Bonny.'

'And men are to blame. I know. Making love? Making hate. You can do that while you're screwing as well, you know. Do you know?'

'Has there never been anybody special?'

'Once,' Bonny said. 'But she was married. Her husband was a nice bloke and there was no way she was going to upset her two kids.'

'You don't see her any more?'

'No. Her old man got a leg-up and a move. She went with him. Tearful, swearing she'd never forget. But she went. There's always something, isn't there, in everybody's life? If only this chap had taken that job in Australia. If only that one had met that particular woman a few years earlier. What is it with you and Eileen, eh? If only she could have a couple of kids?'

'It is disappointing, but it's not the end of the world.'

'Is that what you tell her? Well, I'll tell you, our kid, you want to keep an eye on her. I don't know her very well, but I'd say she's broody.'

'She's always quiet.'

'That just makes it harder to know when she's brooding.'

'I thought it was Eunice she didn't much care for.'

'Oh, Eunice. What are we going to do about Eunice? Do you think I've blown it altogether?'

'Better wait and see when she comes back. Is it important?'

'I don't know.' He took the bottle and gave me and himself what was left of the champagne. 'Cheers.'

'Cheers,' I said. 'Here they come.'

The women came across the room. Eileen did not speak as they sat down.

'Sorry about that,' Eunice said. 'If you'd like me to leave now, I'll go.'

'My fault, Eunice,' Bonny said. He patted her thigh under the table. 'Forget about it. I'm going through a rough patch.'

Eileen asked for China tea. I got up to go to the lavatory and gave the order to a waiter on the way. When I came out of the lavatory, Bonny was using the telephone in the passage. He took my arm, to keep me.

'Hullo, Criterion Hotel? . . . Could I speak to Mr Grint, please? . . . He isn't? . . . Oh, Mrs Grint . . . Dickinson's the name, Jimmy Dickinson. I met a friend of his in Manchester and he suggested I call in and see him. I didn't want to turn up on his night off . . . No, nothing important, just social . . . He's what? . . . I'm sorry to hear that. Is it serious? . . . I see . . . I see . . . I see . . . Never! You're not safe inside your own four walls nowadays . . . Well, I'm pleased about that, anyway. I'll pass the message on. He'll be relieved to –' At that point Bonny gently depressed the receiver rest and severed the connection in mid-sentence. 'I didn't want her to start asking *me* questions,' he said.

'What's the news, then?'

'His condition's apparently satisfactory.'

'That's something worth knowing.'

'I feel a lot better,' Bonny said.

7

Bonny played the car radio on the way home. Random selection of a wavelength gave us a violin sonata on Radio 3. I didn't know Bonny's real taste in music, or whether, in fact, he had any real taste and didn't simply, as most people did, accept what was currently peddled in the pop field. I was mildly surprised, though, when he didn't switch to another station. The music played in a pleasant counterpoint to the steady forward motion of the car. The car's smooth ride gave little indication of speed, though Bonny was nudging the limit on each stretch of road. The radio panel added its glow to that of the instruments and silhouetted in a dim light Bonny's head and shoulders and those of Eunice, who was sitting in front again. In the back, I murmured to Eileen, 'Are you all right?'

'Uh, uh.'

I let my hand rest on her thigh, feeling a fastening of her suspender through the thickness of her skirt. Like most women, she preferred the convenience and comfort of tights; but she knew that, like most men, I preferred a woman in stockings, and she had worn stockings tonight not to be outdone by Eunice. Yet she had seemed not to want my attention. Now she let her hand rest in mine, but with no responsive pressure. Just a small answering squeeze would have told me that everything was all right. Or at least, that her quarrel was not with me. My feeling of unease came back. Had we been lovers still, and not man and wife, I should have suspected her of trying to tell me she didn't want me any longer. But we were lovers as well, weren't we? Only two nights ago she had been desperate in her physical need of me. How quickly, I thought, apparently solid ground can start to shift.

There had been some talk about whether we should go on to a disco-nightclub. Though Bonny didn't want the exposure, neither did he urge the curtailing of the evening because of that. Not wishing to go myself, and sensing that Eunice did, I pointed out that none of us had a membership card for any of the places we knew of, while believing, but not saying so, that payment of an admission charge at the door would have got us entry to one of them. Our lack of enthusiasm was too much for Eunice. Eileen had offered coffee at home, which I could supplement with whisky.

As the headlights of the car swung into the drive, Eunice gave a little exclamation.

'What's wrong?' Bonny asked. 'Have you lost something?'

'No. I thought I saw something.'

Bonny flashed up full beam, illuminating the channel of the drive between boundary wall and house as far as the garage doors. 'What did you see?'

'There was somebody standing in the drive,' Eunice said. 'She must be round the back of the house.'

'She?'

'It looked like a woman.'

I opened my door. 'I'll go and see. Keep your lights on, Bonny.'

'Here, take this.' Bonny reached back and handed me a small battery torch.

I walked to the corner of the house and shone the beam of the torch over the lawn. Nothing moved. I heard a car door close as someone else got out. I was about to turn away when something foreign to the shapes of the garden registered in my eye-corner. It was in a space between the back of the garage and the rear boundary wall where, under the low branches of a crab-apple tree, we threw garden and household waste in a careless hope of creating compost. I swung the torch and went nearer. A figure was sitting in a heavy, rusted metal wheelbarrow which we had inherited from the previous owners of the house. I let the beam illuminate the face for a moment, before an arm came up to cover it.

'Mrs Norton?'

She had a coat over what looked like a nightdress or a long frock in a pale material.

'What are you doing here, Mrs Norton?'

I hardly knew her, having only occasionally passed the time of day with her, wondering as I did so whether she recognised me as her neighbour. Eileen appeared at the corner of the house. I called to her, pointing the torch beam at the ground as she came to me.

'Who on earth is it?'

'Mrs Norton.'

'Good heavens! Is she—?'

'I don't know. Look, Bonny's still got my latchkey. Ask him to go in and put some lights on, then you come back.'

She went away. There was a light, I saw, showing through curtains, in a downstairs room in the back of the Nortons' house. Mrs Norton was now bent forward, her face still hidden in her arm. As I spoke to her again she began to sway the top half of her body slightly, at the same time making little mewing sounds in her throat. Eileen came back.

'What should we do?'

'We'd best get her inside.'

I bent and took her elbow. 'Mrs Norton, you can't stay out here, love. It's bitterly cold and you'll catch your death. Come on, now, let's have you up.' I took a grip on her arm as she began to comply. Her feet were off the ground and the barrow tipped as she struggled out of it. I grabbed her with both arms round and got the stench of her breath in my nostrils as I supported her and pulled her upright. 'Take her other arm, Eileen, will you?' We began to lead her off the lawn.

'There's a light on in their house,' Eileen said. 'Shall we take her straight round there?'

'No!' Mrs Norton said. She pulled back between us.

'All right, all right,' I said, keeping a firm hold on her. 'You can come into our house with us. We'll be nice and warm there while you tell us what it's all about.'

We took her into the living-room and sat her in an easy chair near the gas-fire, which I lit, though the central-heating radiator was still on. 'Just toast your toes in front of that, Mrs Norton, and Eileen will bring you a nice hot drink.'

Bonny and Eunice followed Eileen and me into the kitchen.

'Who on earth is she?' Eunice asked.

'Our next-door neighbour.'

'But she's only got slippers on her feet, and isn't that a nightgown under her coat? Is she ill?'

'Or drunk, or both,' I said. 'She's a wino and it's rumoured her husband knocks her about.'

'Charming!' Bonny said.

'Charming, indeed.'

'All the same, her husband ought to know where she is, didn't he?'

'She just nearly threw a fit when Eileen and I suggested taking her round home. We'll let her get warm, while we think of something.'

'What can we give her?' Eileen asked. She had already filled and plugged in the electric kettle.

'Better be coffee. I caught a whiff of her breath outside. God knows what she's been drinking and how much, but I daren't give her any whisky.'

'Coffee might make her sick,' Eunice said.

'When and where though?' Eileen asked.

'Make it anyway,' I said. 'She might not take it. She's obviously still got a will of her own. Of a kind, anyway.'

'Talking of whisky,' Bonny said. 'It's the very thing I could do with. If I'm not being cheeky for asking.'

'I could use some myself. I'll get the bottle.'

I went to the drinks cupboard in the living-room. Mrs Norton was sitting very still and upright on the edge of the chair, looking at the fire. Those weird, haunted eyes, which were what I mostly remembered from previous encounters, were hidden from me now. With the light from the lamp behind her laying a shadow across the angle of her cheek, and the thick dark coils of her hair, she looked quite young. And unless she was older than her husband she could, in fact, hardly be described yet as middle-aged. I took the bottle and left the room without speaking to her. She gave no sign of having noticed me.

I poured a whisky for each of us except Eileen, who declined.

'I wonder if she needs a doctor,' Eileen said.

'We can hardly call one in without telling her husband.'

'But why isn't he out looking for her?' Eunice said. 'Does she do this as a regular thing?'

'Not to our knowledge.'

'Perhaps he thinks she's tucked up in bed,' Bonny said.

'Is he on the phone, do you know, Gordon?' Eileen asked.

'I don't know.'

'I think we ought to tell him where she is.'

'Let's offer her the coffee first and see if she'll tell us anything.'

Eileen poured boiling water over the coffee-bags in the pot and dunked the bags with a spoon, to speed the brew.

'How d'you think she'd like it?'

'Try it with a little milk and no sugar.'

'Did she take to the bottle because her husband knocked her about?' Bonny asked. 'Or did he start knocking her about because she was on the bottle?'

'We don't know,' I told him. 'We've no first-hand knowledge that he does bash her; only street talk.'

'They lost a boy, apparently, in his early teens,' Eileen said. 'Leukaemia. Perhaps that brought it on.' She gave the coffee a stir, then poured some into a cup and added just a colouring of milk. 'I'll see if she'll have this.'

I followed her into the living-room and watched as she stood over Mrs Norton, offering the cup.

'I've made this coffee, Mrs Norton,' she said clearly and steadily. 'Can you drink it? It might do you good.'

Mrs Norton didn't answer. She bowed her head and began to sob.

'Oh, now,' Eileen said, 'it's surely not as bad as all that. Is it?'

She reached out her right arm as though to lay her hand on Mrs Norton's head, then suddenly gasped and withdrew it, straightening and turning to face me. The cup rattled in the saucer as she began to tremble. I moved towards her and took them from her. 'What's wrong?' Eileen went quickly past me, one hand now to her mouth.

When I got back into the kitchen she was leaning over the sink, tap running as she splashed cold water on her face, with Bonny and Eunice both watching her. She turned round as I put the cup down.

'What's the matter?'

She shuddered and swallowed, forcing out the words. 'It's her hair. I saw it under the light. I nearly touched it. It's swarming, Gordon. It's alive.'

My spine turned cold. I remembered how close to Mrs Norton I'd been outside.

Eunice said, 'U–gh!' and screwed up her face.

'Fetch somebody, Gordon,' Eileen said. 'We can't cope with her here. She needs attention.' She lifted her hands and buried her fingertips in her own hair. 'God! How can she bear it?'

Bonny got off his stool. '*Are* they on the phone, or had we better go round for him?'

'I'll look in the directory.'

I went into the hall. The side door of the house, through which we'd entered with Mrs Norton, stood open. I knew before I glanced into the living-room that she would no longer be there.

'Look for that number,' Bonny said, 'while I have a shufti outside.'

I found the Norton's telephone number in the directory, jotted it on a pad, then went to the door. Bonny had clambered on to the dividing wall and was standing looking round from there.

'Any sign?'

'None at all.'

'Is that light still on in their house?'

Bonny walked a few steps along the flat top of the wall. 'Yes.'

'Come in, then, and I'll phone him.'

I dialled the number. I heard the telephone ringing at the other end. Five, ten, fifteen, twenty. I decided to give it another ten, then let it go to twenty. Norton must have fallen asleep in his chair. I put the receiver down.

'Nothing doing?' Bonny asked.

'No. This is all bloody odd, Bonny. Don't you think so?'

'What do you want to do – shut the door and forget about it?'

'She could go wandering about all night.'

'And if he gets her back he might leather her,' Bonny said.

'All the same, I'd better go round and wake him up.'

'I'll come with you. We don't want him starting on you for interfering. Where did you put my torch?'

'It's here, on the hall table.'

'Right. I'll just tell the girls where we are.'

We walked out through the gate and up the Nortons' drive on the other side of the wall. There was no light in the front of the Nortons' house and though that in the back showed clearly through the curtains, the curtains had been closed too carefully to allow any view into the room from outside. The Nortons had no garden at the back, but a paved area with a park bench of cast iron and wooden slats, and a few flower tubs. I knocked on the back door. Bonny, having shone his torch over the yard, stood back and looked up at the house. 'You say they live on their own?'

'Yes.'

'I suppose a biggish family could turn this into a bright and cheerful place.'

I knocked again, with more force.

'C'mon, wake up, you bugger,' Bonny said. He stepped forward and listened at the window. 'He's got the telly on.' He rapped suddenly on the glass. 'P'raps he's round at the boozer and his missus just got lonely.'

'I don't think he's a pub bloke. I could be wrong. I don't have much to do with him.'

'Try the door.'

I did so. It didn't give. 'It's locked.'

'Are you sure? Stand back a minute.'

Bonny took the knob in one hand, turning it as he put his shoulder to the door. It opened with a jarring groan of warped and sticking wood. He pushed it back, shining his torch along the dark passage inside. I stepped past him and called.

'Mr Norton! Are you there, Mr Norton? It's Gordon Taylor from next door.'

The passage ran away towards the front of the house, turning at a jutting inside wall by the foot of the staircase and connecting with the front hall. A narrow strip of light fell across the patterned floor tiles from the slightly open door of the back room. I went and knocked on that door and called again, stepping aside then as if in anticipation of the door's being flung wide and the sudden emergence of Norton's bulk.

'Mr Norton!' Bonny bawled. He leaned past me and put the length of his arm across the door to push it open, at the same time motioning with his other hand for me to enter.

I hesitated. 'Go on,' Bonny said, then, lifting his voice, 'Hope you're decent, Mr Norton, 'cos we're coming in now, ready or not.'

I went in. Michael Parkinson was talking on the monochrome television set to a woman film star whose name for the moment escaped me. The studio audience laughed. What had been a good fire was falling away in the grate. On the hearthrug in front of it lay a long iron poker with a pointed and curved projection near its end, for adjusting the lie of wood and coal. It pointed directly at Norton's slippered feet and the cuffs of Norton's trousers. The rest of Norton was hidden behind a worn leather armchair over which he had presumably pitched and which it occurred to me later, might have toppled under his weight had it not been so heavy and stable.

'Jesus!' Bonny said at my side.

I didn't want to look over the chair, but I forced myself to do so, just to make sure. Then I made my way quickly into the fresh air.

'They'll want to talk to all of us,' I said to Eunice, 'and goodness knows how long that will take. Maybe it'll be best if you let Eileen make up a bed for you here.'

'The spare beds are both in Bonny's room,' Eileen pointed out.

'Oh, I'll kip here on the sofa,' Bonny said.

'While you're making your minds up,' Eileen said, 'I'm going to wash my hair and have a shower. My skin is crawling from head to foot. And I shall want you to do the same, Gordon, before you come into bed with me. We can put our clothes out for fumigation and cleaning.'

''Leen, you're imagining things, love.'

'I know what I saw.'

'I'm not doubting that, but ...'

'We both touched her. And they could be in that chair now, for all we know.'

'I think we've got some DDT powder. I'll spray it along the seams of the cushions.'

'Do it now.'

'But it's out in the garage, and the police—'

'Never mind. We don't want to have to fumigate the whole house.'

'Okay. Off you go.'

'D'you remember the old soldiers' trick from the First World War?' Bonny said, when Eileen had gone. 'They used to run a lighted match along the seams of their clothes.'

'Christ! What are we yattering about?' I said. 'There's a bloke with his head bashed in next door.'

'I know there is,' Bonny said. 'Can I have some more whisky?'

The police arrived with a squeal of brakes followed by a peremptory shrilling of the doorbell. As it happened, the ambulance which I'd also asked for, and which came as Bonny and I were taking the two constables round to the Nortons' house, was more immediately important. For Norton, to our surprise, was pronounced to be still alive and was rushed away as soon as the police officers had noted exactly where he had lain and replaced the armchair from where the ambulancemen had found it necessary to move it in order to give Norton emergency aid and get him on to a stretcher.

One of the officers had gone to their car to radio for assistance. 'There was nothing we could have done for him, I suppose?' I said to the other man.

'No. You wouldn't know.'

'We thought he was dead.'

'You would do.'

'Perhaps one of us should have stayed with him, but neither of us fancied it.'

'I'm not surprised.' This officer was very young. Perhaps, I thought, it was also his first experience of this kind of violence. 'You didn't touch anything?'

'I turned the telly off,' Bonny said. 'It was on when we came in. Mike Parkinson.'

The constable looked at him. 'I keep thinking I know your face. Do you live round here?'

Bonny told him who he was.

'Oh!' The lad looked impressed. 'I used to play a bit myself. Rather fancied meself at one time. But there's all the difference, isn't there?'

'There's all the difference,' Bonny confirmed.

A light had been switched on in the passage and we were standing there, outside the back room. The paintwork was dark, the walls colourwashed in a dingy green. There was the foreign smell of someone else's house overlaid by an additional odour which stuck in my throat. I wondered who cleaned the place, and how often.

'Do you need us here any longer?' I asked the young officer. 'Couldn't we go round home?'

'Perhaps you'd best wait till the sergeant arrives, sir.'

The sergeant arrived within five minutes. He was the man who had visited us the previous night to question us about Grint.

'It's you two again,' he said as he came through the Nortons' back door.

'Only we used a poker on this one,' Bonny said.

The sergeant frowned. 'You what?'

Bonny shrugged irritably and turned away. The young officer looked puzzled.

'You'd bettter tell me all about it,' the sergeant said to me.

It all took considerable time. The police had several things to do. They sent a man to the hospital to enquire about Norton's condition and remain there in the chance of getting some word from him. A search was launched for Mrs Norton, who could not have gone far on foot, but nevertheless could be anywhere within a radius of, say, a couple of miles. The room where we had found Norton was thoroughly examined, then locked. Bonny and I, having told the uniformed sergeant what we had seen and heard, were questioned again, in detail, along with Eileen and Eunice, by a plain-clothes officer of the C.I.D.

Eventually, in the early hours, after it had looked more than likely that my house would be commandeered as a base of operations, I closed the door on the last of them, having got an assurance that we could go to bed without being disturbed.

'Do you want to go home, Eunice?' Bonny asked. 'I can easily run you there, if you do.'

'I'd rather stay, if it's no bother.'

'Given you the creeps, has it?'

'Well, I'd rather not be on my own tonight,' she admitted.

'I've heard people say,' I said, at one point, 'that real-life murder is nearly always domestic, dingy and banal.'

'It's not murder, though, is it?' Eileen said. 'Not yet, anyway.'

'It'll surprise me if Norton pulls through. I didn't see how he could be alive.' I shivered as a chill touched me again.

'I suppose she must have reached the end of her tether,' Eunice said. 'What do you think they'll do to her?'

'Put her into an institution, I expect. As far as that's concerned it probably won't matter whether Norton lives or dies.'

'You haven't done anything about that chair, Gordon,' Eileen said.

'Oh, Christ!' I said. 'I'm not searching the garage for DDT at this hour. There's no upholstery to worry about, so I'll just take the cushions out there and deal with them in the morning.'

8

Norton died in the night. A newspaper reporter told me on the telephone. The telephone woke me out of a restless, dream-laden sleep. I forgot most of my dream as soon as I woke, but clearly retained was a picture of Eileen, clad in a long white gown, sitting very still on a straight chair in a bare room with bars on the window and a green gloom as if from sodden trees in full leaf outside. I touched her warm buttock beside me as the telephone rang persistently downstairs. 'Oh, piss off, will you!' I said under my breath.

When the bell stopped I got out of bed and put on my dressing-gown and parted the curtains to look out at a grey morning. There was a police car in the street. The house was still and quiet as I went down into the kitchen. As I passed the living-room I opened the door and glanced in. The curtains in there were closed and Bonny was under a blanket on the sofa. In the kitchen, I filled and plugged in the kettle and set out four cups, a small bowl of sugar and a small jug of milk.

A little while later I went back upstairs, carrying a tray. Eileen was lying on her side, as if still sleeping; but when I put one of the cups on her bedside cupboard and reached out to touch her I saw that her eyes were open and looking directly, unblinkingly ahead.

'A cup of tea, Eileen,' I said, when she made no acknowledgement of my presence.

'Yes,' she said.

'Don't let it go cold.'

I left her and went across the landing to the spare room, where I tapped on the door, pushing it half open and looking round it before going in.

'Good morning, Eunice,' I said, warning her of my presence from the doorway. She stirred under the sheets as I went towards her. There was a nightdress I recognised as one of Eileen's lying over a chair and as Eunice turned and raised herself she exposed bare plump shoulders, one hand holding the sheets up over her breasts.

'I've brought you a cup of tea.'

'Oh, thanks.'

'I couldn't remember if you took sugar.'

'No, thanks. That's lovely. What time is it?'

'Just after nine. Did the telephone wake you?'

'No.'

'If you want to go back to sleep you can do. But I'll be starting breakfast soon.'

'Fine. Would you mind drawing the curtains for me?'

'Not much of a morning so far,' I said from the window.

'Never mind.'

Without her glasses her eyes looked darker and unfocused. I wondered if she always slept naked and, if so, why she hadn't refused the offer of the nightdress. Then I remembered Eileen's saying she would make up the second bed and Eunice telling her not to bother, she didn't at all mind sleeping in Bonny's sheets. With the recollection came once more that unbidden stir of private flesh.

'Well,' I said, suddenly aware that I was lingering, 'breakfast when you're ready. And there'll be plenty of hot water, if you want a bath.'

'Thanks.' She reached for her glasses and put them on. I felt immediately then that I was being scrutinised and assessed.

'See you.'

The telephone rang again as I reached the foot of the stairs. I walked past it into the kitchen and picked up the pot to pour tea for Bonny and myself. Bonny appeared in the doorway, one hand lazily scratching under his ribs.

'If you don't answer it you'll have 'em on the doorstep.'

'Oh, Christ!'

''Course, if you do answer you'll still have 'em on the doorstep, but maybe you'll be able to pick the time.'

Bonny stood aside as I brushed past him. 'There's fresh tea in the pot. Pour me a cup, will you?' I picked up the receiver.

The reporter was from the regional office of a national daily. He told me about Norton, and that the police had found Mrs Norton. 'I understand it was you and your brother who discovered the victim.'

'Yes.'

'I'm right in believing that your brother is Bonny Taylor?'

'Yes.'

'When would it be convenient for me to come over and have a word with him? And you, of course,' he added.

'He won't talk to you about himself. He came here for a bit of peace and quiet.'

'I appreciate that, Mr Taylor, but this is news and—'

'Surely the police know all there is to know.'

'Oh, normally we'd just slip a paragraph on an inside page, if that. I mean, it happens every other day. But your brother's a celebrity, and I'll be surprised if we're the only people to contact you. Has anybody else been in touch yet, by the way?'

'No.'

'Good. Well, if you'd give me a time to call you could use that to fend off the others. Tell them you've already spoken to us and you've nothing else to say. ...'

'We've got nothing else to say now.'

'Who is it?' Bonny asked. He put my tea on the telephone table.

'The *Globe*. Norton's dead. They want to talk to us.'

'You'd better let him come. I don't think we can duck this one.'

'That's what he says. He says if we talk to him – if *you* talk to him, he means – we can forget about the others.'

'And that gives him an exclusive.'

'Yes. What time shall I say, then?'

Bonny looked at his watch. 'Eleven?'

'That poor bugger comes to a violent end and it's only news because you happen to have found him,' I said, when I'd hung up.

'Oh, they just want an excuse to get to me. I shall have to play it by ear.'

'I'll get breakfast started. What would you like – sausages, eggs, bacon, mushrooms, fried tomato?'

'No fishcakes?'

'No fishcakes.'

'I'll make do with whatever's going,' Bonny said. He went past me and up the stairs.

I heard the murmur of voices from Bonny's room. Bonny was presumably getting his clothes. I wondered if Eunice was still in bed. Naked between Bonny's sheets. I drank my tea standing in the hall and looking at the telephone, as if waiting for it to ring again.

Eunice came into the kitchen, dressed, as I was frying and grilling.

'Can I help?'

'You can lay the table.' I showed her where things were. 'How did you sleep?'

'Very well, though I dreamed quite a bit.'

'So did I. Norton died. A man on the phone just told me.'

'Have they found her?'

'Apparently so.' She was at the open cutlery drawer, taking out knives and forks. I reached past her for a spatula, one hand on her far shoulder. She seemed to sway back slightly then, as though accepting a proffered embrace, and turned her head to glance up at me. I stepped away from her. 'Could you keep an eye on this lot for a minute while I go and speak to Eileen? Plates warming in the oven. I'll fry the eggs when everybody's ready to sit down.'

I went upstairs.

'Breakfast's ready, Eileen. You haven't drunk your tea.'

'That poor woman,' Eileen said. She closed her eyes. There were tears on her cheeks.

'Don't dwell on it, love. She'll be looked after now.'

'You mean they'll lock her away somewhere, now that it's too late.'

'Listen,' I said. 'I've had the press on the phone. I'm afraid I can't fob them off this time, so there'll be some coming and going this morning. Why don't I bring you your breakfast on a tray, then you can stay up here out of the way for as long as you like?'

'Mr Norton's dead. Isn't he?'

'Yes, he is.' I didn't know her. She was like someone on the edge of a trance. 'Will you eat your breakfast, if I bring it?'

'I don't want anything just now.'

She turned away from me and drew the duvet up behind her head.

I took the cup of cold tea and went back downstairs.

'Don't you get a Sunday paper?' Bonny asked at breakfast.

The newsagent with whom we had an order for a daily newspaper and a couple of magazines did not deliver on Sundays, so after Sunday breakfast I usually walked down to a small shop on the main road. I knew that it cost me more that way – I should have had delivered one of the posh Sundays only – but it was hard to resist the selection laid out on the counter and I more often than not bought two, as well as whichever of the popular papers took my eye. Occasionally I would clip a human interest piece from the latter, as a possible basis of a story or novel. I'd read somewhere that Chekhov had got a lot of his ideas from the popular press. I had a box-file full of cuttings which I every now and then glanced through. But I had never found enough enthusiasm to make a start.

I wanted some fresh air, but I was disinclined to run the gauntlet of neighbours wanting the gory details of what had happened next door.

'We can go in the car,' Bonny said. 'Or, better still, if you tell me where it is, I'll go while you hold the fort.'

'Okay, you go.' I gave him directions.

'What do you want?'

'Bring a *Sunday Times* and an *Observer,* and whatever else you fancy.' I was still in my pyjamas. 'My money's upstairs. I'll pay you when you come back.'

'Be my guest,' Bonny said.

When he had gone I went upstairs to get dressed, while Eunice cleared the table. I went into the bedroom for my clothes. Eileen appeared to be sleeping. The curtains were still closed and I parted them and looked out. A car, without distinguishing markings, pulled up across the street. The driver, a burly man in overcoat and soft hat, walked over to the uniformed officer who, on seeing him, had got out of the police car parked by the Norton's gate. They exchanged a couple of words before the burly man went on up the Nortons' drive. The telephone began to ring. I ignored it. I took my clothes to the bathroom, closing the bedroom door so that Eileen would not be disturbed.

I'd showered last night to appease Eileen, so now I merely washed and shaved along the edges of my beard before dressing in my weekend uniform of sweater and slacks. My movements were slow as I brooded.

Eunice had washed-up when I went down. She had even wiped over the Formica tops. 'I don't know where everything goes,' she said.

'That's okay. Thanks.'

How easy it was to tidy at the edges of someone else's life. I was willing to bet that her own flat was like a tip.

'The telephone rang again.'

'I know. I should have told you to ignore it.'

'Oh, I did.'

She was holding one hand up, palm down, fingers straight, and rubbing the nails with her other thumb. I wondered where she had got this sudden care for her appearance – vanity, almost. Perhaps, it occurred to me now, that was really how she was. She had perhaps come to my classes in what she thought was the guise of a real writer. Like a theatre director I'd once heard say in an interview, that if he turned up for rehearsal in a tie none of the cast would take him seriously. I became aware that I was watching her again.

'How's Eileen?'

'She's asleep.'

'Does she like a lie-in on a Sunday?'

'Sometimes.'

'That woman really upset her last night.'

'Yes. It's all strange . . . and upsetting.'

'I must admit that I still can't quite believe it.'

'No.'

'They're still coming and going next door.'

'Yes. There's a reporter coming here at eleven.'

'I know. He really wants to see Bonny, doesn't he?'

'Oh, yes. What are your plans for today?'

'I usually do my wash, clean the flat, then settle down to my writing.'

'Do you get lonely?'

'Oh, I have friends. But I like Sunday. It's all mine.'

'We've upset your routine.'

'Not you. In any case, I can go as soon as I start getting in the way.'

'I didn't mean that. Stick around, if you want to.'

'Thanks. We'll see.'

I wondered why I'd said that. At breakfast I'd hoped she wasn't going to hang about all day.

She looked aimlessly about the room, then started to leave it. I took her arm as she passed me and turned her to face me. When I pulled her in to kiss her, she let me, until my arms tightened round her and I tried to prolong the embrace. Then she put her hands on my chest and pushed me away.

'What brought all that on?'

'I just suddenly felt like it.'

'Do you always do what you just suddenly feel like doing?'

'It depends how much I feel like it.'

'And whether you think you'll be taken seriously?'

'Sorry.'

'Don't apologise. What's a little kiss and a cuddle between friends?'

I wanted to tell her that I didn't need her, that I'd acted more out of curiosity than wanting; that my sex-life was more than satisfactory and there wasn't an ounce of frustration in me.

'I mean, you're not serious are you? You don't really want to, do you?' She brushed the back of one hand lightly down the front of my trousers. 'Are you telling me you'd really like to?'

'You go steady,' I said. I took her hand and she drew it away.

I was staggered by her complete self-possession. No wonder Bonny had goaded her in the restaurant. Now, both brothers within forty-eight hours. I felt my face colour.

'I'll bet you're a real Grade-A bitch,' I said.

'And you like to play around,' she said. 'Or do you sometimes go through with it?'

'If you want to think of yourself as just another piece of skirt.'

'You mean there really is something special about me?'

'I don't play around,' I said. 'I leave other women severely alone. I just wanted to see what you'd do.'

'Well,' Eunice said, 'now you know.'

She had left me. I had moved down the kitchen and was standing with both hands holding the sink, cursing both her and myself, when the doorbell rang. The burly man I had seen going into the Nortons' was on the front step.

'Mr Taylor?'

'Yes.'

'I didn't know whether to come to back door or front.'

'That's all right.' I was suddenly seized by the alarming notion that he could have seen me embracing Eunice through the kitchen window.

'I'd like a word with you, Mr Taylor.' The man produced a warrant card. 'Detective Chief-Inspector Hepplewhite.'

'Come in.'

'You'll be Mr Gordon Taylor, I believe?'

'Yes.'

'I thought I'd know your brother's face. I've seen him play, and interviewed on the television. Is he about at the moment, by the way?'

'He's out buying newspapers. He should be back any time.'

'Then perhaps I can have a word with you first.'

I took the man into the sitting-room. 'Sit down. I don't know that I've anything to add to what we told your colleagues.'

'No, probably not. But this is a serious matter and I'd like to hear it all myself. So, if you could start at the beginning . . .'

I began with the car turning into the drive and Eunice glimpsing Mrs Norton in the headlights.

'It was you and your wife who had actual contact with Mrs Norton?'

'Yes. My brother and Miss Cadby no more than saw her as we brought her into the house.'

'We don't seem to have any record of what Mrs Norton actually said to you and your wife.'

'That's the point. She didn't say anything.'

'Was your wife alone with her at any time?'

'No.'

'Is Mrs Taylor about, by the way?'

'I persuaded her to stay in bed, and she's still sleeping. I don't want to disturb her. It seems to have upset her.'

'That's understandable. It would be even more unpleasant for you and your brother.' Hepplewhite shifted his position slightly, sitting forward in the chair, neat hands resting lightly between thick thighs.

'Will Mrs Norton be fit to plead?'

'Plead?'

'It's obvious she did it, isn't it?'

'There were no other fingerprints on the poker,' he admitted. 'Only hers and her husband's.' He paused, as if reluctant to accept so ready a solution. 'I expect she'll be charged.'

'I wonder why she did it.'

'Who knows what goes on inside four walls, between man and wife? There are stories that he knocked her about.'

'We've heard that.'

'She had bruises on her body when she was examined. She's alcoholic, probably mentally disturbed clinically, as well. She reached the end of her tether and went for him with the weapon to hand. It only takes a minute, the act itself, though it had probably been preparing itself for years.' We heard the outer door open and close. 'Would that be your brother now?'

'I expect so.'

'Perhaps I could just have a word with him.'

'I'll get him.' I stood up. 'By the way, we're being pestered by reporters. My brother's a celebrity, you understand, and he's been in the news lately.'

'Once Mrs Norton's charged, the case becomes *sub judice*,' Hepplewhite said. 'They can't print anything but the bare facts. Perhaps you can use that to put them off.'

'Thanks,' I said. 'I'll get Bonny for you. Do you want to talk to him alone?'

'If you don't mind.'

Eunice had got one of the papers and was reading it, sitting with her feet tucked under her. I supposed that Bonny, in my place, would have turned her out of the house. But I felt curiously detached now about the incident in the kitchen. I knew I'd made a fool of myself and given her an advantage I should regret, but for the moment I didn't care. She was a bitch though. There had been ways of turning me down without the almost gentle mockery she'd employed.

I picked up a colour magazine and flipped the pages. There were advertisements for carriage clocks in brass, document cases in leather, another series of silver medals, this time commemorating famous battles and regiments, and a fashion feature with the models photographed in some remote Greek village, while incredulous peasants who would probably have murdered their own women for flaunting themselves in such clothes grinned in the background.

The telephone rang. I began automatically to rise, then subsided into my seat again.

'Wouldn't it be simpler to take it off the hook?' Eunice asked.

'Then it'll be engaged if friends ring.'

'If you're not answering, what's the difference?'

'I'll answer it when I feel like it.'

'And they accuse women of being illogical.'

'But not you, Eunice, not you.'

'I wish I thought that was a compliment.'

'I don't think you care one way or the other.'

She shrugged. 'All right, then.'

I put the magazine aside and reached for an arts section. My gaze slid over the columns, taking in little I could have quoted. What I wanted now, more than anything, was Eileen to walk into the room, rubbing her eyes and smiling. 'Goodness, I could have slept till next week. Who'd like some coffee?' Then everything would be back to normal. I had never realised just how much I'd come to rely on her; how she gave shape and reason to my life. I wanted to blame Bonny's coming for it; everything had been all right before Bonny came. But how could Bonny be responsible for what had happened next door? Eileen must have been paying out rope for some time, and I had not noticed.

The cloud was breaking up; a gleam of weak sunlight lit the window. It was time we redecorated this room. The heavy pattern of brown and cream on the wallpaper depressed me. It was twentieth-century Jacobean. Most of the house had been done in a similar style by the previous owners, who seemed to have taken their cue from the imitation-oak panelled dado in the hall. Eileen and I had worked through most of the other rooms, but as this one had been newly done we'd left it till last and somehow never got round to it.

I felt in a state of suspension, devoid of choice, my next move to be determined by events. It was like my interest in the current arts. I looked more closely at the paper now and saw that there was a series of six innovatory plays by a cult dramatist coming on television, a science-fiction film from the States causing a stir in London, a new book by a young and much interviewed English novelist, a feminist novel by an American woman. . . . It all happened regardless of me; I could only react, like or dislike, be honest in admiration or let envy bring forth sour grapes. I hadn't the creative energy to force whatever talent I might possess myself. I should never influence anybody. I should always be the onlooker. Even in my teaching I mostly peddled received values. I was a nonentity, with what passed for a good education; the good son who caused no bother, the good citizen with all the right liberal notions, coasting along till pension time.

There was that pile of essays on my desk to be read and marked. To hell with them. I might do them later. If I didn't I would flannel my way through the class tomorrow. How would I tell my colleagues the story of Mrs Norton, of finding Norton? Lightly, offhand (what odd neighbours one can have)? Or with an attitude of caring and concern? The trouble was I couldn't define my feelings towards either of them, the dead man or his demented wife. Oh, the circumstances had made my skin crawl; but the *people,* both of whom I'd known, if only slightly? They were not wholesome, attractive. My concern couldn't encompass them. Some of my colleagues became involved, often messily, in the lives of pupils from deprived homes, and those who were emotionally or psychologically upset. I didn't think that was my business. I taught them what I had to teach them; the rest was the province of parents, social workers, the medical profession, the police. Why should I feel guilty because I didn't take on burdens I was not equipped to carry? I couldn't, today, even think all that through coherently.

The telephone rang. I decided to answer it this time, but stopped on my way to the door as it cut off. The outer door opened and closed. I sat down again. Bonny came into the room.

'Phone for you, Gordon. Bloke called Branch, would it be?'

'Ted Branch.' I got up again. 'Has the copper gone?'

'Just now.'

I went to the telephone. 'Hullo. Ted?'

'Gordon. If you've got company, don't bother, but I wondered if you were free for a lunchtime pint.'

'Hmm. I wouldn't mind one, but I don't know.'

'Was that your brother, the illustrious Bonny, who answered the phone?'

'Yes, it was.'

'Bring him with you, if you like. I'd like a bit of advice about something.'

'It's a bit tricky this morning, Ted. Where will you be?'

'The Weavers.'

'And you'll be going there anyway?'

'Oh, aye. I usually do.'

'I'll try to make it.'

'Do your best, then. About half-twelve.'

I went upstairs to look at Eileen. This time I thought she really was sleeping. I left the room.

'Ted did that picture you were admiring, on my study wall,' I said to Eunice. 'The snag is, I don't want to disturb Eileen, but I don't want her to wake up and find the house empty.'

'I'll be here,' Bonny said. 'What are you doing, Eunice?'

'I'll go as soon as you want rid of me.'

'Why not stay and hold the fort with me, while Gordon goes for a drink with his friend? I can run you home this afternoon. Or we could go somewhere.'

'I'm easy,' Eunice said.

'You could have fooled me,' Bonny said.

'Don't be facetious.'

'Oh, let me be facetious, Eunice. It does me good to be facetious.'

'You don't know when to stop though, do you?'

'What did Hepplewhite ask you?' I said to Bonny.

'What he asked you, I expect. He took a bit of time out for football.'

'Does he know anything about it?' Eunice asked.

'Not a lot.' Bonny lifted one of the newspapers, open at the sports page. 'But then, not many do.'

9

'When are you going to get your hair cut?' Ted Branch asked.

'If you tell me who did yours,' I said, 'I'll have him duffed.'

Ted was leaning with one elbow on the bar counter of the Weavers as he rolled a cigarette with practised fingers. He wore a long, square-shouldered raincoat open over a tweed jacket and brown slacks. His hair-style was severely short back and sides, trimmed every three weeks by the same barber. You would not have been surprised to learn that he was a painter and decorator by trade; more so to be told that he was a talented and sensitive artist. He was in his middle thirties. We had been friends for several years, though sometimes we would not see each other for months.

'What you havin', then?'

'A half of bitter.'

'Pint.'

'A half,' I said. 'I've got the car outside, and I'm not matching pints against those.' I pointed to the glass of bottled Guinness on the counter by Ted's elbow.

Ted ordered. I looked round. I seemed to remember there being cream paint in places, but tobacco smoke had darkened it to a thick yellow. Through an archway, men were playing darts, and a couple of tables of dominoes were on the go. There were few women to be seen. I came in here only when meeting Ted. It was his local, but some way from my house. Ted didn't run a car, though he drove the firm's van, and he disliked pubs which he said were all cravats and cashmere. Besides, he swore that the beer here, drawn through the traditional hand-pumps, was the best on this side of town, though he rarely drank it himself.

'What've you been doing with yerself, then?' Ted asked.

'What a tale I've got to tell you!' I said. 'We've had a murder next door.'

'Gerraway!'

'True.' I gave him a résumé of last night's events, while he listened impassively.

'Bloody Hell! I'd better not tell our lass, in case it gives her ideas.'

'How is Betty?'

'Oh, baffled, as usual. She thinks if I've got to paint I ought to get in on something lucrative, like Christmas cards. I suppose the newspapers'll be pestering, especially with your kid being involved.'

'We had a reporter round this morning. The *Globe*. He tried to get Bonny on about his troubles, but Bonny wouldn't bite.'

'It's a pity he can't keep his nose clean,' Ted said, 'because he's pure magic on a football field. *I* don't think there's anybody else in the game today got what he's got. Poetry in motion.'

'It doesn't seem to be enough.'

'For him, you mean?'

'Yes.'

'So he's keeping his head down at your house. At a crucial point in the season.' Ted shrugged. 'Doesn't make sense to me.'

'Nor to anybody else. Least of all to Bonny himself. Anyway, it's his life.'

'You don't take much interest in the game yourself, do you?'

'Not much. But I'm interested in talent, and it screws me to see Bonny fucking his up. And talking about talent, what have you been up to?'

'Oh, this and that.'

'I'd like an estimate for decorating my living-room. Will you get me one?'

'Oh, ring the gaffer up,' Ted said. 'I spend more time looking at ceilings than bloody Michelangelo. I'm up to the back teeth with all that. That's why I wanted to see you.' He took a folded newspaper from his pocket, pointing to a display advertisement as he passed it over. 'There's this arts association offering a couple of grants to people working in the visual arts. I thought I might apply.'

'And chuck the job, you mean?'

'They wouldn't give me the brass on top of my wage, would they? It's not the extra money I want, it's the time it'll buy me.'

'How long do you think three thousand quid will last you?'

'Long enough mebbe, to find out what I'm really made of, before it's too late. I don't need much in the way of luxuries, and Betty's in a job.'

'Will she back you up?'

'She can please herself. What she doesn't like she can lump. And what she doesn't understand she can keep her nose out of. You were talking about your kid's life; well, this is mine, and it's galloping by.

It fair bloody terrifies me, sometimes, to think how it's galloping by. It's time I did summat I want to do. I've got a trade. I can likely go back to it if all else fails. On the other hand, p'raps I won't need to.'

'Well,' I said, 'I can't advise you, old lad, if that's what you want. You've got to make your own mind up about this one.'

'Will you be one of me referees, though, if I do apply?'

'I'll do that for you, and willingly.'

'Thanks.' Ted took a swig of his Guinness, stubbed out the soft and splitting end of his cigarette and got out the materials for rolling another. 'Now we come to the big question. There'll be a lot of smart lads who've been through art college on the grab for this one, so I want to be sure I'll not make a fool of meself by goin' up against 'em. D'you think I'm good enough?'

'I don't see why not. I mean, you're not breaking new ground, but . . .'

'You mean I'm not nailing laths to sheets of hardboard or making significant arrangements of lavatory seats?'

I laughed. 'No, not quite that, Ted, and you know the difference. But what you are doing is solid and sturdy. You've got a style, and it could probably develop, given a period of concentration. That's just an opinion, of course. I'm not an expert. The visual arts are not my field.'

'No. But you're one of the few intelligent people I can talk to about it, Gordon. I don't get about much in artistic circles.'

'Which could be to your advantage.'

'I've always thought a bit that way.'

'How I see it is this way,' I said – we had moved to a table now, where we could talk about such matters without raising our voices to be heard above the monosyllabic assertive exchanges going on along the bar counter and the ordering of drinks – 'if you find your own real way of looking at things you'll also find an audience that takes particular pleasure in the way you paint because there'll be no one else doing it in quite that way. A talent should be exercised. You've got a duty towards it. There's no more beautiful thing in this world than talent, Ted. And nothing sadder than a talent that isn't being used.'

'You're right, of course,' Ted said. 'It's just hard to keep faith at times. I mean, when you're on your own and nobody seems to care.'

'Oh, there'll be no great hole left in art if you stop painting. Nobody will miss what Ted Branch doesn't do. But quite a few people will be grateful for what he does do.' I got up to fetch some more drinks.

'Are you doing any writing?' Ted asked, when I came back.

'Nothing of any consequence.'

'Can't you take your own lessons to heart?'

'*I* haven't got a talent, Ted, just a facility. Everything I do turns into a third carbon of somebody else.'

I realised that not only had I never said this before, I had not honestly admitted it to myself. I sat there, suddenly sombre, as though something I had subconsciously come to rely on – a dream, however peripheral – had been abruptly taken away from me.

'Do you remember what the shitty little bastards said about Lowry, when he died?' I asked after a silence. 'Do you remember how they did him down; said in the sphere of world art he was a provincial, and an English provincial at that? And do you remember that girl – I can't recall her name – who took them all to task and said whatever Lowry's shortcomings, one thing he did, and that was to add to the visual stock of a nation?'

'Oh, aye,' Ted said, 'and I'd settle for being a Lowry, but I'm not.'

'Have a go, Ted,' I urged him. 'Fail if you've got to, but don't fail before you've tried.'

Ted sighed, then relit the dead stub of his fag. 'You're good for me, Gordon lad. You give me new heart.'

'I can't do the work for you, though. You're on your own with that. Have you sold anything lately?'

'Not exactly.' Ted looked at his heavy metal-cased wristwatch. 'How much time have you got?'

'I mustn't be too long.'

'Would you like another drink?'

'I'm not gasping. What's the rush?'

'There's something I'd like to show you. Can we use your car for half an hour?'

'Sure.'

We drank up and went outside. The pub stood on a hill. Fifteen years ago a dozen streets of terraced houses had climbed up to it, rank upon rank, on one side. Now open weed-grown ground fell sharply away to a rash of newish council houses along the valley bottom. The haze in the valley was luminous in an unexpected bonus of sunlight. Taking directions from Ted, I drove down through the centre of town.

'There are days when this raddled old hag of a place looks positively beautiful.'

'Stone and trees,' Ted said. 'That's the best combination. But once the stone goes the trees won't save it.' He slumped lower in his seat. 'I try to get as much of it down as I can. What I haven't the time to paint I take photographs of. I'm not sentimental, you understand, about the crap-houses people used to have to live in, and the hours they worked in all those mills for bugger-all except crooked backs and consumption. But it had style. Where's the style in concrete and plate-glass?'

We crossed the river, drove alongside it for a way, then began to climb again. A narrow twisting side road took us up past winter meadows with the lushness of parkland and clusters of sturdy well-painted villas standing among oak and elm and sycamore. All here in spring was a cool green shade. Now the sun glowed briefly in window-glass, dazzling me at intervals, so that I had to pull down my visor to keep a view of the road. Here, as children, Bonny and I had sometimes been brought on picnics. We would pick blackberries for jam in season, or throw a ball, explore copses, finding secret places in the underbrush, while our parents sat content in desultory conversation and, away below, trains hooted along the valley and the mills and factories and warehouses by the river were quiet in the weekend sun. Even then, Bonny had been the restless one, tiring quickly of shared games and wandering off, searching, never afraid to trespass, more than once having to be looked for when it was time to go.

We turned off yet again, running along between a high wall of dressed stone and an iron fence, through a tunnel of horse-chestnut, and emerged on to open ground. Set back from the road on a built-up platform on the rim of a steep meadow was a long stone-and brick-built semi-bungalow, brand new, not yet occupied, dabs of whitewash on its windows, its garden turned-up clods of earth.

On Ted's instructions I pulled into a specially constructed lay-by and stopped the car. Ted had proffered no information about where we were going or for what purpose, beyond a brief, 'I've been doing this job for a feller,' and I had curbed my curiosity. We walked to the house now along a newly laid, raw-edged concrete path and Ted, producing a key, opened the door. The interior was bare, but painted and scrubbed clean, ready at any moment for occupation.

'This has cost somebody a packet,' I said, catching a glimpse as we passed through of a big square kitchen lined with fitted units, fridge, washer, infra-red cooker.

'He's in the business,' Ted said. 'Built it for himself.'

He opened an inner door and led the way into a sitting-room with a fifteen-foot picture window. It was the window, and the clear view it commanded of the valley and the hills on the other side that took my attention, so that it was not until Ted, from behind me, said, 'What d'you think of this?' that I turned and became aware of what I'd been brought to see. I gasped.

'Jesus!'

'Aye,' Ted said gravely, but with a quick glint of humour in his eyes as he glanced at me, 'that's Him.'

It occupied almost the entire space of the end wall of the room, painted directly on to the smooth fresh surface of the plaster, a Madonna and Child, in the manner of an Italian Renaissance composition, but set against a stylised grouping of some of the more impressive Victorian and Edwardian buildings of the town, the mother and child receiving the homage of local dignitaries – a mayor in chain of office, a priest – as well as that of women with shopping-bags and men in overalls caught as though on their way from work. As I looked its colours were suddenly ablaze in sunlight. I was overwhelmed, stunned into silence.

'And you ...?' I said finally. 'You did this, Ted?'

'Aye.'

'But who...? How...?'

'It's an Adoration of the Magi. He saw one in Florence, took photographs, bought reproductions and wanted me to blow it up to the size of his wall. I persuaded him to let me do my own free rendition . When he saw a couple of preliminary sketches and a first stab in colour, he agreed. It was very brave of him,' Ted added dryly. 'He seems happy enough with it now, though.'

'He should be. It's bloody marvellous.'

'You sound as if you didn't know I was that good.' He grinned shyly, his gaze flicking from my face to the wall and back again.

'I confess, Ted,' I said. 'I own up. I didn't. Not that good.'

'The future of the world resides in every child that's born,' Ted said, suddenly grave. 'I haven't any kids meself, don't especially want any, but I know that much.'

I was suddenly on the edge of tears. I turned away, walked to the window, swallowed hard and took several deep breaths. I turned round and looked at the wall from further along the room.

'What an idea, though ... I mean the commissioning of it. ...'

'He wanted something to commemorate a girl he lost. She was killed, young, so I understand. He was on holiday in Florence – he's a Catholic, of course – and he suddenly had the idea. He looked round here for a local painter and came across me. I don't come too expensive, y'see.'

'What's his business? You say he built the house himself?'

'Yeah. He's in the trade.'

'His name's McCormack isn't it?'

'That's right.' Ted didn't ask how I had known. He probably thought he'd dropped the name himself on the way here.

''Course, it's held him up a while getting in, but he doesn't seem to mind that.'

'No, no. You don't get something like that with every new house.'

Neither of us heard a car pull up outside. We were standing looking in silence when the door we had entered by opened and heavy footsteps sounded on the bare boards. Ted looked round as McCormack walked into the room.

'Mr McCormack ...'

'Now then. I saw the car. Wondered who it could be.'

'My friend ran me up. I hope you don't mind. I wanted him to see it. He knows a bit about these things.'

'Does he?' McCormack looked at me. I was mildly surprised to realise that Frances's father had not recognised me. But it was years since we'd met, then only briefly, and I had, of course, since grown a beard. 'So what do you think of it?'

'I think it's tremendous.'

'Aye, tremendous. I think you could say that.' He turned and stood, feet planted, legs apart, and surveyed his possession. 'I wanted summat different, summat special.'

'You've certainly got that, Mr McCormack. The only thing that would bother me is, how do you take it with you when you move?'

'I'm not moving anywhere,' McCormack said. He pushed his hat off his forehead, took a spectacles case from his pocket and put his glasses on. 'I've built this house as me an' the wife wanted it and this is where we're going to stay. If ever I can get moved in for this chap an' his painting,' he added with heavy humour.

'I've just got it to varnish and it's done,' Ted told him.

'Aye,' McCormack said. 'When me and the wife've gone they can do with it what they like. Till then it's mine to enjoy. Did he tell you what it was all about?' he said to me.

'Yes. I knew Frances, Mr McCormack. You don't remember me, but I'm Gordon Taylor, Bonny's brother.'

That was a slip. Bonny's brother? What, so far as McCormack knew, had Bonny to do with Frances?'

McCormack had swung fully round and was surveying me closely.

'I didn't remember you till you said. Now I can see you behind your beard.' His gaze lingered on me till I felt impelled to speak again.

'It's a long time ago.'

'It seems like only yesterday to me,' McCormack said. 'Only yesterday she went out and never came back.'

'I met your daughter Mary,' I said after an uncomfortable moment in which no one spoke. 'She's remarkably like Frances would have been.'

'People say so,' McCormack said. He was silent again, brooding, gazing at the mural. 'Our children, you know,' he said suddenly, 'we lose 'em anyway. They grow up, change, move away, don't need you any more.'

But you can keep Frances, I thought. You can keep her forever as she was, embalmed in memory, the beautiful girl of eighteen, the sweet clean child betrayed by a person unknown.

'You've got photographs of it, Ted?' I asked him.

'Aye.'

'You show them to that arts association and I don't think you'll have any bother.'

McCormack stirred out of his thoughts and his contemplation of the mural. 'I'll put a cheque for the rest of your fee in the post this next week,' he said. 'If there's anything else I can do for you – give you a leg-up – let me know. I'm very pleased.'

We left him in the house.

'Obsessive feller,' Ted said as we drove back towards town. 'Single-minded. A good bloke to have on your side, I'd say, but a bugger to cross. I'll bet he's a sod to work for.'

I explained how I'd known Frances, leaving out Bonny's association with her and that she'd been pregnant. Remembering McCormack standing in the room, I felt uneasy in my knowledge; yet at the

116

same time I was elated by what I'd seen. I took Ted to his house, declined an invitation to 'pop in and say hullo to the wife', and drove home. I knew Betty Branch only slightly. She was an uncomprehending woman who loved the simple comforts and safety of her own backyard. I wondered if she had seen Ted's mural and what she had made of it. I wanted to talk to somebody about it. I felt like getting drunk.

Bonny and Eunice were drinking coffee and finishing sandwiches of tinned corned beef and tomato.

'We helped ourselves,' Bonny said. 'I hope you don't mind.'

I did, but didn't know exactly why. 'Of course not. Any sound from Eileen?'

'Not a peep. Have a pleasant drink?'

'Yes. Any more telephone calls?'

'It rang a couple of times. I took no notice.'

I pulled out a dining-chair and sat down. 'I'd better get those cushions in from the garage.' They were both intruders now. I wanted them out of the place.

As if on cue, Bonny said he was about to drive Eunice home. 'Is there anything I can do? Or any time you want me back?'

'No, no. Please yourself. We shan't be going out.'

When Bonny had gone upstairs for his coat, Eunice put together their plates and cups. She lifted the coffee-pot.

'There's some coffee left. Would you like me to heat it for you?'

'I'll perhaps do it later.'

Eunice looked round the room at floor level, as if idly searching for something she had dropped. 'Well ... thank Eileen for her hospitality.'

'I will.'

'I hope she'll be all right.'

'I expect she will.'

'And I'll see you at the class, if not before.'

'Yes. You'll work on that poem?'

'I'll perhaps put it aside for a while; come back to it fresh, later.'

'As you think best.'

She held the crockery. 'I'll just wash these before we go.'

'Leave them. There's not enough to bother about.'

She made no move. 'I – um ... I hope I didn't hurt your feelings this morning.'

I hesitated for a moment, then opted for frankness. 'You did.' She said nothing. 'There are ways of doing things.'

'That's what I thought,' she said. 'As well as a time and a place.'

She took the pots and got up and walked out of the room. Christ! I thought, she's telling me the door's not closed. She's hoping for another chance to put me down.

I wasn't hungry. I didn't want coffee. When Bonny and Eunice had gone I poured myself some whisky and thought about Ted's mural. I would beg a photograph of it; for the thing itself would be almost as inaccessible as an old master locked in a millionaire's vault, a sight of it available only to McCormack and his family and visitors to his house. I felt again that urge to talk about it, and with that came a desire to do something myself, to create something peculiar to myself. Perhaps I could write a poem about Ted and his work. My hand was holding the whisky bottle again, when I stopped myself. It was still only the middle of the afternoon; no time of day to begin caning the hard stuff.

I went upstairs, taking off the telephone receiver as I passed it. The house was silent. I went into the bedroom, where the curtains were still closed. Eileen's breathing was deep and regular. 'Come out of it,' I said to her, in my mind. 'Come back to me. I want to talk.' I stripped naked and got in beside her, drawing close to the accumulated heat of her. She lay without moving. I palmed the stuff of her nightgown up the length of her thigh and over her hip, then found and supported the weight of one relaxed breast. As my hand began to knead, Eileen mumbled something incoherent and swiftly, with the decisiveness of unconscious reaction, turned her back on me. I could not persuade: I didn't know how. It was all familiar except her response. She should be holding me now with sleepy good-humoured languor.

I left her and padded barefoot along the landing to my study. I took the magazine off my desk and went into the bathroom. I slipped the bolt and flicked through the pages of posed flesh. A girl's eyes mocked me while one silver-varnished fingertip delicately probed her pink labial cleft. My own fingers worked on blood-stiffened flesh. But she was plastic, a one-dimensional doll. Eunice was real. Standing over her, offering her morning tea, I watched the sheets fall away from her rising body, bed-warm breasts exposed to cool room air. 'I thought you were never coming,' she murmured. With her weight on one elbow she reached out at her shoulder-level to fumble then take hold, drawing me to where the tip of her tongue flickered, waiting.

I sagged, trembling after a moment as my skin cooled. It was the first time since I'd married. No, there had been that fortnight when Eileen's mother was ill and Eileen was called away in the middle of term, leaving me alone. But that had been different.

I went back to my study. There, I tore the magazine several times across and dropped the pieces into the waste-paper bin. I walked along to the bedroom and once more got into bed beside Eileen. She lay as I had left her. I tucked up behind her, close but without pressure, my hand resting lightly on her hip. After a time I began to sweat in the heat of her and I turned over, drawing in my buttocks till there was no more contact. A little while after that I slept. When I woke it was nearly dark and the doorbell was ringing. I was aware that it had been ringing for some time.

10

My father's car was standing behind the Mini, under a streetlamp. I put on my dressing-gown and went downstairs, switching on lights. My mother and father were walking slowly away down the drive. They turned as they heard the door open.

'We thought we'd better come round and see what was going on,' my father said.

'You've heard about it, then?' I stood aside and let them past me.

'Well, talk,' my father said. 'We didn't know what to make of it all, so we thought we'd better come round.'

My mother eyed the dressing-gown and my bare legs. 'There were no lights, but we saw your car. Isn't Eileen here?'

'She's having a lie-down. I was just going to take a shower. We were up late last night.' I led them into the living-room.

'Has Bonny gone, then?' my father asked.

'No, he's out for an hour with a friend. Sit down and make yourself comfortable. I'll get dressed and wake Eileen in a minute.'

They sat side by side on the sofa. I saw my mother looking at the cushionless easy-chair and realised that I would rather not have to explain it and tell her about Mrs Norton's hair. Her own hair, dark and not yet showing grey, looked as if it had recently been cut and set. My father was dapper in a raglan-shouldered tweed overcoat that, because of his hours at the shop, he had hardly any occasion to wear. My mother was wearing her chinchilla jacket with a grey skirt and sheer black tights and high-heeled shoes.

She looked round the room. That look, could, to strangers, seem imperious. I had often thought that, given a different background and education, she could have carried herself in any company, and it had amused me to realise from the sidelong glances of some of my colleagues when she had attended a school function that she was still a fanciable woman; though I could imagine her brushing aside any ill-conceived advance with a dismissive laugh and a deflating 'Don't be so daft, you cheeky devil.' She and my father always seemed content together. I could never quite imagine them making love, though no doubt they had their moments of gruff tenderness, she happy enough, like most women of her class, with an affection that did not run to excess.

I speculated thus because I suspected that my mother thought they had interrupted a session of Sunday-afternoon sex.

'What have you heard, then?' I asked my father.

'Nay, we heard somebody had been murdered up here.'

'Tales about somebody getting their head bashed in,' my mother added.

'I'm afraid it's true.' I told them about it while they sat straight-backed, side by side, not yet relaxing, my father still holding his hat of narrow-brimmed tweed with a yellow feather in its band that matched the lemon-yellow of the cashmere scarf Eileen and I had bought him at Christmas. They were silent when I'd finished, taking it in.

'Look,' I said, 'I'll go and put some clothes on and wake Eileen.'

I wondered, as I stood over her for the fourth or fifth time that day, whether, if left, she would sleep forever. Resentment rose in me. Why had she withdrawn like this, shutting me out? If we were lovers as well as man and wife, weren't we also friends? I shook her shoulder with gentle pressure. 'Eileen.' I pressed harder. 'Eileen.' She stirred.

'No, Gordon.'

'For Christ's sake!' I said, softly explosive. 'I don't want to fuck you. My mum and dad are downstairs.'

She opened her eyes, shifting position. 'What?'

'My mum and dad are here.'

'What time is it?'

'Going up to seven. You've been in bed for fifteen hours.'

'All right.'

'All right what? I'm only telling you.'

'All *right*.'

'Will you come down?'

'Who's there?'

'Just mum and dad. Bonny's taken Eunice home.'

'I'll come down.'

She was sluggish, slow to come round. I took my clothes to the bathroom and dressed there, splashing my face with cold water before going downstairs again. Everything was strange, out of rhythm. My father was standing, taking off his overcoat. I took it from him and hung it in the hall.

'I'll put the kettle on.'

'Don't bother for us,' my mother said. 'We've had our teas.'

'Eileen will want some, and I could drink a cup.'

'Is Eileen all right, Gordon?' My mother's unerring instinct for irregularity.

'Oh, yes. She was tired, and she seemed upset about Mrs Norton.'

'She must have been out of her mind, that woman. D'you remember that cousin of Hilda Fairfax's, Alec, how she went into a decline? A lovely smart woman, she was, till she went downhill. Melancholia, it was.'

'She didn't knock anybody on the head,' my father said.

'She put herself in the river though. She'd had a go before, with tablets, but they found her in time. She made sure of it, in the end. We've got a lot to be thankful for.'

My father got up as Eileen came into the room. He always did that in our house, if his first encounter with her happened so. He was quietly approving of his daughter-in-law and ready, wherever they were together, to pay her little attentions. My mother smiled, her glance missing nothing as it raked Eileen from head to foot.

'We nearly went away,' she said. 'Gordon just opened the door in time.'

'We were very late to bed and I didn't sleep well, so I got up and took a pill,' Eileen explained. 'I suppose Gordon's told you all about it.'

She hadn't looked directly at me yet, I noticed.

'I was just going to put the kettle on,' I said.

'I'll do it,' Eileen said. 'Is anybody hungry?'

'We've had ours,' my mother said. 'You don't take sleeping-pills as a regular thing, do you, Eileen?'

'No, I got a prescription once when I was marking exam papers late at night and couldn't sleep after it. Gordon must be famished. Did you have any lunch, Gordon?'

'No. I went out for a drink with Ted Branch.'

'He's a grown man, Eileen,' my mother said. 'If he goes hungry, it's his own fault.' But she was bending to Eileen. It wasn't her philosophy. She believed that men should be fed regularly and that it was a woman's place to ensure it. It was a system that failed only because of incapacity or illness. 'You shouldn't let other people's troubles upset you too much,' she went on. 'Have some feeling, by all means, but don't let get on top of you what you can't mend.'

'What sort of chap was he, Gordon?' my father asked.

'He knocked his wife about,' my mother said. 'What more do you need to know? Mind you, some women ...'

'I can see any man trying it on with you,' my father said.

'But we're not all alike, are we? You remember how Christine Linford's husband used to bray her? Every Saturday night, it was. He'd be at one pub, her at another, and when they both got home he'd leather her black and blue.'

'She were nowt no more than a little tart.'

'Yes. And she fought back, kicking, scratching, biting. But she got a leathering. The funny thing was how they stuck together, as though they couldn't do without one another. You remember Christine Linford, don't you, Gordon? They lived two doors away.'

'Yes.' A thin woman with hennaed hair and a perpetual cough. I'd known her reputation too, but she'd never given me a sidelong glance and I'd been unable to see her attraction. Except that to some men, of course, availability was an attraction in itself.

'He broke her nose for her one weekend,' my mother went on. 'There were bloodstains all over her three-piece. I know, because she took me in and showed me. Not that I used to go in, you know, Eileen, but I couldn't refuse her when she asked me. A tidy house she had, as well. I was surprised. I'd expected a pig-sty. There was a funny smell, though, so I expect she never bottomed it. All top show, like herself. I always suspected she was mucky underneath. You never saw much underwear on her washing-line: just the same two or three flashy bits every Friday. They went to live somewhere Bradford way, in the end. I expect they're still carrying on like they always did.'

'And what was all that in aid of?' I asked, when my mother relapsed into silence with a little chuckle.

'I'm just telling you – it takes all sorts. You've got to live your own life and not take too much notice.'

'I'll go and make some tea,' Eileen said. She went out.

'Has Bonny said how long he's stopping?' my father asked.

'No.'

'What do you think he's going to do?'

'I think one part of him would like to chuck it all, and the other part can't live without it.'

'He's spoiled,' my mother said. 'Spoiled rotten.'

'I'm fed up of thinking about him,' I said.

'He's your brother, Gordon,' my mother said.

'Okay, I've given him a place to hide for three days, but what else can I do? I can't live his life for him. I've got enough problems of my own.'

'What problems would they be?'

I should have known better. My mother was watching me intently now.

'I suppose you think my job's a doddle.'

'Have you been having some trouble at school?'

God! She was so literal-minded. 'Not specially.'

'There's nothing wrong between you and Eileen, is there?'

'No, Mother, there's nothing wrong between me and Eileen. All I'm saying is that my job has its problems and its difficulties, which I usually try to take in my stride without making a song and dance about them. And it's a job I happen to consider more important than booting a piece of leather about a field in front of thousands of people, a good proportion of whom are morons who we were only yesterday – God help us – trying to educate and provide with some sense of values.'

'What sense of values do you find in a dole queue?' my father asked. 'Most people lead pretty dull lives anyway. They like to see something exciting on a Saturday afternoon: people doing things they can't do themselves.'

'So can you blame them when they see their heroes screwing it all up because they're too maungy to stick to the rules and get on with the game?'

My father was quiet for a moment. My mother looked from him to me and back again.

'Have you told Bonny all this?'

'You haven't been falling out, have you?' my mother broke in.

'No, we haven't been falling out, and no, I haven't told him all that.'

'Perhaps it's time somebody did,' my father said.

'The press have had a go, haven't they?'

'Aye. But I meant somebody close to him.'

'Who's close to Bonny nowadays?'

'Don't you get on together, Gordon?' my mother asked.

'Mother, why do you have to worry every remark to the bone?'

'I can ask a question, can't –?'

'Bonny and I get on perfectly well together. That doesn't mean to say I understand him. How the hell do I know what makes him tick? If you'd asked me a few years ago I'd have said it was ambition: a single-minded urge to be up there among the best. Well, he's got that, so what does he want now – a fish and chip shop?'

'If I didn't know you better,' my father said, 'I'd say that was a bit below the belt.'

'What's wrong with keeping a fish and chip shop?' I said. 'It's an honest occupation. You cater for a need and get paid for it. Not as much as Bonny gets paid. But Bonny's different, isn't he? We've always know that Bonny was going on to better things. Where's Eileen with that tea?' She could, for all I knew, be standing outside the door, unwilling to break into a conversation that I myself was surprised I'd allowed to develop in this way.

'I didn't know you were so bitter, Gordon,' my mother said. 'I'd nearly say you were jealous.'

'Jealous! Dear God!'

'You are,' my mother said, seizing on her thoughts. 'You're bloody jealous.'

'What am I jealous of? His money? His big car? His women? Or the fact that he's lost his nerve?'

'You think you could have done better, given Bonny's gift.'

'I bloody well know I could.'

'Well, that's something we'll never be able to prove,' my father said.

Because I was never likely to be challenged at Bonny's level. How I wished I could publish a great novel, an achievement which, without necessarily understanding the extent of it, they would have to acknowledge when the world beat a path to *my* door. But first you had to write it, and great novels didn't get written for the wishing, any more than goals scored for a first-division football team. I was successful at any level of hope my parents – my father one-time semi-skilled workman, my mother sometime factory assembly-line operative, sometime shop assistant, sometime barmaid – could have entertained for their children. But in Bonny had been born that talisman whose blinding light pushed all routine accomplishment into shadow. The most spell-binding revelation of it to me had occurred not on the professional field but during one of Bonny's visits home, soon after his transfer from a second-division side to a first. We were walking together across the corner of a piece of waste ground on which some boys were playing an improvised game of soccer. A wild kick bounced the ball within yards of us and a shout followed: 'Ey, mister! Kick us that ball.' Bonny moved then, a couple of strides bringing it into his control. The next moment the leather was spinning under his feet, which, I wanted to swear, never actually touched the ball as Bonny hovered above it, to all the evidence of eye supported on a cushion of air between the soles of his shoes and the object they were manipulating. Then he dropped, tapped the ball from left foot to right, and deposited it with a precise lob at the toes of one of the lads who, all seven of them, were standing mesmerised in the presence of something they would remind one another of time and time again in years to come. 'Ey, mister! Who are yer?' came a shout as we moved away. Bonny lifted his arm to them and we walked on. The incident had, for a while, made me very happy about my brother: there were things too sublime for jealousy.

I got up and closed the curtains as Eileen, nudging open the door with her behind, came in with a tray on which were teapot, milk and sugar and four cups.

'You'll at least have a cup of tea, even if you have eaten.'

'Oh, I can always drink a cup of tea,' my mother said. 'But don't let us get in your way, if you want to start cooking.'

'I don't suppose we know when Bonny's coming back.' When I offered no answer to her indirect question, Eileen went on, 'And it seems a bit late to start roasting the joint. Perhaps I'll do some omelettes, later on.'

'Oh, anything'll do, any time,' I said. 'It's not as if we'd a houseful of ravenous kids clamouring for their bellies to be filled.'

I never knew why I said it, only that I should never be excused, as Eileen straightened up, the colour flooding her face and neck, then draining from them, her head turning this way and that, eyes blindly seeking, her mouth open as if choking on the gasping moan of orgasm, or a silent scream. She bent then, put down the teapot and left the room.

My father didn't know where to look, but my mother suffered no such constraint. Her glare scorched me.

'Really, Gordon.'

Yes, that *had* been below the belt. 'Oh, Jesus God,' I said, clenching my fists. I felt close to screaming myself.

I I

'Melancholia,' my mother had said, of the woman who had drowned herself. It was a useful general-purpose word, whether or not it was an accepted medical term. A beautiful word, too. Mel-an-cho-lia. I looked it up in the *Concise Oxford Dictionary*: 'Mental illness marked by depression and ill-grounded fears'. 'What would you do if I had to have a breast taken away?' she had asked me. But she had no warning lump – I would have known – and therefore no reason for fear except a morbid dwelling on what might just conceivably come to pass. If she lost her physical charms, what was there in our lives to take their place? Was that it?

I was alone in the senior school staff-room. I stood at the window with the dictionary in my hands, looking out at the swaying tree-tops on the edge of the playing fields. It was a boisterous morning, with occasional slashings of rain in the wind. I had made a telephone call on arrival, leaving a message at the office of Eileen's school, to say she was unwell and would not be going in today. I had asked her if I should do that when I found her still in bed after I'd been through the bathroom. 'You'd better,' was all she had said. 'I don't want to talk about it,' had been her only response to my attempt at apology for the remark which had driven her from the room while my parents were there. When it became evident that she wasn't coming back, and I made no move to go and find her, they had left, ill-at-ease, concerned. I had let my tongue run away with me and my mother and father had witnessed something they need never have known about, an episode of no concern to anyone but ourselves. They had seen friction, and they would brood about it.

Eileen had gone back to bed. She would not talk to me. I realised that I was afraid – of her and for her. But more than this, I was afraid for myself.

After a time I'd scrambled some eggs and eaten them with toast, opening the second of the bottles of wine which Eileen had brought home on Thursday. Thursday, only three days ago. We had been all right then. Bonny had been in the house hardly twenty-four hours. He was the one with the troubles. We could stand back, watch him.

Feel smug, because we ordered our lives better. Bonny. . . . Now he was coming and going as he pleased, using the house like an hotel. I told myself that Bonny had taken Eunice home and talked her straight into bed. While I had been pulling myself off in the bathroom, imagining her, Bonny's neat tight buttocks had been plunging between her parted thighs. And when it was over for the moment she would have been telling him how I had kissed her in the kitchen, bringing Bonny on again with the knowledge that he was possessing what his brother wanted but had been refused.

The telephone rang. When it persisted, I moved sluggishly from the sofa and went to answer it. It was from a call-box. 'Bonny Taylor?' a man's voice asked. 'Who is this?' I said.

'We know where you are, you bastard,' the man said. He rang off.

I watched television, programmes of popular series I'd never seen before flickering across the room, while I drank the wine. By the time Bonny came in there was no more than an inch left in the bottle.

'All alone?'

'Yes.'

'Is Eileen still in bed?'

'Yes.'

'What's the matter with her?'

'She's not well.'

Bonny grunted and came round and sat beside me.

'She got up for a while when Mum and Dad were here.'

'They've been, have they? What did they want?'

'Did they have to want anything?'

'No.'

'They wanted to know what your plans were.'

'They would, I expect.'

'I'd like to know myself.'

'So would I.'

'Do they include stopping here indefinitely?'

'Not if I'm in the way.' I didn't respond. 'Am I in the way?'

'It's too much, with Eileen not well.'

'Is there something wrong between you and Eileen?'

'What makes you ask that?'

'I dunno. Just a feeling.'

'What do you know about marriage, permanent relationships? You just pick up and drop as you please.'

'I only asked.'

128

'These things only become awkward when there are strangers looking on.'

'Strangers?'

'Other people,' I said. 'Third parties.'

'I'm in the way,' Bonny said. 'Why don't you say so, straight out?' I couldn't. I poured the last of the wine. 'When do you want rid of me?'

'Have you eaten?'

'Fuck food,' Bonny said.

'I think it's time you got yourself straightened out.'

'Just like that.'

'Any way you think is best.'

'But not on your patch. You've done your bit for the Bonny Taylor rehabilitation programme.'

'Did you manage it with Eunice this time?'

'Three times,' Bonny said. 'With all the trimmings except the poetry. Not that she's deaf and dumb when she's doing it, but she keeps it simple, so even I can understand. Fancy her yourself, do you?'

'What do I want with a bitch like Eunice?'

'I don't know. But the bitchiness does add a touch of spice.'

'Did she tell you I made a pass at her in the kitchen this morning?'

'No. But I'm not surprised.'

'She more or less invited me to try again another time.'

'Why don't you? I shan't be under your feet for much longer. And she wouldn't be the first bird we've shared.'

'You shit,' I said. 'I never screwed Frances McCormack. It was you made her pregnant.'

'Look, I'll go,' Bonny said.

'Where will you go?'

'Does it matter?'

He got up and left the room. I wished I still smoked. I could have murdered a packet of cigarettes. I thought I heard my brother's voice speaking into the telephone in the hall, and remembered the call I'd taken earlier. Bonny was a while before he came back. I knew, without seeing it, that he'd packed his bag.

'Okay, then,' Bonny said.

'What are you doing?'

'Leaving.'

'Oh, for Christ's sake, Bonny ...'

'For Christ's sake what? Why can't you say what you really mean sometime?'

'You're not driving back tonight.'

'No, I'm not. But what if I were?'

'Why not leave it till morning?'

'I'm going now. And you'll be glad to see the back of me. Until your conscience starts bothering you.'

'Okay,' I said. I was leaning forward now. I knuckled my eyes and let my forearms rest on my knees. 'Just tell me one thing, something that's always puzzled me.'

'Go on.'

'Why did you keep that affair with Frances so quiet nobody ever connected you and her?'

'Because she bored the arse off me, Gordon. I couldn't understand it at first – a willing little cracker like that. But she did. And I didn't want people pairing us off. So I took her to places where nobody knew either of us.'

'She was a cracker,' I said, 'that's true. But she was only willing because she was in love with you. You wouldn't know an honest woman from a kick in the balls.'

Bonny laughed. He stood in the doorway, then turned back. 'You think what you like, our kid. But look after your own. You've had it too good for too long. Thanks for food and shelter.'

Then I got out what was left of the whisky and finished that too.

A voice at my side startled me. I had not heard the door open.

'Sorry, Gordon,' Lucy Browning said. 'I didn't realise you were so far away. You're not in mourning too, are you?'

'What?'

'Another pop-star has met a sticky end. Haven't you seen the papers this morning?'

'No.'

'It was on the late news last night as well.' I had switched channels, looking for more pap. 'Particularly bizarre, this one. He was electrocuted by his own apparatus during a public performance. There's quite a pall of grief over my fifth form. Boys biting their lips, girls dissolving into tears at the most inconvenient moments. "He died doing the thing he loved doing most, Miss," one of the more articulate said to me, sobbing her heart out. It's tragic, and I know one shouldn't be amused, but imagine Menuhin running himself through with his bow, or Rubenstein falling into his piano and being beaten to a pulp by the hammers. It's Tom and Jerry, except it's for real.' She paused. 'But you're still not with me.'

'Sorry.'

Lucy was small-boned, full-breasted, in her middle forties. I wondered if she had had any experience of melancholia, and doubted it. Though a widow, she had a ready and attractive chuckle with which she brought proportion to most of the happenings in the school. She held out a folder thick with exercises written on lined paper.

'I'd like you to look at these.'

'What are they?'

'Those creative-writing exercises you asked me to set.'

'How did it turn out?'

'Interesting.'

A bell had rung for mid–morning break as we were talking. Other members of staff were drifting in, loaded with books and papers, the women with their handbags, and heading for the electric kettle and the big tin of instant coffee on the long table.

'You've got reservations.'

'Oh, I can see its value in one sense; but once we really open them up how are we going to close them down again?'

'Will we want to?'

'Gordon, the relationship between us has got to be one of a certain formality. Easy, based on respect and liking rather than fear, but formal. It's the only posture that makes it possible. You know yourself that the only creative writing worth a light is what looks under stones, discusses what we're often too polite to mention in conversation. How can kids manipulate allegory, extended metaphor, all the devices of the practised writer who doesn't merely record experience but uses it to make significant patterns? They've no choice but to make it personal. It means taking off the masks. Don't kids need masks as much as adults do? More important, in this context, what do we teachers do without our masks? Total honesty of communication isn't possible, because we can't expect total understanding. We have to work here, Gordon, year in, year out. We're not merely popping in to ginger them up, then leaving for the next port of call.'

'Is there any of that in here?' I had taken the folder from Lucy now and was casually glancing at one or two of the papers.

'No. It's new to them yet. They're self-conscious. But the more we break that down and the better they become, the more the problem will arise. What will we do when we get one which tells us how much some boy hates his father? Or some girl describes how she lost her virginity at fourteen to three lads in a ginnel on Bonfire night? What will we do when the first candid portrait with warts of one of us turns up? Where's the limit on freedom in free expression?'

'They've got to be made aware of the possibilities outside syllabus-learning, Lucy.'

'Then we're in for a reappraisal of our roles, too,' Lucy said.

'Why didn't you bring this up when the department first discussed the idea?'

'I hadn't thought it right through. And don't think I'm objecting now. I'm just making a point. Time alone will tell who's right.' She glanced at her watch, then looked over her shoulder. 'Would you like some coffee?'

'Please. One sugar.'

We had been left alone while standing together, apart from the others, at the window. When Lucy moved away, John Pycock came across, stirring the khaki-brown liquid in his cup.

'Ah, Gordon.'

'John.'

'Did the rest of the weekend go pleasantly after we saw you?'

'Hardly that, John.' Pycock obviously hadn't heard. He listened, brows aloft, with interjections of 'Really!' 'Good heavens!' and 'Good grief!' Lucy came back in the middle of it.

'Did you know all this, Lucy?'

'No.' I recapped briefly. When I'd finished, she said, 'So you *were* preoccupied with sudden death when I came in.'

'There seems to be a lot of it about just now,' I said.

'But I'm certain I know that woman,' Lucy said. 'If she's who I think she is, I went to school with her.'

'Are you a local woman yourself, then, Lucy?' Pycock asked. His bulk dwarfed her. She looked up at him, eyes twinkling behind her rather becoming glasses.

'But of course I am, Juno. I thought you knew that. My family came here in the wake of the Ark. Don't tell me you've never heard of Tillotson's toffee. It was the best and most famous in the North of England.' She chuckled. 'Why, I was once offered it as the best you can buy in Devon, of all places.'

'Is it still on sale?' Pycock asked.

'Yes, but now it's one of the many products of a confectionary combine. My grandfather sold out when the problem of capital investment became too much for him. My father got a share when Grandfather died, but one or two ill-judged business ventures saw it off. So it's no use thinking of leaving Monica and running away with me, Juno. I have to earn my crust.'

'I couldn't imagine you twiddling your thumbs on the profits from toffee,' Pycock said.

'No, but a little of that would have come in useful since I've been on my own.'

'What was Mrs Norton like when you knew her, Lucy?' I asked.

'What is she like to look at now?'

'Thin, sallow-faced with dark hair and big dark haunted eyes.'

'You don't know her first name, do you?'

'I don't think I've ever heard it.'

'I think she was Catherine Hetherington. We were at a fee-paying school for the daughters of men of some substance and others with pretensions to gentility. It was a crammer, really. Quite a lot of girls were there because they couldn't pass eleven-plus and get a free place at the high school. Catherine was always a loner. She was never a member of any group, though overtures are always made to people who are aloof. At first, anyway. When it's seen that they're not just hard to get, but impossible, they turn into the target for jokes. Catherine had a really blistering line in verbal contempt for those who tried her too far. She combined fastidiousness in her contacts with an apparent unawareness that she didn't bath or change her clothes often enough. She sometimes smelled.' Lucy chuckled. 'Yes, she did. I remember being mildly surprised when I read the report of her wedding. I wondered what kind of courtship it could have been. I couldn't imagine anyone getting close enough to her for that. I mean her letting anyone near. Certainly not to the extent of fathering a child on her. But then, marriage has always been a mystery, hasn't it? What is it that draws two people together, makes them content to live in such close proximity for thirty or forty years, or willing to endure it when they come to realise they can't abide each other? It's all very strange. I'm sure his name was Norton. You say she was on the bottle, Gordon?'

'Grocer's sherry. Perhaps other things as well.'

'And he tried her once too often. . . .' Lucy suddenly shivered. 'What a way to end up.'

'Who knows what prolonged treatment might do for her,' Pycock said.

'But can she live with the haunting, though?' Lucy asked. 'Knowing what she's done and can never undo. Still, if the boy's dead it won't pass down any further.'

'You mean you think it's hereditary?' I asked.

'I saw Catherine's mother a few times,' Lucy said. 'She was distinctly odd. She had what *my* mother called "a yonderly look" – other-worldly, as though her real communication was with things we couldn't perceive.'

'So what happened was Mrs Norton's destiny?' Pycock said.

'One mightn't have prophesied anything quite so drastic, but don't we all shape our own destinies? There's nothing that surprises me in Catherine's story except the degree of her undoing.'

Pycock smiled. 'I'm afraid that's a little too glib for me, Lucy.'

'No, Juno,' Lucy said. 'We shape what happens to us much more than we realise. I said I was surprised Catherine married at all, but did she have to marry a man who would find it necessary to beat her? All right, suppose she would have exasperated nine out of ten husbands, why did she have to choose the one who would go to such extremes? She was a potential battered wife who found a battering husband. The circle was closed, and it went on and on until, one day – the other night – she ended it.'

'It would have been more fitted to the pattern if she'd been the victim,' Pycock said.

'She broke the circle,' Lucy said. 'Yes. But I'll tell you what – if she's not watched carefully, she'll kill herself now.'

I thought about it when the staff-room had emptied again. I had another free period. There was work I should be doing, but I stayed there by the window, as if unable to break my mood. Two of the participants in a soccer match on the playing-field squared up to each other and began to fight. Butcher, the games master, jogged into sight. They were hefty lads, but he parted them and held each by the shirtneck, at arms' length, while he bawled them out. Butcher was a direct, uncomplicated man whose nature I mostly held in scorn, but sometimes secretly envied. 'That brother of yours,' Butcher had once said to me, 'he could be a millionaire before he's thirty-five, if he plays his cards right. Then he can say ta-ta to the lot of them. Give me his chances, I'd show you.' And so thought thousands, who weren't Bonny.

Someone cleared her throat behind me. I turned. A girl was peering round the door, holding on to it as though she might at any moment need to slam it behind her and run for her life. My first thought was that she was a sixth-former whose features I'd somehow failed to note. But she was too old.

'Mr Taylor?'

'That's me.'

'I've been looking for you.'

'I haven't been hiding.'

A little frown. 'Mrs Dewhurst said to tell you the Headmaster wants to see you.'

She was from the secretary's office; a new girl. As the school had grown, so had the number of women needed to handle the administrative paperwork.

'Did Mrs Dewhurst say when?'

'Now, I expect.'

'Tell her I'll be right along.'

Hewitt would know from the timetable that I had free periods this morning. The girl, in her inexperienced way, had made it sound like a summons, which indeed it was, though Hewitt had no doubt phrased it more like, 'Ask Mr Taylor if he'd mind popping along to see me, when he's got a few minutes free, would you, Mrs Dewhurst.'

I followed the girl through the corridors, recalling my feeling at the age of eleven, when new here, that I would never learn my way about. Since then, in my absence, even more extensions had been grafted on to accommodate the tripled numbers brought in by the reorganisation of secondary education, and there were parts of the school to which pupils did not penetrate until senior years.

Mrs Dewhurst said she was sorry, but the Headmaster now had someone else with him and would I wait. I found a chair and sat down with the folder of exercises that Lucy Browning had given me on my knee. Typewriters clattered, telephones rang. There were desks and tables, with wire baskets full of papers; a bank of filing-cabinets; a duplicating-machine; coloured charts on the wall – one a huge timetable which Hewitt and Pycock laboured over each summer, and of which Pycock, its chief author, was justly proud. Mrs Dewhurst's assistants left and were replaced quite often, but she herself had already become a legend by my time. Bulky, bespectacled, grey-haired now, she knew more about the school than any other single person and was diplomatically close-mouthed about everything except that which affected its smooth administration.

Collinson, head of middle school, came out of Hewitt's room, nodding to me as he passed. Mrs Dewhurst got up and went in, re-emerging in a moment to say, in her habitually formal manner, 'Mr Hewitt will see you now, Mr Taylor.' She had, I could never forget, seen me come through that door fighting back tears after a particularly severe walloping.

I knocked and went in. The two big bay windows of what had once been a mill-owner's drawing-room caught the sunlight. Hewitt said, 'Ah, Gordon. Good of you to come along.' He was lighting a pipe. Hewitt's taste ran to bulky briars of a foreign make. They were a part of his style, as were the dark shirts and brightly coloured ties with which he enlivened his sober, well cut suits. He affected glasses too, though they spent most of their time pushed up into his crinkly greying hair. As he waved me to a chair I caught sight of a paper-backed novel on his desk and guessed why I'd been summoned. Hewitt got his pipe going, pulled his chair closer to the desk and held up the book.

'You've been giving this as extra reading to some of your second-year "A"-level pupils, I believe.'

'Yes.'

'Any particular reason?'

'It illuminates in a powerful and vivid way an area of life I thought they might be better off for knowing about.'

'Drugs and promiscuity, both hetero and homo?'

'It has its own tenderness and compassion, as well as a moral standpoint, and it's well written.'

'You think so?' There were several slips of paper in the book's pages. Hewitt opened it at one of the marked places.

'It's very carefully controlled, technically,' I said.

'Controlled? It uses every four-letter word I've ever heard and quite a few that are new to me.'

'I think they're justified in context.'

'You think it's a good novel, Gordon?'

'Yes. And an important one. May I ask if you've read it yourself?'

'I've looked through it. Sufficiently closely, I think, to form an opinion. At least, as to its suitability for the purpose you've been using it for.'

'And your opinion differs from mine?'

Hewitt turned the question aside. 'You've given it to girls as well as boys?'

'Yes. Girls know as much, if not more, of the messy facts of life as boys.'

'Hmm.' Hewitt's pipe had gone out. He reached for the big box of kitchen matches and lit it again.

'I've had a telephone call from a parent. A long call. He was very upset. He sent his daughter to me with the book on Friday. He says the last place he expects to send filth like this into his home is school, and certainly not at the instigation of a teacher.'

I sighed. 'It's a story as old as writing itself. They persecuted Lawrence. Even Hardy didn't go unscathed.'

'I'm not for one moment suggesting that the man should be prevented from writing what he wants to write,' Hewitt said. 'What I should like you to do, though, is think very seriously about the advisability of putting it into the hands of young people: of *recommending* it and by so doing giving it the imprimatur of the school.'

'I did think about it,' I said, 'and I'd no intention of simply chucking it at them as a piece of spare-time reading. We've had group discussions about its implications.'

'You've found no embarrassment?'

'No. Some of these kids are very bright and perceptive. It's not my fault if they can discuss in group with each other and with me things they can't discuss with their parents. We can't shield young people from life.'

'But need we dole it out to them in such ferociously uncompromising doses?' Hewitt fell silent for a moment. 'Gordon, just how important do you think the reading of this book is to them?'

'Well, it's not *vital*. It's not in the syllabus, though if it has the quality I think it has, I can foresee a time when it might well be.'

'Can you, indeed?'

'We've come a long way in the past ten years. There's no reason to suppose the next ten will be any different.'

'Isn't there?' Hewitt leaned forward, his elbows on the desk, both hands holding the pipe before his face. He looked keenly at me. 'Supposing the pendulum were to swing the other way? Supposing something as apparently unimportant as this were to cause a reaction and we were to lose most of the ground we've captured?'

'Oh, surely . . .'

'No, seriously, Gordon. It might be considered irresponsible of us to jeopardise that. You say yourself that this particular book isn't vital to your teaching.'

'But there's the question of principle.'

'Principle?'

'My considered judgement being called into question by one parent. There is only one, I take it?'

'One is all it needs to start the ball rolling,' Hewitt said. 'And I thought – allowing for one's possible disagreement with his initial premise – that he was rather reasonable about it.'

'You mean he's not demanding my head on a charger?'

'Come, Gordon, there's no question of anything like that. You know how much faith I have in your ability. By the way, have you thought of applying for the English Adviser's job when Tom Noonan moves on?'

'I didn't know he was going.'

'Not many people do yet. Could it be the sort of position you see yourself in?'

'I'll have to think about it.'

'Well, now you'll have time to put out a few feelers before the vacancy is officially notified.'

'You wouldn't be trying to get rid of me, would you?'

Hewitt chuckled. 'It has just crossed my mind to wonder why I should encourage one of my best members of staff to leave me. But I always like to see people get on and assume the responsibilities they're fitted for.'

'Even though there's doubt about my judgement.'

'Oh, none of us is infallible, Gordon,' Hewitt said expansively. He leaned back in his chair now, putting one knee up against the edge of his desk. 'Just so long as we catch things before they get out of hand. I'm a great one for liking decisions to be made inside these walls. Let the others do their job, but not try to do ours for us.'

'And you'd like me to withdraw this book?'

Hewitt suddenly got to his feet. He walked to the bigger of the two windows and looked out across the approach to the main entrance, as though expecting to see somebody. Then he turned and strolled back towards the desk. Still standing, he said:

'What the man said was—'

'Excuse me,' I said. 'Sorry to interrupt, but could I know which parent it was?'

'Mr Bellamy.'

138

'Audrey Bellamy is among the brightest of my pupils.'

'I'm glad to hear it. And I'm sure her education is not going to be jeopardised if she's deprived of the contents of this particular book.'

'But she's not going to think much of our authority if all her father has to do is pick up a telephone.'

'What Mr Bellamy said, Gordon, was that if we withdrew the book he'll be happy to let the matter rest.'

'And if we don't?'

'If we don't, I'm very much afraid he'll feel bound to go to the Governors and then the local papers will get hold of it. We shall witness a right old gathering of the Philistines then. Eh? And I doubt if they'll stop at the issue of this one book. Once the blood's up it'll take some cooling.'

'Don't you think you might be exaggerating?'

'What I'd like you to consider is the possibility that you're doing that very thing,' Hewitt said. 'I can't seriously believe you'd wish to make a last-ditch stand on such a matter. What's the point, Gordon? If they want to read the damn book they'll get hold of it for themselves We're not responsible for what they read out of school.'

'But if they read it with my guidance, and with discussion, they'll get more from it than the cheap thrill of apparently gratuitous sex and violence.'

Hewitt glanced at his watch. He'd given me enough of his valuable time.

'Don't make a rod for your own back, Gordon,' he said quietly. 'Do it the easy way. Drop it, there's a good lad.'

I felt my ears burn. 'I think I'd prefer you to tell me what to do.'

'Order you, you mean?'

'Yes.'

Hewitt sighed. He scratched among his hair with one forefinger.

'I'm sorry about this, Gordon. I really am. I'm sorry it's come to this, and I'm sorry that now it has you feel compelled to adopt this attitude.'

'I'm sorry you don't feel you can back me. It would only be a storm in a teacup.'

'No.' Hewitt shook his head emphatically. 'There are other things I'm working for, and publicity of that kind is something I particularly don't want just now.'

'Only you can be the judge of that, of course.'

'Yes, but you could have given me credit for it without my having to spell it out.'

I stood up. 'I'm sorry.'

'Yes, well ... retrieve all the copies and bring them along here. Make sure they're all accounted for, and put them in a box, or some such, and fasten it. It's not the kind of thing I want Mrs Dewhurst and her helpers dipping into.'

Hewitt turned and walked to the window again. I went out. Hewitt was disappointed in me and he wasn't, I was sure, the man to forget.

12

I telephoned home at lunchtime and got no reply. I didn't think Eileen could be *still* in bed, but she would not have gone out, without the car, except possibly for a walk or to the local shops. She was perhaps fighting shy of taking calls about Bonny. She would be wondering, too, where Bonny was. I perhaps ought to have left her a note about that.

I was late to table. Bill Pine, the woodwork teacher, sitting opposite, had a folded copy of the *Globe* by his plate. 'You've seen this, I suppose?' An industrial dispute was limiting circulation, and I'd failed to get a copy on my way to school. There was a picture of Bonny on an inside page under a heading: 'Soccer star in mystery killing.'

'Oh, Christ!' I said. 'Don't they have a way of tarting things up?'

'You've got to expect these things when you're famous.'

'Tell me something I don't know,' I said. I disliked Pine, who had a way of stating the obvious as though it were original wisdom. I knew of two nicknames in current use by Pine's pupils. 'Pitch' was one of them; but cleverer was 'Porky'. For Pine was a prickly man, not slow to express his own candid opinion, but quick to fancy slights in those of others. The story itself was brief and factual, with an added résumé of Bonny's recent differences with his club.

'He just can't steer clear of it, can he?' Pine said. He was eating heartily from a plate of cottage pie, sprouts and carrots.

'It's hardly his fault if my neighbour comes to a sticky end.'

'It just seems typical of him to be there,' Pine said. 'Where the trouble is.'

'As typical as the delight of smug cunts like you, who just love to see a man pulled down.'

Pine couldn't believe his ears. 'What did you just say?'

'You heard what I said. Back off, will you.' I tossed his newspaper back across the table. Without special aim, I nevertheless intended it to clear Pine's plate and fall in his lap. It dropped on to what was left of his food. Pine pushed his chair back and began to get up.

'Look here, what the hell do you think you're playing at?'

I forced myself to stay seated. When I neither spoke nor looked up again, Pine put his hands on the table and leaned across.

'I said what the hell do you think you're playing at.'

'Piss off, Pine,' I said. 'Go and blunt your chisels somewhere else.'

I thought he was deciding whether or not to come for me, and was wondering if getting to my feet now would be a good idea, when Pycock loomed up.

'What's the trouble?'

'Ask him,' Pine said, making an angry gesture towards me.

'Gordon?' Pycock said.

'I'm sick of people making snide remarks about my brother, John,' I said. 'So I've told Pine that he's a smug cunt and suggested he should go elsewhere.'

'You heard that, didn't you?' Pine said. He was losing face every second he stood there. People along the table were now leaning to see past their neighbours.

'Come on, now, both of you, calm down. We can't have this kind of thing.' Pycock put a conciliatory hand on Pine's shoulder, only to have it angrily shrugged off.

'Christ!' Pine said. 'They think they're the lords of the earth.'

That puzzled me. I wondered what in my own everyday demeanour could have created such buried resentment in Pine. I wondered even as I retaliated:

'When you look at the opposition, is it any surprise?'

I thought then that Pine actually would have reached across to strike me, but Pycock took a grip on his arm.

'Have you finished your lunch, Bill?'

'I haven't had any pudding,' Pine said.

'Well, get some and take it across to my table.'

'I was here first,' Pine said.

I pushed my food away. I had hardly touched it.

'He can sit back down. I'll go.' I got up and walked round the end of the table. By now most of the people in the room were aware of the disturbance and faces turned to watch me. Pycock hurried after me into the corridor.

'I thought you were going to fight.'

'Oh, I don't think it would have got to that, John.'

'What was it all about?'

'I told you, John.'

'Come now, Gordon, you don't often flare up like that.'

'Look, John, do me a favour, will you? Ask Lucy Browning to get somebody to take my classes this afternoon. I'm going home. I should never have come in today.'

'Are you ill, Gordon?'

'Eileen's not well, and I can't raise her on the phone.'

'Well, then ...'

'Thanks, John. He really is a shit, you know, that Pine. I've been wanting to tell him so for months.'

'You're both grown men,' Pycock said reprovingly. 'Balanced men, able to weigh the pros and cons.'

'You've got to be joking, John. Half the pillocks in this place are so full of prejudice and self-importance it runs out of their ears.'

'We can't manage a school on the kind of behaviour I just witnessed in there,' Pycock said.

'Why not? It might show the kids we're human in ways they can understand.'

'You're not being reasonable, Gordon.'

'I don't feel reasonable. You'd better go back in before Pine accuses you of favouritism.'

'I don't need either you or Pine to tell me my job, Gordon.'

'No. I'm sorry, John. But I really think I ought to go home now.'

'Off you go then.' Pycock walked a few steps with me. 'I hope you'll find everything all right. Give me a ring if there's any way I can help.'

Bonny's car, standing outside my house, was visible from the end of the street. I swung the Mini into the drive and parked in front of the garage, then went into the house and opened the living-room door. Bonny was sitting in the easy chair across from Eileen who, in sweater and jeans, had her feet pulled up beside her on the sofa. They were drinking coffee from mugs.

'Hullo.'

'What are you doing home at this time?'

'There was no one answering the phone, so I thought I'd better come and see if you were all right.'

'I took two calls, but they were both about Bonny, so then I ignored it.' She looked normal enough now, with colour in her face.

'And where have you sprung from?' I asked Bonny. 'As if I can't guess.'

'I forgot a couple of things last night,' Bonny said easily.

'Why didn't you tell me Bonny had gone?' Eileen said. 'That you'd asked him to go?'

'I got fed-up of talking to a brick wall. I'm glad to see you back in the land of the living. Apparently there's still somebody you can communicate with.' Again, I thought, I was setting off on the wrong foot. Again, Bonny was in the way.

'Did you find a comfortable bed?' I asked him.

A little smile touched his lips. 'Oh, yes.'

'You're in the paper again this morning.'

'I saw it.' Bonny indicated a copy of the *Globe* lying on the coffee table.

'Did you get any lunch?' Eileen asked.

'A couple of mouthfuls.'

'Do you want anything more?'

'I'm not hungry. Have you two had anything?'

'I made a couple of omelettes.'

'The ubiquitous bloody omelette,' I said. 'What would we do without it?' I looked at my watch. 'Well, if everything's all right here I suppose I can go back and do my work.' I took off my overcoat and sat down. I'd come home hoping she would be up and intending then to sit beside her, taking her hands in mine, and say, 'Look, love, I know something's upsetting you. Tell me what it is and we'll work it out together.' But Bonny had beaten me to it, barring my way. For they had been talking, I was sure: the atmosphere as I'd entered was not that created by people exchanging polite chit-chat. And there was that colour in Eileen's cheeks, as though she would have preferred me not to find them together.

'How do you feel?'

'I'm all right. Or I was.'

'You didn't seem so to me.'

'I was all right before you walked in and started scratching.'

'I came home because I was worried about you. But it looks as if I needn't have bothered.'

'I'm in the way again,' Bonny said. He put his mug aside. 'I'll buzz off and leave you.'

'No, don't go,' Eileen said. Bonny half relaxed in his chair again. 'I don't want you to go.'

'I should never have come in the first place.'

'We've been through all that.'

'It's true, all the same,' Bonny said.

'Carry on,' I said. 'Sort it out between you. Don't mind me.'

'Shall we run away together, Eileen?' Bonny said.

'That's more like it,' I said. 'Now it's getting interesting.' I paused. 'Bonny asked you a question, Eileen.'

'You're a bloody fool, our kid,' Bonny said.

'I may have been. I may indeed. Do you think I'm a fool, Eileen?'

'You're behaving like one now.'

'You know he's sitting there with his prick still wet from Eunice Cadby, don't you?' I said. Bonny shifted in his chair, but didn't speak. Privately, I was astounded. I did not know how matters could have taken such a turn. From Thursday to last night, and now to this.

'Are you wishing it were you?' Eileen asked.

'Oh, let's reduce it all to simple basic envy. That'll explain everything, everything bar what really matters. And that is – what the bloody hell is going on?'

'What's going on is bloody life, Gordon,' Eileen said, with more heat than I could recall her ever using before. 'And it can be messy. You like it all neat and tidy, don't you? All cut and dried. You potter about in the arts and liberal studies, analysing, explaining, loving it all as long as you can put a label on it and keep it in its place – nicely mounted and framed, so that you can look at it without its touching you. Well, there comes a time in some people's lives when they find they've no façade to hide behind, when they look into the pits that you walk carefully round and find they can't see the bottom. Like the hell that couple next door must have lived through. Like Bonny when he loses what's driven him all these years and there's no beauty in the game anymore, only what's wrapped round it: the nightclubs, the women, the drinks and the drugs and the trouble.'

'That's good,' I said. 'You could expand that into a useful lecture.'

'Oh, God!' Eileen said.

'Look,' I said, 'you can fuck everybody or you can fuck nobody. And you can find all you want and need somewhere in-between.'

'If you're lucky.'

'Like we were. Now what's changed? Only what's in your mind. Or is there something else, that I don't know about?'

Bonny held up a small rectangular leather case. 'I forgot my electric shaver. I still had your key so I thought I'd come round for it while there was nobody in. Catch.' He lobbed the key from his other hand. I fumbled it. The key fell to the carpet. I let it lie.

'But you found Eileen at home.'

'Yes.'

'And so you had a good talk.'

'She didn't know I'd packed my bag, so we had a chat about your reasons for throwing me out.'

'Didn't you find my reasons reasonable, Eileen?' I asked. 'It was all right Bonny being here while *we* were all right. But we couldn't stay all right as long as he was here, could we?'

She didn't answer.

'I don't know what's happened,' I said then. 'Honest to God, I don't know.' I paused, then I asked the question. 'Do you two fancy each other? Is that what it is? Is that why you came at me in bed like you did the other night, after you'd been alone in the house with Bonny?'

'He thinks he likes good full-blooded sex, with no holds barred,' Eileen said, her face flushed. 'But it upsets something in him when I make the pace.'

'You know he can take anything he wants?' I asked. 'He could always do that. Didn't you know?'

'No, he can't,' Eileen said. 'None of us can.'

'What is it you want, that I can give you; that I'm not giving you now?'

'I don't want this.'

'Neither do I. I don't want any of it. I want things like they were before.'

'Before I turned up,' Bonny said.

'Yes, all right, then – before you turned up.'

'How do you know things were all right then?' Bonny asked.

'All the evidence pointed to it. It wasn't a subject of speculation. And I asked you last night what you knew about such things.'

'Nothing, mate, nothing. But since I'm being dragged into it . . .'

'Eileen wants a baby,' I said. 'She can't have one. She thinks I'll hold that against her one day, if I don't, subconsciously, already. She thinks there'll come a time when I'll find somebody who can give me what she can't. What she's doing now is building a self-fulfilling prophecy.'

'That gift of tongues again,' Bonny said. 'Why don't you talk plain English?'

'Don't act the dumb footballer with me, Bonny. You know what I mean.'

'Where do I come into it?'

'I don't know.'

'You think Eileen thinks I can give her something you can't?'

'I don't know,' I said again. 'I want Eileen to tell me.'

Eileen moved her position on the sofa a little, but didn't speak.

'Suppose I just clear off, like you said, and we'll forget all this ever happened?'

'It's too late for that,' I said. 'We've lost something.'

'And all you've done since you walked in is chuck it away with both hands.'

I looked at Eileen. She was sitting with lowered eyelids, her face slightly averted from me. Sometimes her gaze had flickered on to Bonny as he spoke, but almost the only time she had looked directly at me was while she was denouncing me for my attitude to life. Always, before, in the presence of a third party, there had sooner or later passed between us that glance, given without reserve, which conveyed a shared understanding: there were the two of us, and then the others. Its absence now, and my inability to see our ever recovering it in any untarnished, instinctive form, appalled me. I was baffled by how quickly it had all come to grief.

A flurry of rain patterned on the window. The room had gone dark. I switched on a standard-lamp, then shivered. 'Is the heat turned down?' I was moving to light the gas-fire when a sudden clatter from behind it startled all of us and made Eileen cry out, 'Oh! What's that?' The black glossy tip of a bird's wing thrust itself through the gap between the fire and the tiled surround. Then it disappeared and the frantic thrashing was heard again.

Bonny was on his feet now, standing beside me. 'Can we get it out?'

'I think the fire will pull out just enough.'

Bonny knelt, close up, as I eased the fire away, as far as it would come without fracturing the pipe from the gas supply. He put his hand into the aperture, fumbled for a moment, then brought it out holding the struggling terrified bird. Eileen pressed back in her seat, her eyes staring, as he turned.

'Its wing's broken,' Bonny said. His hands as he held the bird were surprisingly gentle. It broke free of his soft hold and fell in a flurry of movement to the carpet. I reached down and caught it as it made a grotesque lurching run for the cover of the sofa.

'What will you do with it?' Eileen said.

'Its wing's broken,' I said. 'It's done for.' I took it behind the bobbing head in the circle of thumb and forefinger, then tightened and twisted. The throb of life stilled in my hand.

'What have you done?' Eileen cried.

'It's dead.'

'Did you have to—?'

'It was crippled, Eileen. It couldn't be saved.'

I walked out with the soft warm body in my hand and went to the dustbin. I took off the lid, opening my hand and looking for any lingering life in the bird before dropping it among the household waste. When I went back into the house, Bonny was putting on his topcoat.

'I'll be off, then.'

'Sure you've got everything you came for?'

'Everything I brought with me.'

'Are you going for good this time, or will you be popping in again?'

'We shall have to wait and see.'

'And what do we tell enquirers after your whereabouts?'

'Tell them you don't know where I am.'

'Is there nobody wondering about you? Apart from reporters, I mean.'

Bonny picked up the copy of the *Globe,* folded it and put it in his pocket. 'They'll have seen that. And it's only been – what? – four days. They'll have been glad to have me out of their hair.'

'Where *do* you intend going, as a matter of interest?'

'I'll be in touch.'

'Why don't you just go back, throw yourself on their mercy and get on with what you're paid to do?'

'Haven't I made any impression on you at all?'

'Oh, yes. If you leave unfinished business wherever you go, you're bound to be remembered.'

'Get your nose out of the novels and poems, our kid, and look around you.'

'I don't much care for what I see, thanks all the same.'

'It won't go away, though. You can't shut the covers on it and put it on the shelf.'

'I wish I knew what everybody's trying to tell me,' I said. Bonny turned to Eileen. 'So long, then, Eileen. Take care.'

She was biting a knuckle, turned in again on a raw edge of nerves. 'Yes,' she managed. 'And you.'

148

Bonny nodded to me. 'Be seeing you.' Then he left.

He left a silence in which we sat through a lost trance of time, not looking at each other, brooding, drawn in to our thoughts. Neither of us spoke until I at last got up and began to rummage in a cupboard of the sideboard, when Eileen asked, 'What have you lost?'

Her making the commonplace enquiry surprised me. I could almost imagine that things were normal, that none of it had happened.

'There's a rather complicated answer to that,' I said, 'or a simple one. The simple one is that I'm wondering if I did leave a part packet of cigarettes in here, after all.'

'Do you really want one?'

'Yes, I do.'

She got up and came to stand beside me as she opened a drawer of the sideboard. From under laundered and neatly folded tablecloths surplus to the requirements of her mother and mine, and which we rarely used ourselves, she produced the twenty-packet of Embassy-tipped which I had put firmly aside before going to bed in the early hours of New Year's morning. 'I thought I'd put temptation out of your way.'

She was, I thought, temptation herself as she stood so close. I could feel her body warmth. When I took hold of her elbow – 'Eileen' – she turned away and disengaged herself, her movement releasing to my nostrils the faint tart tang of her odour. I didn't think she could have washed herself properly. Fastidious Eileen. ... My hand tightened on the cigarette packet, crushing it, as she went back across the room. In a moment, I followed her in search of matches. There were four cigarettes in the packet and I had bent and split two of them. What a pity, I thought as I lit one of the good ones, to throw away all those weeks – months now – of will-power successfully applied. The first deep drag made my head spin. I sat down in the chair again, afraid, feeling rather sick.

'Don't you want me anymore?' I asked her.

'You think that solves everything,' Eileen said.

'A warm cuddle? A little kiss?'

'What it's bound to lead to.'

'I always thought you liked it as much as I did.'

'But I can't now.'

'D'you mean not just now, or from now on?'

'I can't now, anyway.'

The taste of the tobacco was strange on my tongue. I could wonder why I had ever enjoyed it. But I knew I should try it again before the day was out. There was the rest of today to be got through, and the night, and tomorrow and the days after that. I could at this moment envisage no routine which would carry us through. You came to that over slow years in which affection cooled and proximity became tolerable only when spontaneity had been banished, separate ground cleared, fences erected, at a time of life when it was easier to make do than to seek alternatives. I was not ready to think in those terms; had not entertained the possibility of its ever being our lot. We had been the ideal couple, with never an irritable word that was not tempered by love. It was a pity we couldn't have a child, but our consolation had been that we had not exhausted our enjoyment of each other.

'You don't want to leave me, though?' I finally managed to ask. I had a feeling that my question, like so much I'd already said, was ill-timed, better not put to her in her present state. But it was the one thing I had to know.

Now she took in air, as though breathing itself was a struggle, then put her hands to her face and wept.

'Oh, God!' she said, and I strained to hear the words. 'I don't know what's happening to me.'

It was now that I should have gone to her, taken her in my arms and offered comfort. But she had rejected my touch once and fear of risking myself again kept me helpless in my chair. Until I could watch her no longer, when I got up and left the room and went into the kitchen where I walked to and fro, touching jars and utensils, picking them up and putting them down, and then, for the sake of something positive to do, ran water into the kettle, plugged it in and waited to make tea.

The telephone rang. I went, without thought, to answer it.

'Bonny Taylor?' the man's voice said.

'He's not here,' I said.

'Just tell the bastard he's got it coming to him.'

'And you go and stick your stupid head up your arse,' I said. I put down the receiver on an already dead line.

13

Faced with the choice of returning to school or obtaining medical authority for her absence, Eileen reluctantly went to see our G.P. I didn't know what she told him, but she came back with a prescription for a mild tranquillizer, a note which said she was suffering from a 'general debility', and instructions to visit the surgery again in a fortnight's time. I looked up 'debility' too: the dictionary said 'feebleness (of health, purpose, etc)'.

I thought it a fair description of my own growing condition. I was surprised and daunted by how quickly everything I had enjoyed began to seem meaningless. Favourite music could no longer hold my attention; I would read a page of a book and absorb none of its content. I taught without concentration, going lethargically through the motions. When I caught myself questioning the value of teaching children only for them eventually, in their turn, to have the props of their lives knocked from under them, I wondered that Eileen's defection could so have blighted every aspect of my existence. I had always thought I'd lived to the full before I knew her, questioning, eager, taking pleasure from my work and outside interests. But now it seemed to me that only my relationship with her had given them coherence and meaning.

When, too, I began in the next few days to get a feeling that I was being watched, I blamed it on the deteriorating state of my nerves. It was like the sixth sense which would sometimes tell me I was being looked at in a pub or a theatre when the house lights were up, and I would turn to find friend or acquaintance acknowledging my presence. But when I looked over my shoulder now, there was either no one in sight or no person I could single out from the other people around me.

Pycock asked after Eileen. I told him she was run down and needed a rest. 'Monica thought she looked a bit peaky, in the Black Bull,' Pycock said. 'She remarked on it afterwards. I wonder we're not all of us round the bend anyway, the things they expect of teachers nowadays.'

The Thursday evening-class came round again. I didn't want to go, but I'd made no attempt to find a deputy or to warn Noonan, who might have found one for me. Numbers were down to less than a dozen. I couldn't understand why: it was a soft, clear evening and there was no big event on television. It gave me fewer excuses to make: there was work I hadn't read, but which I should have been able to comment on. Lazenby was among those missing, though loyal Jack Atherton was there; and I found myself to be mildly surprised when Eunice Cadby came into the room a couple of minutes after the class had settled and I'd begun to speak to them. She murmured an apology and took a seat. Her presence threw me slightly. The faint patronising sense of superiority I'd felt towards her before was lost: she knew too much about me now.

I improvised a group exercise, eliciting through questions, discussion and suggestion outline portraits of three characters – their ages, jobs, backgrounds – building up, as they filled in more details of personality, areas of possible conflict. All this data I wrote on the blackboard, changing it as conversation exposed inconsistencies and more and more information came to light.

'Now,' I said finally, 'I think this is where we should stop.'

'We haven't got a story yet,' Mrs Brotherton pointed out.

'Well, we haven't got a plot,' I acknowledged. 'But I think it would be a mistake to try to superimpose one now on the raw material we've produced. What I'd like you all to do is to use these characters and the possible areas of conflict we've brought out as the basis of a story – several stories, because each of you will have different perceptions of the people involved, and each of you will develop the basic situation according to those perceptions. Your story, Mrs Brotherton, I'd expect to be different from Jack's, and Jack's to differ again from Eunice's. I'd like you to feel that a little mystery in your comprehension of the characters at this stage is all to the good, in as much as it's more likely to lead you to three-dimensional people rather than puppets dancing to some preconceived design. We've got, as it were, still portraits of these people. Now's the time to get them walking and talking, interacting with one another, revealing themselves through action and, in fact, surprising us along the way. They should show us things about themselves that we don't know yet. If they can surprise us, they'll surprise the reader and be all the more alive because of that.' I realised that, for a little while, I had been distracted from my own preoccupations.

Both Eunice and Jack stayed behind when the others had gone.

'Well,' I said, 'shall we have one across the road?' I didn't want Eunice to go without my speaking to her alone, nor did I wish to appear to be cutting Jack out.

'I can't stay tonight,' Jack said. 'I just wanted to ask about my play.'

'I've passed it to a friend of mine who produces for amateur groups,' Eunice told him. 'I'm hoping he'll arrange a reading.'

'I hope you told him to guard it with his life.'

'Oh, yes. And he promised he'd let me know something by this time next week.'

'Is that okay, Jack?' I asked him. I wasn't really bothered about Jack tonight.

Jack was frowning. 'He knows it's not a finished job; that it needs more work on it?'

'I thought that was the idea in trying for a reading.'

Jack looked doubtful. I took him on one side and talked to him. He agreed to leave things as they were and wait for developments.

'A touch of the cold feet there, don't you think?' I said to Eunice as we crossed the road to the pub. I had offered her a lift into town and she had suggested having the drink I'd mentioned first.

'I just hope a reading won't make him change his tune too much. They tell me it can be a pretty heady experience hearing your lines performed for the first time.'

'It's something I'm never likely to know,' I said.

'Isn't drama a medium that interests you?'

I hesitated. I'd meant that I lacked both the talent and the drive to write a play, and my instinct to candour with Eunice surprised me yet again. As if, I thought, I had not already revealed too much of myself for comfort.

'Oh,' I said lightly, 'I feel that it's such a chancy business. The odds against writing a good play, then of getting a production at all, let alone a competent one. The odds after all that of anybody ever doing it again.'

'What do you think Jack's chances are?'

'I think he'll end up putting this one down to experience.'

I bought the drinks and we stood at one end of the bar, waiting for a table we would not have to share with others. Tonight, I noticed as she took her glass, she was even wearing nail polish.

'I hadn't really expected you tonight,' I said.

'Why not?'

'Better things to do.'

'Such as?' She spoke in apparent innocence.

I shrugged. 'I don't know.'

'How's Eileen?'

'She's having a few days off work. She really needs a rest.'

'You perhaps ought to take her abroad and get her into some sunshine.'

'It's an idea; but there's no chance till school breaks up.'

We both fell silent. The old easy, impersonal relationship had gone. It was my fault. And the awkwardness was on my side as well. She seemed as self-possessed as ever.

Some people got up.

'Look,' she said, 'there's a table.'

She moved quickly past me to take possession. I could smell her perfume on the disturbed air as I followed. With my back to the wall now I had a view of most of the room. The red flock wallpaper was scuffed on exposed edges and the carpet looked almost ready for renewal. But it was a pleasant enough place at this time of day, with a good crowd in to give it life. I drank from my pint, the first of the day, and savoured its cool bitter flavour. A man standing at the far end of the bar was looking in our direction. He turned and spoke to his companion, who looked across in his turn. They were both young. One wore a zip-up windcheater of black imitation leather; the other had on a wool coat with a bold check design, like that of a Canadian lumberjack. I didn't think either of them had been there when Eunice and I came in.

'So,' I said, 'how's the research coming along?'

'Research?'

'Into my celebrated brother.'

'Oh, that. He's something of a mystery, isn't he?'

'I don't think I could deny that. Is he behaving himself?'

'I've no idea.'

'I suppose I meant how is he. How does he seem?'

'He seemed all right the last time I saw him.'

'The last time? When was that?'

'Monday.'

'Where is he now, then?'

'Isn't he with you?'

'No. I, er . . . I thought it would be better all round if he moved on. With Eileen not feeling too good.'

'When did you see him?'

'Monday afternoon.'

'And you thought he was living at my place?'

I toyed with a beer mat. 'Well, I . . .'

'Did he lead you to believe that?'

'No, not exactly. But since he wouldn't say where he'd been, or where he was going, I got to wondering.'

She gave a short harsh laugh. I saw that her colour was up. 'I don't know just what you two take me to be.'

'Well, not as shockable as that. Or so easily offended.'

I couldn't make her out. She had thrown me again. I wanted to remind her that she had manoeuvred her own way into Bonny's company.

'What did Bonny tell you about me?' she asked.

'We didn't discuss you.'

'You're a liar. You've all discussed me – you and Bonny, and Eileen as well. You couldn't have avoided it, and why should you want to?'

'Well, if we did it was just casual small talk; the same way you and Bonny must have discussed us.'

'You're family. Bonny doesn't talk about family. In fact, he doesn't discuss personalities much at all.'

'Well, then; you've just answered your own question.'

The man in the windcheater left his place at the bar and shouldered his way towards us. I thought for a moment that he was coming all the way to the table. My heart beat a little faster. Then the man stopped at the huge ornate juke-box standing against a pillar in the middle of the room. It was while he leaned on it with a hand at either end, reading the cards, that he looked our way again.

'Don't look too obviously,' I said, 'but do you know either that chap at the juke-box or his mate, the lumberjack at the bar?'

Eunice lifted her glass of lager and glanced over its rim while she drank.

'No. Why?'

'They seem to have been weighing us up.'

The man at the juke-box fed in coins, pressed some buttons and looked across once more before turning and going back to his place. Music with a heavy, throbbing bass beat into the room. Eunice eased her behind on the seat and tugged at her skirt.

'Stocking-tops are a novelty these days.'

'Were you showing?'

'I could have been.'

'Lucky him.'

'You're easily pleased, aren't you?'

'*I* am?'

'Men are.'

'Easily pleased, perhaps, but not easily satisfied.'

'Oh, I don't think you're ever satisfied.'

'The divine discontent?'

'I wouldn't have called it divine; not what I meant.'

'I should have to know how many men you'd tried to satisfy before I accepted the truth of your contention. And I don't suppose for a minute you're going to tell me that.'

'No. You'll just have to take my word for it.'

'For the evidence of your contention, but not for the contention itself.'

'You're losing me.'

'I mean what you've learned from some men in relation to yourself doesn't necessarily hold good for all men in relation to other women.'

'You can only speak as you find.'

'And what you expect to find is surely what you will find.'

'I don't know. I live in hope of being surprised.'

'I'm glad to hear it. Disillusionment shouldn't set in so early in life.'

I felt quite pleased with myself. I'd done something towards restoring the lost balance between us. But the pleasure touched and fled. For, 'Disillusionment *will* set in, though,' I could have said to her, 'and not all of life's surprises are pleasant ones.'

I emptied my glass. 'Would you like another drink?'

Eunice took her handbag on to her knee and opened it. 'Let me get these.'

'No, no.'

'Come on, I'm a working girl, able to stand my round.'

'I'm not bothered, anyway, unless you want one.'

'No. We can go, if you're ready.'

'I'll just pay a call.'

We stood up together. I went through the door marked with a small silhouetted figure in trousers, in the corner to my right. I was coming out again when the inner door was suddenly pushed open, stopping hard against my foot. I held the door and stood aside as lumberjack came in. The man walked past me with neither word nor look. He came out again as I waited at the table for Eunice. The man in the windcheater drank up as his companion crossed the room; then they went out together, without a backward glance.

I had left the Mini in the yard at the Centre. There was no one about as we stood at the kerb, waiting to cross. Then a car engine started in the pub yard, behind us, and headlights picked us out briefly before the vehicle began to move. We were a third of the way across the road when the car, coming out of the far gate, swung our way and hurtled towards us with a brutal rasp of acceleration. I grabbed Eunice's hand, pulling her after me, as I ran for the opposite pavement. The car roared away down the road, increasing speed as it went.

'Jesus!'

'They were coming straight for us,' Eunice said. 'Just as if we weren't there.'

'Or in the full knowledge that we were there,' I said. My heart was pounding. I took several deep breaths.

'You mean they were really trying to hit us?'

'No, no.' I was recovering now. 'They were just playing silly buggers. Let's make these two punters run for it.'

'Why do you say "they"?'

'I thought there were two people in the car. In any case, it's not the kind of thing a lone driver does, is it?'

'Not unless he's drunk or blind, or both. You didn't catch a number, did you?'

'No.'

'They ought to be reported.'

'Are you all right?'

'Yes.'

She seemed quite composed, if indignant. But then, to her it was no more than an isolated instance of irresponsible behaviour. I unlocked the Mini and let her in. I reached in and switched on the lights then walked round and looked at the tyres before getting in myself.

'What's wrong?'

'I was just checking my lights.'

I was becoming paranoid, I thought as I started the engine. I turned the car and nosed out between the stone pillars of the gate.

'You're a much moodier person than I used to think you were,' Eunice said.

'Being nearly run over does tend to affect a person's equilibrium, rather.'

'I mean in general.'

'We're all moody,' I said. 'You've just been seeing more of me. Since you mention it, though, you seem to keep a pretty even keel.'

'Oh, I have my low moments,' she admitted. 'But I try not to brood about things I can't change, and do something positive about the things I can.'

I had not meant my remark as a compliment. Eileen's erstwhile composure I had always admired and treasured; Eunice's, I thought, was based in coolness, shallowness of feeling and self-interest. Her written work made acknowledgement to feeling, but its images startled while hiding a lack of real warmth. I liked her, I told myself, no more than I'd ever liked her; but my sexual curiosity was still alive, despite my instinctive certainty that nothing but disappointment lay along that path. She would hand out sex, I suspected, as a favour, at a time she deemed appropriate, going through the motions of technical proficiency and incidentally gratifying a mild urge in herself that could usually be sublimated in less compromising activities. I didn't know why I should spend so much time speculating. Bonny had got her number early on.

There was a pair of headlights following at a steady distance. I hadn't noticed them settle into place. I slowed. Other cars slipped into the gap, then passed us, but the lights I was watching came no closer.

'Where do you think Bonny's got to?' Eunice asked.

'I've no idea. Back home, perhaps. Didn't he give you any clue?'

'No. As I said, I naturally thought he was still at your place.'

'Didn't he say he'd be in touch?'

'He said he'd phone sometime.'

Had that seemed reasonable to her, I wondered, or casual, offhand? It depended, of course, on what had happened between them.

The lights were still there, behind. I was hoping for a red light which would bring the other car nearer and offer me a closer look; but tonight, for once, a sequence of greens kept the road open all the way into town. At the entrance to the bus station, I swung over abruptly and braked hard at the kerb. Eunice lurched forward against her safety-belt. I said 'Sorry' and watched a car go by: a green Ford with a five-year-old registration. It was lost to view as it went without faltering, round the next bend.

'Well, thanks again.' Eunice sought the release catch for her belt.

'Hang on a minute,' I said. 'I'll take you all the way home.'

'There's no need for that. It's out of your way.'

'Don't argue. Just give me some general directions.'

'Well, if you're sure ... You really ought to turn round. Or if you drive a bit farther along you could cut across.'

'I think I'd prefer to turn.'

I pulled forward past the entrance, then reversed into it. My feet were still poised, balancing clutch-pedal and accelerator, when a car appeared from round the bend. I gave the engine gas and slammed back between the buildings, again throwing Eunice about in her seat. The green Ford cruised by. I gave it a few seconds before easing forward again to a position from which I could see both ways. A red light was holding the Ford two hundred yards away. I swung left and put my foot down.

'Give me very clear directions and in plenty of time,' I said.

'I thought you were turning.'

'I changed my mind.'

'There's something going on. Would you mind telling me what it is?'

'It might sound silly, but I think we've been followed. That green Ford that passed us, then came back.'

'I didn't notice. But who are they, and what do they want?'

'I'll tell you my guess when we get to your place. Is there a way round without going back through the town centre?'

'Yes. You carry on past the park and turn right up the hill.'

'Moorcroft Lane?'

'That's it. You drop down on to Low Moor Road from there.' She was quiet for a few minutes, as I pressed on at speed. Then: 'You're sure you're not imagining things, or playing some funny game to frighten me?'

'I could be imagining things,' I admitted, 'and I wasn't going to say anything, until I had to take evasive action back there.'

'But what do they want with us?'

'I think they want to see where you go, but it's not us they want.'

'Where *I* go? Who *do* they want?'

'Bonny.'

She sat on that, not speaking again until, five or six minutes later, she pointed out a complex of nine- or ten-storey apartment buildings.

'There's a service road runs round the back.'

I parked in a courtyard between two of the blocks. 'I'll see you in.' As I followed her across the asphalted yard and on to a flagstoned approach, a car moved quietly into sight along the main service road. Its lights went out as it stopped. It was too far away for me to determine its make or colour.

I said nothing to Eunice, but followed her up concrete stairs to the second floor. On each floor a glass door, reinforced with wire mesh, gave on to a lobby with the doors of four flats, the lift and windows in opposite walls. Blank doors, lives shut behind them. It was alien to me, brought up in terraced-living at ground level. Alien, too, to most of the inhabitants, moved out of the cleared rows of back-to-backs and one-up-one-downs which, not so long ago, had crowded the slopes on both sides of the main road. In this smallish town we had not yet produced a generation of flat-dwellers with no memory of street-living. I noted as Eunice felt for her keys that she had in her door a tiny glass Judas through which she could appraise callers before opening to them. Anyone, it struck me, could roam these stairs and lobbies at will.

'I wasn't expecting a visitor,' Euncie said, 'so you'll have to take things as you find them.'

There was a small T-shaped lobby with doors leading off it. She slipped off her topcoat and was reaching for the lightswitch inside the living-room doorway when I took her elbow to stop her – 'Just a minute' – and moved past her into the room and across the uncurtained window. It gave no view of the stretch of service road I wished to see, but I closed the curtains before saying to her, 'All right now.' The light came on to show her smiling uncertainly.

'If you'd wanted an invitation to come here, you'd only got to ask.'

'I'm sorry.'

'You'd better tell me all about it.'

'There's very little to tell. There's been a bloke on the phone to my house a couple of times. "We know where the bastard is." "Tell him he's got it coming to him." That kind of thing. I thought at first it was just casual malice. Somebody having a bit of perverted amusement.'

'But now you think it's more than that?'

'I'm afraid so.'

'Does Bonny know about the calls?'

'I haven't had a chance to tell him.'

'What about Eileen?'

'She hasn't said anything.'

'They couldn't just come through when you answered.'

'No, but ... I didn't want to upset her for nothing. You neither, come to that.'

'Thank you.'

'But if we were followed tonight, I think you've a right to know.'

'Why do you think whoever it was would want to follow us?'

'Do you know where Bonny is?'

'I told you, no.'

'Neither do I. And nor do they, presumably. I think they're just checking on his contacts.'

'Hoping somebody will lead them to him?'

'Yes.'

'But he could have gone back home.'

'They don't know that.'

She said 'Mmm,' looking at me for a moment longer. 'Do you think it was those people who nearly ran us down?'

'Could be.'

'Why should they want to draw attention to themselves by doing that?'

'Perhaps because they're amateurs and they have to keep the adrenalin flowing.'

'Well ... since you're here, can I offer you coffee? Or something stronger?'

I looked at my watch. Eileen would probably have gone to bed. 'What have you got in the strong line?'

'Whisky.'

'I'd like that. But I'd like some coffee as well.'

'All right. Take your coat off and sit down.'

She switched on a table-lamp at one end of the sofa and turned off the overhead light as she left the room. The room immediately took on warmth and cosiness. Most of its contents, I guessed, had been bought from second-hand shops and auction sales. I didn't see how else a young woman on her own could afford to set up house. Eileen had lived in a bed-sitter before we married, with just a few personal possessions to soften the anonymity of the junk her landlord had put in to qualify, in the cheapest possible way, for the designation 'furnished'. Eunice, I saw as I took off my coat and looked round more closely, went in for photographs of people and places eighty or ninety years ago. There were a few of Sutcliffe's Whitby studies among others I had never seen before. I was surprised.

My contemplation of a city street, with a large sign advertising Dewar's whisky on the corner of a building, was interrupted by her appearing with a bottle of that same Scotch and two glasses. I wondered idly how many million gallons of the stuff had been consumed between then and now; how many romantic moments it had made glow, how many fuses of tragedy it had set alight.

'The kettle's on. Coffee will be ready in a minute.' She poured two measures of whisky. 'Do you want water with it?'

'I'll take it as it comes, thanks. I didn't know nostalgia was one of your weaknesses.' I waved my hand at the walls.

'It's an age I feel very much drawn to. I could have lived in it: bustles, corsets, parasols, big hats, horse-drawn carriages ...'

'Bad drains, chamber-pots, T.B. and diphtheria, primitive contraception: have ten, rear six; no Married Women's Property Act, no divorce, no vote.'

'They managed.'

'Some did.'

'I would have.'

'You'd have been chaining yourself to railings.'

'Not me. That was for women who couldn't get what they wanted any other way.'

Eunice reached up and took off the wall a portrait photograph which I had not looked at closely. She handed it to me. An abundance of soft dark hair framed her face under a huge-brimmed hat. Her waist was drawn in tight, the cone-shaped funnel of her bodice pushing up and holding her half-exposed breasts in a cornucopia of glowing white flesh. The smile on her face was precisely the smile she was giving me now.

'I'd say you'd have got what you wanted.'

'Yes.'

'What do you want now?'

'To be me. One hundred per cent me, one hundred per cent of the time.'

'Militant, feminist?'

162

'Only for myself. The others can do what they like.'

'You're honest about it, anyway.'

'Which means you don't approve. I don't think for a minute you like militant feminism but you can, in theory at least, approve of solidarity, women united in a search for the common good. A woman who tells you she looks after Number One undermines your masculine foundations.' Her smile had turned sardonic.

'Perhaps I wasn't so wrong about you, after all.'

She kept that look on me for a moment longer. When I didn't explain I thought I began to detect in it just a hint of defiance, as though she were not as confident in her stance as she made out. Then she turned her head towards the door. 'The kettle's boiling.'

I sat on the sofa as she left me again. I wanted to smoke. I had bought a ten packet of cigarettes, but determining not to add to temptation by carrying them with me I'd left them in a drawer at home. On the low table in front of me was a small oblong cedar-wood box with a porcelain lid. Eunice didn't smoke, but ... I took off the lid, looked inside, then replaced it quickly as Eunice put her head round the door and spoke to me.

'Sorry.'

'D'you take sugar?'

'One, please.'

I took off the lid and looked again. In a moment I gave a snort of laughter that I muffled into the sound of a sneeze. I got out my handkerchief and put it to my face, controlling myself as Eunice brought in two mugs and put them on the table before sitting down against the other arm of the sofa.

'It's only instant, I'm afraid. I've run out of real coffee.'

'It's a hell of a price just now.'

'You're telling me.'

I took another sip of Scotch, leaving the coffee to cool. 'You don't happen to have any cigarettes, do you?'

'Sorry. Didn't you stop?'

'Yes. But I sometimes feel like one. I, er, took the liberty of peeping into the box.'

'That's what it's for. Though it's usually empty, unless I have a party, or somebody leaves some behind.'

I picked up the box. 'There's nothing unusual in providing *fags* for one's guests, but ...' I took off the lid of the box so that Eunice could see the packet of condoms.

'What are . . .?' She took the packet and turned it over in her fingers. 'Is this a joke?'

'I suspect it is.'

Her face was scarlet, more with annoyance than embarrassment, I thought, as she tossed the packet on to the table.

'I'm sorry, but I don't think that's very funny.'

'You'll probably think it's even less funny when you work out how long they've been there. How long is it since you looked in the box?'

'I can't remember.'

'Have you had any other visitors?'

'My mother came round on Tuesday evening. She usually comes on Tuesdays.'

'I don't think she'd put them there.'

'No, but suppose she casually opened the box and . . . look, are you sure you're not putting me on?'

'Eunice, I didn't even know I was coming here tonight.'

'All the same, you could have—'

'Why should I?'

'I don't know. It could be some kind of, well . . .'

'Elaborate sexual ploy? Not my style, love. Who else was here?'

She took a drink of whisky and chased it with one of coffee. Her colour had deepened. 'You know who else was here,' she said finally, 'the bugger.'

I picked up the packet and opened it. It was full. I began to laugh again. This time I sat back and let the laughter take me. 'I think he must be trying to tell you something.'

'Yes, that's all very well, but suppose my mother *had* opened the box, or somebody else?'

'Well, she obviously didn't, unless she went away without saying anything.'

'Oh, she'd say something, all right. She has a very vivid imagination about young women who live alone. She never wanted me to leave home.'

'I expect she misses you. It's understandable. Aren't you an only child?'

'I was. She married again. I've a stepbrother and stepsister, both younger than I am. And a stepfather. There's enough of them in the house, without me.'

'Don't you get on with them?'

'I didn't choose them. She did. All right, she wanted another man. She didn't want to be left on her own when I finally did leave. I'm not blaming her for that, but you can't have things both ways.' She drank again, was silent. It was none of my business and she'd said enough.

'When was Bonny here? Last, I mean.'

'Sunday night. I'd been with him earlier, of course. Then he rang up, said there'd been a bit of friction between you and him and could he come back and spend the night. I'd already made it plain there was nothing else doing.'

'But he still fancied his chances?'

'Of course he did. It was only natural, I suppose. Anyway, I let him come back and he slept here, on this sofa.' She caught my grin. 'What's so amusing? Did he tell you he'd managed it?'

'No, no.'

'But you assumed.'

'I have to be honest and say I assumed.'

'Is he so irresistible, that brother of yours? Do they all drop them at the sight of him?'

'You know as much about that as I do. I'd be surprised though, if they all put up as much resistance as you.'

'Well, I didn't fancy being another scalp on Bonny Taylor's belt.'

'Which is not to say you didn't fancy *him*, of course.'

'Mind your own business, Gordon.'

I was silent for several seconds. I looked at the photograph of her in costume, which lay on the table. 'I suppose what I'd like to know – with as little fuss and embarrassment as possible – is whether you fancy *me*.' I knew the moment I'd uttered the words that I'd made a mistake. That I'd set myself up again.

'Sort of just for the record?' she said. 'Something to warm your vanity on in idle moments of the day?'

'I hadn't thought of it like that.'

'How had you thought of it? As a quick kill, a bit on the side to add spice to married life? You don't know yourself, do you? I don't think you've thought it past idle speculation.'

I took a deep breath. 'Well,' I said, 'you've taken the gay, carefree edge off that.'

'What's carefree about going to bed with a married man?'

'Once you pose the question, the answer's impossible.'

'Yes. But thanks for the offer. If it was an offer. Whether you'd actually go through with it is another matter. I'm not sure that's your style. You like to talk about things.'

I felt myself reddening and was glad of the subdued light. 'You can't cast me as the happy adulterer, then?'

'I'm only guessing. I don't really know you well enough.'

'Ah, well . . . I'll say one thing for you: you can certainly talk the hard off a man, if you'll pardon the vulgarity.'

'Or talk one on, if I feel like it.'

'How often do you feel like it?'

'It depends. Women can wait, Gordon; quite a while, if necessary. Didn't you know that?'

Irritability stirred. I swallowed the rest of my coffee in one long gulp.

'Why do you think those men want Bonny?'

I shrugged. 'He upsets people.'

'You'd have to upset someone pretty badly to bring them after you.'

'Men like Bonny breed hatred as easily as they inspire love. You've only got to hear people talk. There are some who can't stand the sound of his name.'

'I'd call that resentment rather than hatred.'

'Oh, I don't know.' I felt a great weariness now. 'Perhaps I'm imagining things.'

'You didn't imagine the phone calls.'

'No, but perhaps they were no more than I thought at first. Just a malicious joke.'

I got up, felt for my car keys and took my coat. 'Thanks, anyway, for the refreshment.'

'You're welcome. I'm sorry I couldn't be more – um – hospitable.'

I grunted. 'You'll let me know if you hear anything from Bonny?'

'Yes.' She was standing herself now. She bent and picked up the packet of condoms. 'Would you like to take these with you and find a use for them?'

I shook my head. 'They're no use to me. Eileen can't conceive. Didn't you know?'

Outside, on the landing, with her door closed and the sound of a bolt going home, I felt vulnerable again. Keeping close to the wall, I crossed to the window. From here I could see the shape of the car standing on the service road. I was making up my mind whether to use the stairs or the lift when someone got out of the car and began to walk towards the building. It was a girl. I smiled as the car's head-lights came on and it moved silently away.

I passed the girl on the stairs, between the first floor and ground level, giving her a polite good-night. 'Oh!' she said, startled. There was a clown-like patch of orange make-up on each of her cheeks. 'Good-night.'

I went out to the Mini, got in and started the engine, and drove home.

I found Eileen, in a thick wool dressing-gown, sitting crouched over the gas-fire in the living-room.

'They've been ringing up again, Gordon.' She trembled violently. Her voice was near to breaking. 'You've got to make them stop it.'

14

Lucy Browning lived in an adjoining town, an independent borough before local government reorganisation had made it part of a larger authority. 'We grumble,' Lucy said, 'as I expect you do, about loss of identity and having to apply to strangers several miles away for permission to use facilities – like the town hall, for instance – that were our own; but it's all too late. We live in changing times.' Her flat was in a mansion standing among other mansions and villas on a hill still referred to by older people as 'Brass Park'; where the money had been when the wool trade was in its heyday, and even rag merchants made fortunes. Few could maintain them as private houses now; fewer still would choose to when the motor car could whisk them out to the Dales where, among limestone fells, they could put out of sight and mind the debris of the industrial revolution which still littered these millstone-grit valleys. It was, I speculated as I followed Lucy into a big empty entrance hall, no doubt the kind of house Eunice Cadby imagined herself living in in that *fin de siècle* dream of hers; whereas I knew only too well the likelihood that *my* lot then would have been twelve-hour shifts six days a week in some local mill or pit, and scratching for what education I could get through the sparse patronage of a mechanics' institute.

The wide stairs were uncarpeted. Some sense of visitor's deference made me tread lightly; but Lucy's tread rang out in the lofty well as she went up briskly, sometimes a couple of steps before me. She might, I thought, be trying to recall in what state she had left her rooms and unconsciously attempting to hurry ahead and repair any omission. I had never been here before. I noted that her brown court shoes had heels just a height to show off her trim ankles and calves. Lucy was always well shod. On one landing, a pram and a child's tricycle in chipped scarlet and white paint stood outside a closed door. At the top of the house, where the territory was no longer communal but Lucy's own, the stairs narrowed and were covered by a length of carpet in some indeterminate pattern in mid-brown. The stairs ran up through the doorway of the flat, terminating in a railed-off lobby-cum-landing. We entered Lucy's kitchen first and from there, turning right through a partition wall whose upper half was panes of clear glass, came to her living-room. It was a room of some size – as big as any one-and-a-half of mine – with a semi-circular window in what the steep pitch of the roof allowed of wall.

'They did their servants rather well, didn't they?'

'Oh, things have been knocked about quite a lot,' Lucy told me. 'They'd be poky little holes up here in those days.' Though the weather was now mild she bent and lit the gas-fire then turned down the flame to miser-rate. 'The chief drawback is the poor natural light. That's why they put in this paned wall, to get what could be got from the kitchen as well.' She slipped off her tweed jacket and tugged down her thin grey jumper. Her bosom – covered and supported, at any rate – was really rather fine. *'Would* you like some tea?'

'Please.'

'If you'll switch on that standard-lamp, I'll go and make it.'

'I ought to ring Eileen,' I said. 'Tell her I'll be a bit late.'

Lucy waved her hand. 'You can see the telephone. Help yourself.'

I switched on the standard-lamp as she, almost simultaneously, turned on an overhead fluorescent tube in the kitchen. There was an oval mahogany table with let-down leaves in one corner. A photograph, in a silver frame, of a dark-haired man with a clipped grey moustache stood on a low mahogany sideboard against the back wall. A couple of big chintz-covered armchairs and a sofa flanked the hearth. Bookshelves were built to chest-height on one side of the chimney breast. On the coffee table lay a green-jacketed book-club edition of John Fowles's *Daniel Martin,* with a marker in its pages. I looked round for the telephone.

'You can't go on like this,' I'd said to Eileen. 'You've got to let me help you, and I can't unless you tell me what's troubling you.'

'I just can't cope any more.'

'But why? What's changed? What is it that's different?'

'I'm different. Inside my head.'

'Would you like to visit your mother for a while? Have a little holiday?'

'She can't see me like this. It's best if she doesn't know.'

'What can I tell *my* mother?' I asked her.

'I don't know.'

She took a sleeping-pill. I didn't stop her. While she slept she was free of everything except her dreams. I lay wide awake beside her for a couple of hours, then got up and lit the gas-fire in the living-room and chain-smoked cigarettes from the packet I had bought and put away. Eventually I dozed off, to wake stiff and raw-eyed, with a pale dawn light beyond the curtains. I pondered the wisdom of leaving her alone. But it was Friday. I would finish the week. I made tea, then went to look at her while it brewed. She lay as if she had not moved all night, her face calm, eyelids still. I went quietly away from her after stealthily opening drawers to find clean socks and underwear. My wardrobe was running low. I should have to visit the launderette, and also shop for fresh food. Before I left the house I rang up the telephone supervisor, who agreed to have incoming calls intercepted by the operator for the next two weeks.

There was a thin mist and a smell of cool damp earth. Crocus heads, bright as splashes of paint, lit a border by the garage. A fat blackbird, foraging on the lawn, took to flight at my coming, as though recognising in me a killer of its kind. It was time to clear up winter's leavings: to turn over soil, spike, rake and feed the lawns. I should do more. I had told myself I would, this year. A man needed something outside the life of the mind. But when all the mind could apprehend was futility ... 'A pipe for fortune's finger to sound what stop she please.' Where was my Horatio? There was no one I could confide in; nothing I could confide without being asked questions I couldn't answer. When I flipped through my mental file of friends, acquaintances, colleagues I found none with whom I was intimate to the extent of sharing secrets. I had given all that to Eileen.

Lucy Browning was ahead of me, on foot, among the swarms of young people, as I turned into the road leading to the school. I was surprised that she did not appear to have drawn a group round her. When I pulled in alongside her and called, she bent and looked in at the passenger's window I had opened. 'It hardly seems worth it.'

'Get in,' I said. 'You can use that five minutes.'

'I can always use an extra five minutes in the morning,' she agreed as she settled beside me. 'I mis-timed it this morning. One bus full, the next one late. I'd intended to be there twenty minutes ago.'

'Where's your motor?'

'In dock. Again. It's cost me a small fortune in repairs this last twelve months. I'm afraid I've got to face the fact that it's clapped-out.'

I smiled. Lucy had got her occasional slang expressions from her late husband who, ten years older than she was, had served in the army in World War Two. She had once, in a staff meeting, made Hewitt blink by referring to suede boots as 'brothel-creepers'.

'These are nice little runners, aren't they?'

'Reliable, economical and they don't cost a packet to service.'

'I shall have to charm my bank manager.'

'I'll bet you do it all the time.'

Lucy chuckled. 'I'm afraid it's a necessary technique these days.'

'I didn't mean it that way.'

'I know you didn't. You were flattering. And in the cold grey light of dawn.'

Slowly as I was now moving, I had to brake at the entrance to the drive as a bicycle swung from behind a knot of older pupils and across my front. At the same time I threw out my left arm to stay the firm cushion of Lucy's bosom as, beltless, she jerked forward in her seat. I wound down the window and bawled after the lad. 'Hey! You ... The little sod,' I said, 'he's not stopping.' Rider and bike were lost to view as they wove a path through the pedestrians in the drive. 'They're told to wheel their bikes up here. And he's brazen enough not to stop and take his chastisement. Did you know him?' Lucy said no. 'And you wouldn't know him again, I expect? No. Neither would I. He's safe.'

'It wasn't a major offence, Gordon.'

'Of course it wasn't. But it's a damn fine thing when a school's so big a malefactor can lose himself in the crowd, and he's cheeky enough to know it.'

I crawled at five mph along the drive and turned into the car park.

'How's your wife?' Lucy asked, as she opened her door.

'Oh, tired. The doctor's given her some mild tranquillizers.'

She waited for me as I reached into the back of the car for briefcase and raincoat, then locked the door.

'I hear you had a difference of opinion with the Great White Chief,' she said when we were walking.

'Oh?'

'Over suitable – or unsuitable – reading matter for young impressionable minds.'

'Now how the hell did that leak out beyond his four walls?' I said.

'You withdrew a book. The kids can put two and two together.'

'They're not in your year, though.'

'Some of them have brothers and sisters or friends who are. You don't think that book stayed solely in the hands you put it in, do you? It's spicy stuff. One or two of my kids bought their own copies.'

'They walk into a bookshop with legal tender and choose from the shelves.'

'Then take it home and when it's questioned say it was recommended at school.'

'Oh Christ, Lucy, don't you start.'

'I'm just pointing out life's ruthless logic.'

'Which is partly what I was trying to do when I gave them the book.'

'There are ways and ways.'

'And my way was the wrong way.' I waited. 'Eh?'

'I think, perhaps – with respect,' Lucy said, 'your enthusiasm was a trifle misguided in this particular case.'

'Lucy, any time now most of those kids will come of age, be able to marry without asking permission and fight in a war.'

'One of mine particularly liked the bit where they get the girl down and rape her with a beer bottle,' Lucy said. 'He pretended to be horrified, but his eyes were shining and he couldn't quite keep the glee out of his voice.'

'Then he's a disgusting little pervert whose parents have already marked him for life. He'll make a good recruit for the secret police when the take-over comes.'

'We must have a care for the less stable elements in our midst, Gordon.'

'And we'll know better how to deal with them when we meet them if we already know they exist.'

'There's a great deal of life that isn't learned from books.'

About to push open one of the double doors of the main entrance, I stopped and turned to face her. 'Lucy, you surprise me. And you a teacher of English.'

'I simply meant that to some people it's for real. Have you had a chance to look at those writing exercises?'

'Yes.'

'Do you want to talk about them?'

My mind moved sluggishly as we stood like an island in the stream of people dividing to flow on either side of us. I'd lied. I hadn't read them. Perhaps I could manage a glance through them in the lunch break.

'I've got a full timetable today.'

'So have I.'

'I'll tell you what, though,' I said. 'Since you're without transport why don't I give you a lift home? We can have a chat on the way.'

The operator answered. 'What number are you dialling, caller?' I told her. 'It's all right. This is Mr Taylor. I'm ringing my own home.'

'Dial the number again, please. I'll clear the line.'

I did so and heard the ringing-tone. 'Come on, girl,' I eventually muttered. I replaced the receiver.

'No answer?' Lucy was coming in, carrying a tray with a teapot under a knitted cosy and white china cups with small blue flowers. 'She's probably popped out.'

She's not popping out anywhere these days, I wanted to say. She wasn't answering because I hadn't told her what I'd arranged with the Post Office.

'I expect so.'

The tea was smoky, fragrant. 'Earl Grey?'

'Lapsang. D'you like it?'

'Yes. It's good.'

'I like an occasional change from the average char.'

I sat back in one of the chairs, cup and saucer on the arm beside me. 'This really is a very pleasant flat, Lucy. I wouldn't mind a place like this myself.'

'But don't make the mistake I made,' Lucy said. 'When Eddie died I thought the house was far too big for Donald and me. He's away at university now, of course, and probably won't ever live at home permanently again. So when I heard through a friend that this was to let, I sold up and moved. That was before inflation really got under way and now I've lost my most valuable capital asset; the money's tied up in unit trusts that have hardly held their face value, let alone kept up, and I'm paying rent every month with nothing to show for it. In any case, it's no place for anyone starting a family.'

'We shan't be having a family,' I said.

'Oh? Is that your choice?'

'No.' I'd assumed Lucy knew. 'Eileen can't.'

'Does it trouble her?'

'Quite a lot.'

'What about you?'

'Not as much. Not yet, anyway.'

173

'Well . . . I just had Donald. Then a miscarriage a couple of years later, a prolapse not long after that and an early hysterectomy. That was my lot.'

'You've got the boy, anyway.'

'Yes. I'm grateful for that. He's a good lad.'

She offered the teapot and poured me a second cup when I nodded. 'Thanks.' I wondered what she did about sex. Whether it bothered her. 'Women can wait; quite a long time if they have to,' Eunice Cadby had said. Was it true that a hysterectomy removed appetite as well, or was it that the operation, coming usually later in life, often coincided with a falling off in desire and provided a convenient excuse?

'By the way . . .' Lucy got up. 'I threw out a lot of stuff when I came here, but . . .' She was at a drawer of the sideboard. She took photographs from a manilla envelope, selected a few and came to perch beside me on the broad arm of my chair, her thigh spreading under her skirt as it took her weight. 'Do you see anyone you know among that lot?'

It was a school group: a dozen or so young girls in gymslips, blouses, striped ties. I pointed. 'That's surely you.' Grinning, round, the glasses already there, but plain, unflattering. 'You were carrying a bit of weight.'

'I was. A proper *boule de suif*. Just puppy fat, though. I lost it later. Most of it, anyway,' she added dryly.

'It would have been a pity to lose the most becoming parts of it, Lucy.'

'My, we *are* having a flattering day,' Lucy said. 'It's easy to see who misses his mother.'

'Oh?'

'Men who favour big bosoms.'

'Is that so?'

'It's a well known theory.'

'Is it? Like men who smoke pipes?'

'My husband smoked a pipe.'

'There you are, then. What about *his* mother?'

'He never remembered her. She died when he was tiny and he was brought up mostly by grandparents.'

'There you are again.'

'But the fact was that all the women who took his eye, who turned his head on the street, were on the small side there.'

174

'You were watching.'

'Enough to notice.'

'What a pity.'

'I don't mean he ran after them.'

'Nor did I. I just meant that while he was looking at small breasts, other men were no doubt admiring you. The human race is never satisfied, is it?'

'Oh, Eddie and I got along,' Lucy said comfortably. 'And how did the conversation take this turn anyway?'

'I don't know.'

What I did know was that it had charged me with sexual tension, that she was very close and I was holding down a growing urge to slide my arm round her waist and press my cheek against her. There would, I thought, be an enormous comfort in that. She put her finger-end under another face: a thin dark face framed by thick dark hair.

'Do you recognise her?'

'No.'

'That's Catherine Hetherington. Could she be your Mrs Norton, d'you think?'

'It's hard to say. She's not unlike her, I suppose.'

'I wonder if they'd let me see her.'

'Do you want to? Were you close?'

'No, but . . . she might be all alone in the world now, with no one to call a friend.'

'I'd be prepared for her not to remember you, and not to want to talk.'

Lucy sighed. 'I think I might try, though.'

'I don't even know where they're keeping her,' I said, 'but there's a Detective Chief-Inspector called Hepplewhite. I should think he's the man to talk to first.'

Lucy shuffled through the photographs. 'I thought there was another one of her; but never mind.' A smaller picture displaced itself from the others and slid across the steep incline of Lucy's skirt. As she instinctively grabbed for it her thigh lost its purchase on the chair arm. I felt her go. The lift of my arm, over and round, to encircle and save her, was quick and automatic. Not so my decision to leave it there, my hand resting lightly on the slight protrusion of flesh above the waistband of her skirt. How simply, I was to think later, a moment can present itself. My heart thumped. I did not want to speak because my throat was thickening and I was afraid my voice would falter. She turned her head and looked down at me. I couldn't see her expression because her face was slightly behind as well as above me, and I had leaned forward a little in the act of helping to save the other photographs.

'I think we ought to talk about those exercises.' But she did not move.

'Lucy, I have a confession to make.'

'Oh?'

'I haven't read them.'

'Why didn't you say so?'

'I wasn't thinking straight this morning, and you put me even more off-balance.'

'With what I said about that book?'

'Yes. So I thought I'd look through them at lunchtime. Then I had a session with a sixth-former who came to me with a work problem. So ...'

'You could have told me when we met after school.'

'Well, I'd offered you a lift anyway.'

Lucy tapped the photographs into alignment on her knee.

'Had you ... had you already got something else in mind?'

'Cross my heart and hope to die.'

'But proximity and privacy worked the trick, um?'

'What trick, Lucy?'

'Am I letting my imagination run away with me?'

'I think mine's already way ahead of yours.'

'What is it you want?'

Now I dared to tighten my hold, the pressure persuading a slight turn and inclination of her torso which my head went to meet, until my cheek was against the warm resilience of her breast.

'This,' I said. 'Just this for a moment.'

She moved her arm across my shoulders, her fingers touching the hair covering my ear. My other ear heard the inner resonance of her voice as she spoke.

'Is this a hobby of yours, or doesn't your wife understand you?'

'I don't seem to understand her any more,' I said.

She gave my hair a little tidying stroke and pat, then gently extricated herself. I watched her as she went unhurriedly to the sideboard and replaced the photographs, then took her original seat on the sofa. She drank the last of her tea and put down the cup. I

176

leaned forward and put my own cup and saucer on the tray. She was regarding me now, elbows on knees, chin on her hands, with a direct and appraising gaze which I found I could only intermittently return.

'This is ridiculous,' she said, at length.

'Not ridiculous,' I said. 'Unexpected, perhaps, but far from ridiculous.'

'I suppose it wouldn't surprise you to know how many so-called happily married men have offered to bring comfort to my lonely bed since my husband died?'

'I'm not surprised you've had offers.'

'But I must say this is the first time I've ... I've been propositioned by someone young enough to be my son.'

'Don't exaggerate.'

'Near enough, anyway.'

'Have I shocked you?'

'No, I'm not shocked. But I'm mightily surprised. One ordinary Friday afternoon. I accept a lift home from a colleague and here we are.'

'Just like that.' I waited through a silence.

'It's not on, you know.'

'That's a shame.' I could even manage a small smile now.

'How could we possibly work together afterwards, behave as if nothing had happened?'

'We won't know if we don't try.'

She caught her breath on a little sigh. 'I did give in once ... with one of those who offered. Oh, I'm human and I haven't a nun's vocation to support me. It was messy, inadequate, frustrating and afterwards we couldn't look at each other.'

'You made a bad choice.' Again I waited.

'You're expected at home.'

I shook my head. 'No. There's no one in. I remembered after I'd tried to phone.'

'Are you good at lying?'

'The occasion won't arise.'

'Hasn't it before?'

'No.'

She shook her head now. 'No. That's what winded me. I've never thought of you as ... What I mean is, you're one of the last people I'd have expected to make this kind of ...'

'Who are the first ones?'

'Oh ... you know how thoughts pop into the mind.'

'As long as there's no one else you'd prefer to be sitting here now.'

'Oh, there is. There's someone I often long to see sitting there. But he'll never come back.' She turned her face away and fiddled with her cup.

'Lucy ...' I said eventually. When she looked at me I met her gaze directly. 'Lucy,' I said again. I didn't want actually to say it, but I hoped my eyes would say it for me: 'Please.'

'Women of my age look better with their clothes on,' she said.

'Nonsense,' I said. I turned her to face the dressing-table mirror. 'Look. Give yourself the lie.'

Her tights contained her plump but trim belly and behind. Her breasts, released, had dropped a little and sprung apart, clearly separated. I ran my hands down from her shoulders, over and under, then lifting, till each palm weighed surprisingly taut flesh.

'Look,' I said again; but she had closed her eyes and turned her cheek to my chest. How tiny she now seemed beside me.

An ice-cream van entered the street four floors below, its carillon jingling out the opening bars of a familiar melody whose name I could not bring to mind: *Ba-dee da di-dom di di dom da-dee, di-dom da-dee di-dom dah.*

'Come,' Lucy said, 'where it's warm.'

I took off the rest of my clothes and laid them on a chair. With the sheets to her chin, she watched me between half-closed eyelids as I walked towards her. The last remnant of my own diffidence gone, I stood over her for a moment.

'Come in,' she said, 'and stop showing off.'

I was laughing as I stretched the length of my body beside her and drew her to me. Her lips had softened into a candid admission of hunger. She held me to her, the sigh of her breath on my face. Her breath smelled of milky tea. As though eager now to please me, her hand began almost at once to search; but its touch was heavy, unpractised. I released myself from it and, ducking under the sheet, sent my mouth to explore through that dark warm cave the terrain of breasts, belly, thighs until, with hair against my lips, she took the hair of my head in her hand to restrain me. 'No.' 'Yes.' I gripped her wrist and prised open her legs, crouching between them, tongue probing through to moist flesh whose sap called her liar. Then she gave in, lifting in a spasm of delight to thrust at me while my two

178

hands cradled her buttocks and held her poised to lunge and her head rolled on the pillow.

'God, you're sweet!' I said, when she cried out. 'How sweet you are!'

Her body sagged. 'No more, no more.' Her hands took my head and drew me up into the light. I placed little kisses on the crows' feet at the corners of her eyes and nuzzled my lips against the roughened skin by her nostrils.

'Oh, nobody ...' she murmured, on a sigh.

'Nobody what?'

'Nobody's ever ...'

'Sweet, sweet Lucy,' I said. 'Lovely little Lucy.'

She lay for several moments of kisses, eyes closed, then: 'We haven't got the time. And I'm ready now.'

'Now, Lucy?'

'Yes, yes,' she said. 'Please, now.'

Her finger-tip traced the line of my mouth between moustache and beard. 'Don't fall asleep.'

'No ...' Her voice came to me from a distance.

'Gordon ...'

I opened my eyes, bringing myself back with an effort. 'No.'

'Thank you,' she said, 'for not dashing straight away.'

'I want to stay.'

'Hmm. But you can't.'

She rolled on to her back and stretched, one arm behind her head, as she looked round the room to which I had now added my mark.

'Well,' she said on a sigh, 'it's done now.'

'Yes.'

'There's no wiping it out.'

'No.'

'So long,' she said, 'as you don't get an attack of conscience and try to purge it by confessing to your wife.'

'No.'

'I don't want to be the cause of trouble between you.'

'You won't.' I ran a hand flat over her, taking the sideways sag of her breast and straightening it on her rib-cage in the arc of thumb and forefinger. 'You're not sorry, are you, Lucy?'

'No. So long as we've had pleasure without harm.'

'It was pretty special, wasn't it?'

'Was it?'

'Oh, yes. Wasn't it for you?'

'Yes. It was wonderful. I hope I can make it last.'

'Need you?'

'I must. There's nobody else, and you can't come here again like this.'

'What a pity.'

'But you can't,' she said, suddenly intent. 'You know that, don't you? It's impossible. We couldn't possibly carry it off.'

I sighed. 'I'm afraid you're right.'

'I know I am.'

'In that case . . .' I moved up close and reached across her to support my weight.

'Gordon, you've got to go.'

'Yes, yes. In a little while now.'

'There's no future in it,' she actually did say before, transferring on a finger a kiss from her lips to mine, she let me out, the nakedness she had surrendered to me, and which she was at pains to make me understand I could never see again, covered now by a thick, quilted dressing-gown of the most utilitarian and unseductive design.

'We must never,' she had said earlier, 'by any word, look or gesture give anyone the slightest suspicion that we're any more to each other than we've always been: amiable and friendly colleagues. And if you should happen to catch me in private repose looking like the cat that's been at the cream, please pretend that it's for some other reason altogether.'

'You'll allow yourself the memory, then?'

'Oh, yes, Gordon. Be sure I shan't forget.'

'Goodbye, Lucy,' I said. 'My friend and sweet love.'

It was almost dark. I sat quietly in the car for a few minutes, the engine ticking over. My limbs were totally relaxed. It was done now, as Lucy had said. There was no wiping it out: an act I had never thought I would be guilty of, for had I not possessed all I needed inside the walls of my own secure castle? But when I opened my mind to the possibility of remorse, none touched me. I felt instead older, calmer, wiser, as though Lucy in lending me her body had, in that short time, taken me through to another level of maturity. In drawing strength from a source outside my life with Eileen I felt for the first time since her decline the possibility of my being able to see us both through.

There were other cars in the yard now, but Lucy had thought to tell me how to park so that I should not be blocked in. I put the engine into gear and gently trundled out on to the road, pausing in the gateway for a second to choose the best route, then turned towards home.

There was no light on in the house and the door was locked. I let myself in with my latch-key and with apprehension blossoming through fear into full-blown panic, began to go through the house, switching on lights as I went. The bed was made, the duvet drawn up neat and tidy. Outside the closed door of the bathroom I stood for a moment, mustering the courage to go in. The room was empty. I slumped on to the stool. The sweat cooled on me till I suddenly shivered and pushed my hand inside my coat to stay the pounding of my heart.

I found the note on the table in the living-room, the writing still neat and legible but showing stress in the unfinished loops and uneven pressure of her hand. My own hand trembled as I held it. 'My dear Gordon, I'm going away for a while to see if I can get myself sorted out. Don't look for me and don't frighten my parents by asking for me there, as they won't know where I am. I'll be in touch as soon as I feel able. In the meantime, watch out for yourself. I'm truly sorry about all this. Love, Eileen.'

I5

Young girls that spring were wearing man-style jackets in tweed, with suede patches on the elbows. There was one such among the half-dozen people waiting to be served along the counter of my father's shop. Though smaller, she reminded me from the back of Eileen in the way her dark hair touched the high roll-neck of her white sweater. Her face, when she turned to leave with her parcel of fish and chips, was fresh, unwritten upon. She looked altogether untouched, waiting for joy, not knowing what sacrifice the world might demand of her.

'Hullo, Clarice.'

'Hullo, Mr Taylor.'

'How're things? How's the little one?'

Something deep at the back of her eyes lit her whole face with pleasure. 'Getting bigger.'

'Mam looking after him?'

'She spoils him.'

'I'll bet she does. Take care.'

She had had an abortion at fifteen, then left the sixth form at seventeen to bear a child whose father she refused to marry.

My mother served the customers while my father stood over the pans, pushing the fish around in an occasional movement and lifting one clear for inspection with the fine judgement that, with no lack of competition, had brought him so much trade. Though it was early, my mother's fingers were already blackened by the printing ink from the sheets of newspaper she used as outer wrapping. As soon as she had a free moment she would wash them under the tap in the back. Fastidious, afraid of carrying on her person outside the shop the after-smell of fried fish, she bathed regularly and scrupulously kept her work-clothes apart from everything else she wore. She inclined her head, inviting me to go through, and I walked to the end of the counter, lifted the flap and went behind. My father had transferred his attention to the chip pan, lifting the fried potatoes in a wire open-mesh scoop whose handle he banged smartly on the edge of the pan to release excess fat before throwing them with a thud into the serving-compartment above. 'Now,' he said as I passed him and he became aware of my presence.

Mrs Bolster, the middle-aged woman with fluffy gingerish hair who helped to serve at the busier times, was buttoning her nylon overall in the back room. She smiled as she greeted me and asked how I was keeping. 'I'll go and relieve your mother,' she said, 'and let her have a minute.' She had a tic which, at intervals, turned her head to one side in two or three little jerks. It was something she herself no longer seemed aware of. An electric kettle was hissing up to the boil. My mother sustained herself during the long sessions with snatched gulps of tea. Mrs Bolster made the tea before going into the shop, and left it to brew.

'Now then.' My mother appeared and went straight to the sink to scrub the black ink from her hands. 'Are you shopping, or is it a social call?'

I realised that I was hungry. 'I wouldn't mind a bite.' My wanting to eat outside the house at this hour was odd enough to give me a lead into the lie I was going to tell her.

'Haven't you had any tea?'

'I didn't bother,' I said. 'Eileen's gone to visit her mother for a few days.'

'Isn't she at school?'

'The doctor told her she was run-down and needed a rest.'

'Oh, well. A change might do her good, then.'

She took a large plate into the shop and returned with two portions of fish, some chips and a helping of mushy peas. 'Bread?' When I nodded she sliced and buttered a tea-cake and put it beside me, before pouring cups of tea for both of us. I had pulled out a chair and was sitting at the Formica-topped table. The fish was crisply battered and flaky inside. My mother leaned against a cupboard and sipped her tea as she watched me wolf.

'You eat like a chap who's had nowt for a fortnight.'

'Delicious,' I mumbled, my mouth full. 'They're that good they make you hungry.'

'Aye, your dad's got the knack.' She twisted her head to glance at the electric clock on the wall behind her. Before long all help would be needed out front and there would be no time for talk. 'Where's our Bonny got to, then?' she asked.

'I don't know. Haven't you seen him?'

'Nay, we've not seen him since you were both at our house last Friday. Has he gone back?'

'I don't know,' I said again. 'He just took his hook last Monday and said he'd be in touch.'

'Last Monday? Well, he never called to see us.' She said it as though it were not surprising. But there was hurt in it. 'Perhaps he was too timid,' she said after a moment.

'What?'

'Where did you go to after you left our house last Friday?'

'What d'you mean?'

'You know what I mean, Gordon. When you keep a shop you see a lot of people and hear a lot of news. Did you clout that landlord an' all, or was it just our Bonny?'

I swallowed a mouthful of food and chased it with tea.

'Well, he shouldn't have done it, but the bloke really was obnoxious.'

'I thought you were supposed to be looking after him.'

'In what way was I his keeper? I gave him a bed to sleep in and a roof over his head. I don't rule his life.'

'All the same—'

'It was over in a second, Mother. He'd dropped the bloke before I could move.'

'Landed him in hospital as well, so we heard. Lucky he didn't kill him. Lucky he's not up for manslaughter.'

'How was Bonny to know he had a heart condition?'

'If he'd controlled his temper it wouldn't have mattered.'

'True, true. Why should I defend him? How is the landlord, anyway? Did you hear that?'

'He's not dead, at any rate, as far as we know. But there was some nasty talk going on at that pub, among the regulars. Talk about some of 'em finding Bonny and giving him a dose of his own medicine.'

'Oh, men like to talk. Especially with ale inside them. Anyway, Bonny's gone now.'

'And you've no idea where he is?'

'No. I told you.'

'Haven't you tried phoning his flat?'

'Why should I? He said he'd be in touch and I expect he will be, when he's ready. You know he goes for months at a time without a thought for home. A couple of tickets for a match and a scribbled note and he thinks he's done his duty.'

'Perhaps we can put up with that in normal times. But—'

'Whenever have times been normal with Bonny?'

'Escapades are one thing. All this could be the end of his career.'

'I told him,' I said. 'I told him why didn't he get a grip on himself, go back and talk to them and get on with the job. Perhaps that's what he's done.'

'Aye, and perhaps not.'

My father put his head round the door. 'Dot.' She went out and in a moment he came through, wiping his hands on a towel. 'Your mother'll fry for ten minutes, before the rush starts.' He watched me chase the last few scraps round the plate. 'Have you had enough to eat?'

'Yes, thanks. They were delicious. Smashing. When you retire you'll have to do like Harry Ramsden and flog your batter recipe.'

'Nay, there's nowt secret about it. The secret's in the touch of the chap who mixes it and fries.' He was pouring himself tea. 'Where's Eileen tonight?'

I told him what I'd told my mother. The sequence launched, I went through virtually the same conversation with him.

My father brooded for a while. Then he pointed to the wall telephone. 'Ring his flat,' he said.

'We shan't catch him at this time, in any case,' I said. 'He's bound to be out somewhere.' I didn't want to talk to Bonny until I'd thought out exactly what line to take. Nor did I want the sound of my father's voice, or my mother's, to jolt him into believing they knew more than they did and giving it away by defending himself. But I couldn't stop them from ringing up from home.

'I want to know where he is,' my father said. 'Can you remember his number, off-hand?'

I got out my pocket diary, looked up the number and went to the telephone and dialled. I heard the click of an answering machine, then Bonny's recorded voice: 'This is Bonny Taylor's residence. Mr Taylor is not here. If you wish to burgle the place, ring off and come round now. If you wish to leave a recorded message, do so and Mr Taylor will ignore it on his return. . . .' I broke the connection, dialled again, then held out the receiver to my father. He listened, stony-faced, then hung up.

'Bloody hell!' he said, without a change of expression.

I buttoned my jacket. 'I'll be off. Thanks for the food.'

I'd come to provide an explanation for Eileen's absence and to get any news I could of Bonny's whereabouts. Now I wanted to be alone again so that I could think, though I had little hope that the process would be any more constructive than it had proved so far.

'You look shagged out,' my father said, appraising me. 'You want to watch yourself.' I could almost have smiled at his choice of phrase, remembering Lucy in my arms only a couple of hours ago. 'Are you worried about Eileen?'

'She'll be all right.'

'Well, we're worried about her – your mam an' me. It's not like her, is it? She's always been so steady.'

'Some people are not as strong as they seem to be. I think she must have been tired for some time. And then that business next door really got through to her.'

'You look after her, that's all we've got to say. They don't grow on trees, women like Eileen.'

Oh, but they do, Dad, I wanted to say. All over the place. In great fat bunches, shiny on the outside and rotten at the core. 'I know.' I should have to let him harbour whatever suspicions he might have that I'd upset her in some way. For the time being, at least. I pointed to the back door. 'I'll go out this way.'

'Hang on a minute,' my father said.

I waited. 'What?'

'Wasn't Bonny talking at one time of buying a place in the country, where he could rest and lie low? Do you remember that?'

'I believe so. Did anything come of it?'

'He went to look at a cottage. I'm nearly sure he did . . .'

'Where was it? Can you remember?'

My father shook his head. 'Damned if I can. Didn't he mention the Cotswolds?'

'Nay, I don't know. He said he liked Somerset once, when Eileen was talking about it.'

'Hasn't he any special mates in his club?' my father asked. 'There must be somebody he's close to.'

'He'd keep a thing like that to himself, surely. I mean, one careless word, the press on to it and his cover's blown.'

Now I was resorting to the language of spy novels. But Bonny must have a contact. There must exist a channel for messages, because although he didn't care now, in normal circumstances his team manager would surely not tolerate his absenting himself without some means of communication.

186

'And if he had got himself a place,' my father mused, 'why didn't he go there instead of coming to see us?'

'He wanted to see us,' I said. 'That's understandable.'

'Aye, aye. But he got no satisfaction here, so he buzzed off without leaving an address.' He paused. 'Did you two have a scrap, made him go off like that?'

'The press were on to him. They wouldn't leave him in peace. Everybody knew he was here.'

'You've not answered my question, Gordon. Did you have words?'

I sighed. 'Oh, I got impatient with him. You saw it coming on. It was nothing serious, but I couldn't pat his head and say "Poor Bonny" any longer. So he left.'

'In a temper.'

'That's too strong. But he wasn't in any mood to leave forwarding addresses. So I just assumed he'd gone home. For all we know, that's where he is.'

'I shall try him again in the morning.'

'You'll catch him then, more than likely. If he's answering the phone, that is, and doesn't have that machine on permanently.' I put on my topcoat. 'Well, thanks again. I'll be seeing you.'

It came to me as I was sitting watching television, a glass of whisky in my hand, only partly comprehending what was on the screen, but reluctant to go to bed and face my undistracted thoughts. Bonny's solicitor: the man whose home telephone number he carried; the man he'd been going to ring about possible repercussions from the incident with Grint. Simpson? Simmons? His name had appeared in the papers when he'd defended Bonny on that breathalyser charge. Bonny was exhausted, the man had pleaded, his nerves still wound up after an important league match in which he'd saved his team from defeat by scoring two goals in the last ten minutes of play. That had been in the days when people still made allowances for him, when his brilliance on the field more than outweighed his growing reputation as a hell-raiser off it. With more than double the statutory limit of alcohol in his bloodstream, Bonny had seemed to think a year's driving ban and a £100 fine a satisfactory outcome. Simons! But what was the name of his firm?

I was up early on Saturday morning, after managing to doze uneasily for a couple of hours. I cut up an orange and sucked at the segments while tea brewed and I waited for the morning paper to arrive. When it did, the football league fixture list told me that Bonny's team were playing at home. I got the club's number from directory enquiries, then, a few minutes after nine, rang and asked for the manager's secretary.

'I wonder,' I said at the sound of the woman's voice, 'if you can give me the address and telephone number of Mr Bonny Taylor's solicitor.'

'Who is this speaking?'

'This is Mr Taylor's brother, Gordon Taylor. Bonny was staying with me last weekend, but now he's left. I don't know just where he is at present, but he asked me to pass on some information through his solicitor, only rather foolishly I've mislaid the piece of paper he wrote their details on. A Mr Simons, I believe it is.'

'Hang on a minute, would you?'

I waited. She came back. 'Here it is . . .' I wrote the information down as she read it out, then asked her to repeat it. 'I've already left a message with them, asking them to tell Mr Taylor that Mr de la Rue wants to speak to him as soon as possible,' the woman said. 'Perhaps you'd be good enough to tell them again while you're speaking to them.' I said I'd do that. 'You say you don't know where he can be reached?' she asked.

'No. There's an answering machine switched on to the phone at his flat.'

'I've heard it,' she said dryly. 'Would you let me have your own number, Mr Taylor, in case Mr de la Rue wants to speak to you.'

'Certainly.' I gave it to her. De la Rue was the team manager. He it was who had bought Bonny from a Midlands club for a £450,000 fee, two seasons ago. He it was who had somehow failed to keep Bonny happy, and whose own reputation had suffered accordingly.

I rang the number the woman had given me, praying that Simons's office would be manned on a Saturday morning. Another woman answered, a younger woman, from the sound of her voice. I asked for Simons.

'I'm afraid Mr Simons isn't in this morning. Can I help you?'

I told her who I was. 'I believe Mr Simons negotiated the purchase of a country house for my brother.'

'Oh, yes?'

Cagey bitch. 'I wonder if you can find the address and telephone number in his file.'

'I'm afraid it's strictly against the firm's rules to divulge information about clients.'

'Yes, I can understand that. And you're probably wondering why his brother doesn't know it. Well, Bonny has a secretive nature, even where his family's concerned, but it's imperative that I contact him.'

'I've no proof that you even are who you say you are.'

She was well-trained, this one. She probably wouldn't let on what kind of lavatory paper they used in the bogs. 'Our father's name,' I said, 'is Alec. My mother's name is Dorothy. He calls her Dot.' I gave her my address and telephone number. 'If you like I'll hang up and you can ring me at that number, just to be sure.'

'That's all right, Mr Taylor. I apologize. But you'll understand how careful we have to be. I'm here on my own at the moment and in Mr Simons's absence all I can do is offer to pass on to your brother any message you'd like to leave with me.'

'Suppose you don't reach him? Are you prepared to travel to see him? This is a family matter of the gravest importance and urgency. I must speak to my brother today.'

'Well . . .'

'If you can't oblige,' I said, 'I shall have to have an emergency radio announcement broadcast. I don't think he'll like that.'

'No,' she said. 'Wait a moment, will you, while I get the file.'

A couple of minutes later I had what I wanted. It could, for all I knew before I got it, have been an address anywhere in the British Isles, or even the northern departments of France, a country Bonny was fond of. But what I'd written down was not in a place Bonny had found on his grown-up journeying, but one we had once both known with an intimacy not of extended and deepening acquaintance, but of a kind imprinted briefly in impressionable years, which could ever after summon out of memory the sights and sounds and odours of the dawdling afternoons of childhood summers.

I got out maps. On his demob from the RAF my father had gone back to the Sheffield steelworks in which he had started his working life. At weekends, he joined a cycling club in runs into the Derbyshire countryside. Performing some small service for them, he had on one of these trips been befriended by a middle-aged couple who ran a small farm. He got into the habit of calling to see them. When, later, a change of job took him farther north, he kept going a spasmodic correspondence. Later still, after he had met my mother, married and fathered the two of us, he one Sunday, on impulse, packed us into his second-hand Ford Popular and set out to show us his old haunts. The Henshaws were delighted to see us. Their relationship with my father was one of the respectful, polite and almost formal acquaintanceships still common in those days. In their sixties by this time and childless, they seemed to find some special spring of pleasure in Bonny and me, and they suggested that we be allowed to spend some weeks of the summer holiday with them on the farm.

It was on our second and last visit that I fought Bonny for a girl. Her name was Sonje Elisabeth Wales; at twelve years old a honey-pot with curly dark hair, dark lustrous eyes, already budding breasts and long bare downy legs flawed only by a mole above her right knee. Once aware of their presence, she came up regularly from the village to show herself to these two new males. I fantasised before dropping off to sleep about rescuing her from the perils of the countryside. Bonny till then had been scornful of girls, but when I became aware that he was a rival for Sonje Elisabeth's affections I faced him in a blaze of resentment whose ferocity surprised us both.

Already, Bonny was adept enough with a ball to have become a favourite and to have overshadowed me, two years his senior but lacking his physical grace, more interested in books and making only a duty attendance at games. Having introduced him into the school and kept an early eye on him, I had by now become Bonny Taylor's brother. So when, with the appearance of Sonje Elisabeth, he seemed ready to accept the kind of feminine worship he had previously shrugged aside, I fought him. He met the challenge, but we were at just the stage where his agility was no match for my two years' advantage of height and weight. I beat him, and I went on after I'd beaten him until I'd marked him. The Henshaws, whose chief characteristic was a grave kindliness, were horrified by this savagery, this brutality of brother to brother. Our parents were summoned. It wasn't necessary: the rupture would have healed enough for us to have finished the holiday; but they knew little of young people and still less of what sibling relationships could produce and withstand. So it was treated as an emergency. Our parents arrived two days later, on receipt of the Henshaws' letter. A low-voiced conference took place in the farmhouse parlour. Shamed, my father and mother took us home where my mother – not my father – her anger stoked anew as she sought words strong enough to condemn my behaviour, finally laid hands on me.

And what of Sonje Elisabeth, the dark-eyed honey-pot, in the meanwhile? I saw her just once, in the village street where, walking with a friend, she ostentatiously ignored my presence. As for the Henshaws – he died the following year, his wife the year after that.

I looked at the map. Once, it had seemed as distant as the other side of the moon; now it was no more than a sprint down a six-lane motorway, there and back before lunch, if need be. It was not, I'd have thought, a place Bonny would especially want to be reminded of. But there was, in our present circumstances, a pretty irony in his choice.

16

I had not been back. Other places where one could weekend, walk, or camp claimed my allegiance: Wharfedale, Wensleydale, Swaledale, in that remote spur of the West Riding now, under the local government reorganisation Lucy Browning had complained of, officially North Yorkshire. And beyond that the Lakes, from sleek, urban Windermere to wild, dour Wastwater. That was the way I, and later we, had always gone, leaving Derbyshire to escapees from Stoke, Stockport and Sheffield, relegating it to a tug of child-hood memory in a life looking forward as as I glanced west along the iron valleys from the M1: the slope of a meadow, a quarry face, the shoulder of a fell, the ever widening corner of a wood; the smell of new bread in a farmhouse kitchen, a slippery-seated pew and the wheeze of a harmonium in a three-quarters empty chapel, while somewhere outside Sonje Elisabeth Wales sauntered in Sunday even-ing sunlight, offering nothing except the whim of her presence for the worship that was her due.

We spoke not one lewd word about her, though our vocabulary was well enough equipped. She was at once more to us and less than that. She represented a mystery that would, from then on, have to be taken account of in our lives. Bonny began keeping company with a succession of girls. That they changed so often showed there was no one who especially interested him. But they were all the most pretty and sought-after. He was testing his muscles; telling me that brute force proved nothing and won less. He could have anyone he crooked his finger at. He'd been doing it, one way or another, ever since.

I drove down through a morning of brilliant sunshine alternating with showers of rain that sometimes thickened into sleet. In Buxton I bought an ordnance survey map of the district, then went into a pub and ordered a pint of bitter. While the landlord was drawing the beer I asked him if he served bar snacks. He said no, only Monday to Friday. 'Not even sandwiches?' He said no again, he hadn't got the staff.

'How much staff do you need to make a sandwich?'

He gave me the look he probably reserved for awkward customers. 'Make one, I end up making a dozen.'

I was, as it happened, the only person in this room; though it was still early.

'And the profit's not worth it?'

'I haven't got the staff,' he said again. 'And at weekends I haven't got the food.'

I'd made a wrong choice, but the pint was pulled so I took it to a table, where I reflected on the hospitality of the English inn and opened my map. After a moment I pushed it brusquely aside, took a drink and put the glass down hard enough to cause the landlord to glance in my direction. It could have been interpreted as anger; but it was, in fact, an expression of the sudden bafflement which swept over me. What the hell was I doing here? How could the foundations of my life have crumbled so in little more than a week? It didn't bear thinking about, and so, while going through the motions, I had refused to let my mind face squarely what I still could hardly believe.

The landlord came out from behind the bar and picked up a couple of empty glasses from a nearby table. I felt him give me a sidelong look before he turned his back. It was the exterior that had deceived me. It looked like the pleasant old-fashioned coaching inn it probably once had been; but some brewery architect had remodelled the no doubt hopelessly impractical interior into a hopelessly gloomy and depressing new one. When I reached for my map, which had fallen across the bench seat, I noticed for the first time a foot-long gash in the PVC covering. Somebody had expressed his opinion with a directness I for once envied.

I drank up and went out. Down the road a neon hotel sign was fixed to the front of a house in a Georgian terrace. From the overnight bag I'd packed with a change of clothes, I removed my binoculars, locked them in the Mini's boot, then walked to the hotel and went in. It was with some vague idea of securing a base that I asked the girl in reception for a single room for the night. The one I was directed to, at the end of a thickly carpeted upstairs corridor whose floor creaked under my weight, contained two large single beds, with a reproduction watercolour of old Buxton over each. I washed my hands and face in the basin and, leaving my bag, went downstairs and found the dining-room, where I ate steak and kidney pie, washed down with another pint of beer, before walking back to the car.

Fifteen minutes later I was looking at a sweep of ploughed land, the rays of a fitful sun glinting in the standing water in its furrows. There was no house. No building of any kind on that side of the road. I looked for landmarks. Over that brow should be the quarry. Up there to the left, the wood. Yes. But still bare in this early spring, when we had known only full-leaved shade. 'O Unicorn among the Cedars/To whom no magic charm can lead us,/White childhood moving like a sigh/Through the green woods.'

I drove on to the village. The nameboard of a sheet-metal firm was fixed to the wall of the chapel to which the Henshaws had asked our lapsed Church of England parents for permission to take us. Farther along the main street of dour greystone buildings I stopped to make a purchase. I had the door of the general store half open before I saw the name on the glass: 'F. W. Wales'. My heart tripped in its beat. I wanted to back out and think about it, but the man behind the counter was already waiting for me. I swung a revolving rack of paperbacks to give me a moment. Could it be?

'Can I help you?'

He was in his fifties, thin faced, with heavy dark-framed glasses and smooth still-dark hair cropped severely at back and sides.

'What have you got in small cigars?'

He waved a hand at the shelf. 'Hamlet, Manikin, John Player's Mild. Special offer on them.'

'They'll do.' I paid him. 'What happened to the Henshaws' farm, back over the hill?'

'The Henshaws?' He gave me the smile of one who delights in encountering the totally ignorant. 'You're going back a bit, aren't you? They've both been dead for fifteen years.'

'I know that. I couldn't see the house.'

'Oh, they levelled that. Put a bulldozer through it and ploughed straight across. More economical use of land, so they made out.'

'I see. You didn't keep the shop in the Henshaws' time, did you?'

'Oh, no. I bought the business when the quarry shut down and I was made redundant. You knew these parts then, did you?'

'I visited the Henshaws a couple of times.' From the corner of my eye I saw a woman enter the shop from a back room and bend down to look under another counter.

'What you lost this time?' the man said, past me.

'Darren's gloves. He's hidden 'em again 'cos he doesn't like to wear 'em.'

'There was a girl lived in the village. Sonje Elisabeth Wales. Could she have been a relative of yours?'

The man's eyes narrowed as they took me in more closely. Then that cold, knowing smile came again. There was something cold and knowing about him altogether and I was ready to bet he had a reputation for tightness among his customers. His gaze flicked beyond me and as I began to turn he said:

'She's looking at you now.'

The woman had straightened up at the sound of her name and was appraising me. I felt my ears begin to burn.

'A young feller asking after you, Sonje.'

Her blue nylon overall hung loosely on her slim body. I was surprised, remembering the signs of its early development, to note that she had hardly any bosom at all. I took in wedding and engagement rings.

'Should I know you?'

I didn't even think her pretty now. The skin of her face lacked lustre. The flesh was puffy under narrow eyes, as though she had recently wept, or slept badly and not washed since. Her mouth, whose shape she had inherited from the man behind me, was thin, turned down at the corners, as though not naturally made for smiles.

'You won't remember me,' I said, 'but I used to come and stay at the Henshaws' farm in summer. You'd be about twelve or thirteen then.'

She was taking stock of me with a total lack of self-consciousness. 'There were two of you,' she said after a moment. 'Brothers, weren't you?'

'That's right.'

'I wouldn't have known you. P'raps it's your beard.'

'It was a long time ago.' I didn't think I should have recognised her in any other context. I looked in vain for the vivacity, that glow of inner mystery, which had given her such allure as a child.

'You liked a scrap,' she said.

'Oh, I don't know,' I said, at a loss for the moment.

'I remember that,' she said. 'You went at it hammer and tongs. Are you the older one or the young one?'

'The older.'

She nodded, still watching me. 'How's your brother?'

'He's okay.'

The clatter of something falling in the back room jerked her head away. 'Darr-*ern*! The little devil. He's always into something.' She hurried out.

'Helps me out in the shop,' Wales explained. 'The wife passed on a couple of year ago. Her husband's away a good bit. Oil rigs. Have you business yourself in these parts?'

'No. I'm just passing through.'

'What is your line?'

'I'm an English teacher.'

'Ah! Thought it must be summat like that.' He stroked his clean-shaven chin with a thumb and forefinger. 'The whiskers.'

He said it, I thought, without the least intention of giving offence. He was merely attaching a label in that curiously uninformed way of all whose habit it is to attach labels while priding themselves on their knowledge of human nature. I wondered what his and Sonje's reaction would be if I were to tell them who my young brother had turned into. A customer came in. I left.

Was it McCormack, I reflected, back in the car, who had said we lose our children because they grow up and change? Frances McCormack would always be beautiful and eighteen. Catherine Hetherington would live in Lucy Browning's mind as she had known her until she met poor demented Mrs Norton. And then she would, like pretty little Sonje Elisabeth Wales, be erased from existence by the woman she had become.

I was stalling. I'd made the detour partly out of an understandable curiosity, but mainly because it gave me an excuse to postpone the object of my journey. I still had not worked out a plan of action. An unexpected appearance in the role of the wronged and outraged husband did not appeal to me. I was still more baffled than angry, looking for complexities below the banal surface of the situation. To accept its banality was to condemn myself as inadequate, to face the fact that I'd been living in a dream world. All right, I had never thought it would touch me, the other world out there of creation, performance, achievement and failure; of work and sweat and professionalism, of pain and affliction and frailty. I was one of the well-informed, had read, seen, heard. I hung it on walls, tucked it away in collected editions on shelves, stood it in neat sheets of vinyl in colourful sleeves. I talked about it, added my pinch to the bushels of judgement, and knew nothing, because I had not lived it. Eileen had been right when she'd accused me of living on the sidelines, the perpetual observer. But how much of that outburst had been hidden self-justification? And in what way did the truth of the indictment oblige me to lie down and let them feed off me?

Sonje Elisabeth, in blue anorak and trousers, came out of her father's shop and walked away along the pavement, holding by the hand a small boy of two or three, with whom she stopped every few yards to remonstrate. Eventually, she reached down and slapped his behind, then set off at a brisker pace, dragging him behind her at a trotting run.

I had expected Bonny's place to take some finding. It was one of those addresses that could have you searching endlessly within a three-mile radius. The map, large scale though it was, wasn't much help. I should, of course, in other circumstances, have rung up and got precise directions. When, after half an hour of driving, I came on a mail van standing on an upland road while the driver emptied a post-box set into a stone wall, I stopped and got out of the car.

'Changed hands,' he said, after he'd given me a few landmarks as guidance. 'Weekenders. Keep themselves to themselves.'

'Friends of friends,' I told him. 'Don't know them myself.'

He transferred the meagre contents of the box to his bag and walked round again to the driver's door. He cocked his head. 'Watch your back.'

He'd heard it before I did, a car coming very fast beyond the shallow but blind brow of the hill. Too fast for the width of this road. I stood back between the van and the Mini as it flashed by.

'Bloody lunatics,' the postman muttered. 'Think it's the M1.'

I said yes as I stepped out and looked after the car, which was already disappearing over the next rise with no slackening of speed. I'd caught only a glimpse of it as it hurtled by, but I was almost certain it was Bonny's Jaguar. I was almost equally certain that it had not been Bonny at the wheel.

17

The lane to the cottage was sunk between a wood of larch and birch and a high sloping meadow. Water from some gorged spring poured in a narrow torrent down a gully on one side. The ground was moist between the stones that saved the lane from becoming a mire. It would, under any reasonable fall of snow, become impassable by car.

I'd left the Mini in a clearing by the road at the top of the lane, preferring to approach on foot and unannounced. A bend and a rise in the lane before it continued its descent gave me my first view of a roof. At the same moment the sun broke through in a brilliant shaft of light. I went on, keeping well into the bank, until the house itself became visible. It was a sombre grey two-storey building, its window frames picked out in white paint. As I observed it the sudden, unexpectedly intense warmth of the sun began to draw a thin steam from the roof slates. Bonny's car was parked by the house, its boot lid open. I drew back instinctively as Eileen appeared, carrying a suitcase. When she had struggled it up into the boot and shoved it into place she drew the back of her hand across her forehead and stood peering about her. I put the glasses on her. Sweat pasted her hair to her brow. At one point, as her head turned, she seemed to be looking directly at me, her eyes full of apprehension.

As she went back round the corner of the building I took to the meadow, climbing the slope and swinging in an arc until I judged I was on the other side of the house. Then I went down through the cover of a stand of beech trees to approach the building from what was virtually a blind side. The only windows here were the frosted ones of the bathroom and, on the ground floor, what was probably a pantry. A moment or two later I was standing on a flagstoned path and peering cautiously into a big square kitchen. Its door stood open, giving a view into the hall. Eileen, who had made another journey to the car, walked by from the front door and went out of sight again. There had been only one person in the car. So where was Bonny now? Possibly, I thought, observing me performing this elaborately surreptitious manoeuvre and waiting for the crucial moment to appear and render it ridiculous.

I moved round the corner and on to the front of the house. The sun was hot here and as I stood with my back to the wall by the open door I felt myself begin to sweat under my top-coat and thick sweater. I prepared myself, like a soldier about to storm an enemy strongpoint, and turned and stepped into the doorway.

Eileen was just coming out. Her reaction as my shape, the sun behind me, barred her way was one of pure terror. She yelled and, dropping the things she was carrying, turned and ran across the hall. As a flushed rabbit will, she hesitated momentarily once, her body swaying to one side, as though she would choose one of the downstairs rooms. Then she held her course and fled up the stairs and out of my sight. I heard a door slam and a key turn.

I followed as far as the foot of the stairs, then called her name. I had to call twice more, each time louder, before the door opened again and slow footsteps came along the landing. She turned the corner, looked at me, then subsided on to the top step and, putting her hands to her face, began to cry in uncontrollable sobs.

I went up until my face was on a level with hers, then stopped, making no attempt to touch her.

'What's the matter? Are you here on your own? Where's Bonny?'

She couldn't speak. I waited.

'Why were you so terrified?'

'I thought ... I thought they'd come back.'

'Who? What are you doing here on your own? You were packing the car. Where's Bonny?' I asked again.

'He's not here.'

'Where is he? Where has he gone to without his car?' A chill touched me now. It was not entirely due to its being much cooler in here than outside in the sun. I shivered. 'Were you packing up to leave yourself?'

She nodded. 'Yes.'

'What's been going on?'

She sniffed and wiped her nose with the back of her hand. Her throat was thick as she spoke.

'It was last night. I went to bed. Bonny said he'd have a breath of air and a look round outside. When he didn't come back, I —'

'What d'you mean, when he didn't come back? Were you waiting for him to come to you?'

'No. We'd agreed on that.'

'Oh, had you?'

'I must have dropped off for a while. When I woke up I just knew he wasn't in the house. Don't ask me how, but I did. I got up and looked in his room. He wasn't there and his bed was still made. The lights were still on downstairs. I was making up my mind to go out and call for him. I . . . I'd somehow lost track of the time. I didn't know how long he'd been gone.'

'What time was this?'

'The early hours by now. We'd sat for a long time talking, after supper, and Bonny had drunk quite a bit. I wondered if he'd fallen in the dark and knocked himself out. And then . . . I was just walking to the door when I heard a . . . a thud. Something falling against it. It was Bonny, on his hands and knees on the step. Partly on his hands and knees, anyway, because his leg . . . Oh, God, his leg . . . But it was his face I saw first, all puffed and swollen, and his clothes, torn, mud all over them. I got him in somehow and on to the sofa. What a sight he was! What a terrible sight!'

'They were here, then,' I said, half to myself.

'Who? How do you know?'

'What did Bonny say?'

'He said he strolled some way from the house and suddenly two men were there.'

'Did he say he knew them?'

'No, but they knew who he was. One of them called him by name.'

'And they beat him up and left him.'

'Oh, God! You should have seen him, Gordon. I did all I could for him and I wanted to phone for help, but they'd pulled the wire out somewhere, and Bonny said to wait till morning and see how he was then. He sent me to bed, but I couldn't sleep so I went back and sat with him. His leg. It came up in the night till his knee was like . . . like a football. He said that himself once. "It's like a bloody football," he said. And the pain he was in! He ran in sweat. All he wanted was hot tea. I made pot after pot and I couldn't seem to satisfy his thirst.'

'Is his leg broken?'

'Yes. He said it probably wasn't. He could bend it, you see, in a fashion, though it obviously hurt like hell to try. This morning I wanted to fetch a doctor and the police. He said no, he didn't want strangers down here. He said the press would crucify me if they found out I'd been down here alone with him and you didn't know where I was.' She hugged her knees and put her face down to meet them, rocking slightly. 'How did you know?'

'A bit of detective work. Go on. . . .'

'So this morning I got him into the car and drove him to hospital in Buxton. They looked at him and said he'd be better treated in Chesterfield.'

'And that's where he is now?'

'Yes. It all took so long. Hanging about waiting, then driving from one place to another; then afterwards when they were deciding whether they ought to keep him in and if they had a bed . . . and all the time he was in agony . . . I didn't want to come back here again, but somebody had to get our things. . . .'

I sat down a couple of steps below her and lit one of the cigars I'd bought from Wales. I waited till she'd finished crying again.

'Do you think you could try to tell me why you came here?' She didn't answer. '*How* did you come to be here, then?'

'Bonny rang up yesterday afternoon. He told me where he was. He just wanted to see if I was all right. I said I'd come to him. I caught a bus to Sheffield, another one from there to Chesterfield and he met me in the car.'

'Are you in love with Bonny, Eileen?' I waited. 'Don't you love me any longer?'

When she still didn't answer I got up and stepped past her and walked along the landing. The door of a bedroom stood open. I went in. There was a double bed with a duvet. Eileen's coat lay across it and her case stood nearby. I was at the window when I heard her come into the room behind me. She looked terrible, but my flesh stirred where my heart wouldn't.

'Is this where it happened?'

'What?' She seemed genuinely puzzled.

'The consummation of your adulterous passion, I'm talking about. Your incestuous passion, it would have been called at one time.'

'I've told you we didn't.'

'Oh, yes, you'd agreed. Why did you agree?'

'It was a step we weren't ready to take. One there was no turning back from.'

It's done, Lucy Browning had said to me in her bed. There's no wiping it out.

'Is Bonny in love with you?'

'They're just words, Gordon. They don't mean anything.'

'Tell me some that do mean something.'

'He needs me.'

'How long has he needed you?'

'I think probably a long time.'

'What a pity he didn't see you first. But then, that's the kind of minor technicality that's never bothered Bonny.'

'Gordon, I'm so terribly sorry. I never wanted any of this.'

'But you feel it's something bigger than all of us? Is that it? What the hell happened to you and me? that's what I want to know. We had it so good. You were fretting because you couldn't have a child. You were flaying yourself because you thought you'd let me down. How is it different with Bonny?'

'It doesn't come into it.'

I dropped the butt of my cigar on the stained floorboards under the window then moved towards her. 'For God's sake, Eileen, where did it all go to? Nothing as good as we had can crumble so fast.' My hands were holding her shoulders now. Tears welled, then ran over down her cheeks. I kissed her hot face and took her tears on my tongue. 'Eileen, Eileen ... we were on a winner.'

I lowered my hands to her breasts, then gently but firmly turned her and moved her the two steps to the bed. She went down without resistance and lay with her eyes closed in a hot flushed face as my hands pulled zips and drew away clothes to free flesh. Her flesh burned. She had the smell of the last twelve hours on her, the exertion, the anxiety, the terror. It was strong, alien. I almost gagged on it as I found and penetrated her. 'We bathe,' someone had once said, 'to hide the fact that we stink.' And we built the routine of our lives on the assumption that the crust we trod would not give way and show us the chasm beneath. . . . She was tight, nearly dry, resisting, while making no voluntary effort to resist. I thought that I should last seconds, but as I reached then fell back from the spasm and the sweat started on me again, I knew that my failure was to be even more ignominious.

'For God's sake,' she cried. 'For God's sake, get done. Please.'

I drew away. 'I can't.' I left her. I stood at the window again, until I heard the rustle of her movements. How I loathed this place, this hideaway, this haven from the cares of the world. This place where my wife had finally become a stranger.

A movement of cloud darkened the window-pane and gave me

her reflection as she sat on the edge of the bed, head bowed, her hands in her lap.

'If you tell me what's to go I'll put it into the car,' I said. 'The Mini's at the top of the lane. I'll drive the Jag and you can follow me.'

'I wasn't running away,' she said, flatly, without emotion. 'I was going home this morning.'

'Were you, indeed?'

'We'd agreed about that. Last night. Before ...'

'What now, then?'

'You realise,' she said, 'that Bonny will probably never play football again.'

'Then that's one of his problems solved for him,' I said.

Oh, sweet Jesus, I thought. What a foul, unfeeling thing to say.

She was silent. I waited, still not looking directly at her.

'If Bonny won't go to the police, those men will never be punished.'

'Does he know who they are?'

'No ... do you?'

'The ones who were ringing up, I expect.'

'But do you know what they look like?'

'Yes. Yes, I think I do.'

'God knows,' McCormack had said. McCormack who had lost a daughter. 'He knows and He'll punish him.' Was this how that prophecy had worked itself out, in the atrocious overkill of someone else's petty revenge?

'Gordon ...'

'Yes?'

'I've got to ask you something. I don't want to, but I've got to know.'

'What?'

'Did... you send them here? Did you tell them where Bonny was?'

I turned to face her. 'Did he say that? Did he put that idea in your head?'

'No, but —'

'Christ Almighty, what kind of man do you think I am?'

'I'm sorry. I don't believe it, but I had to ask. I couldn't see how, otherwise ...'

'Eileen,' I said. The look on my face then must, I thought, resemble that of Wales when I'd asked him about the Henshaws: the look of a man to whom any kind of ignorance is a stupidity to bring perverse delight. For it had come to me earlier, the only way it could have happened, while she was talking on the stairs. I'd not been going to tell her, but now I said:

'Eileen, they followed *you*. They did the easiest thing in the world and followed two scheduled buses until you met Bonny. You led them to him.'

18

When we had taken the rest of the stuff out to the car, emptied the fridge, turned off water and electricity at the mains and drawn curtains on the empty rooms, we locked the door and left the place. The routine reminded me irresistibly and achingly of Eileen and me leaving a cottage we had rented for a couple of weeks one summer in Patterdale, not long after we were married. There we had tramped the fells, often in long silences, storing our talk for the evening when we sat after supper or drank beer in the pub and then made love in a strange bed with a mattress so highly sprung it imposed its own rhythms on ours and led Eileen, giggling, to confess that it had created in her an unseemly curiosity to know what it would be like done on a trampoline. That was when we were still capable of discovering things about each other: 'I didn't know you liked that!' or 'You never told me you'd done/met/been to so-and-so.' When we could delight each other afresh at any hour of the day or night.

It was a season which could never return. Now we knew too much about each other. We knew too much and yet did not know the important things that were still to be learned. For there was no going back. Things had been said and done which could never be forgotten. My need to re-establish possession in that assault on her body had mocked all the tender times gone by. And when, in the pain of loss and her suspicion of my perfidy, I'd thrown at her that she had brought Bonny's destiny to him and seen her tremble in the knowledge, I knew that I had gone too far; that there must be an end to wounding. I must, whatever the outcome for me, step back from that brink where one false move could launch her on a journey of the tortured spirit from which she might never return.

For she was precious, this girl who sat so still beside me, yet not relaxed; still, yet strung out taut and quivering. Precious, I saw now, in the very meaning of her troubled mind and divided self.

And yet, as we reached the road and I turned to pull in beside the Mini, my loss and the fear of its everlastingness savaged me with a renewed onslaught so fierce I couldn't for a moment speak or even draw an unforced breath.

'Gordon ...'

I couldn't answer. I was seized by the appalling fear that today might be the last time I should ever be alone with her. The violence of it made my teeth chatter.

'Gordon ...' She put her hand on my arm.

A car whooshed by with a salute from a musical horn. I took precarious hold of myself.

'I'm all right ... Listen. I took a room in an hotel in Buxton. I've got a bag there. Follow me down and we'll talk about what's to be done today.'

I gave her the keys. She got out. I turned the Jag and waited for her. When I heard the engine start I moved off, driving steadily, slowing after every bend and rise until the Mini came in sight. Brave little Mini, doggedly, bravely following.

The light was pure now, bathing the vast landscape of fells and villages and lonely farms. Steadily we drove down between walls which had patterned this country for centuries: a pattern of survival and livelihood drawn by men and women long gone. Not far away was a village whose courage had become legend and given children a rhyme they still chanted three hundred years later. At the time of the Great Plague, when it was seen that an innocent roll of cloth had brought the contagion to Eyam, their vicar went to his people and said that they should isolate themselves, let no one in or out, and so ensure that it would not be carried further by them. This they did, and the plague ravaged them:

> Ring a ring o' Roses,
> A pocket full of posies.
> Atishoo, atishoo
> All fall down.

It was as well to think of courage. There would be no hiding what had befallen us. Already news of where Bonny was would be out, and the rest would surely follow. And that would be only the beginning of it. After all that there would still be the question. After the scandal, the gossip, the speculation, after the scorn and vilification and outrage the question would remain. What was to become of us, the three of us? How were we to be saved?